"They're right behind us!"
Mildred yelled

Ryan heard the boom of Ricky's Webley hand blaster echo out of the stairwell, and started moving toward the window.

"Looks clear," Jak said, peering around the edge of the empty frame. He promptly slipped from out of his cover and fled to the street.

Securing escape was more important than discouraging the stickies from following, and Ryan raced for the front door. The other companions were hot on his heels.

Ryan burst out of the building. The humidity hit him in the face like a wool blanket soaked in hot water. Quickly he took in how profuse the vegetation was, grass and flowers pushing up through big cracks heaved in the pavement.

Then he noticed the tall, skeleton-thin woman with an electric-green Mohawk strolling around the corner of the building across the street. But there was nothing casual about the way she whipped up the M16 she'd been carrying and aimed it at Ryan.

JAMES AXLER

DEATHLANDS®

Desolation
Angels

A GOLD EAGLE BOOK FROM

W☉RLDWIDE®

TORONTO • NEW YORK • LONDON
AMSTERDAM • PARIS • SYDNEY • HAMBURG
STOCKHOLM • ATHENS • TOKYO • MILAN
MADRID • WARSAW • BUDAPEST • AUCKLAND

First edition July 2014

ISBN-13: 978-0-373-62627-4

Special thanks and acknowledgment to
Victor Milan for his contribution to this work.

DESOLATION ANGELS

Printed in U.S.A.

We first crush people to the earth, and then claim the right of trampling on them forever, because they are prostrate.
—Lydia Maria Francis Child,
1802–1880

THE DEATHLANDS SAGA

This world is their legacy, a world born in the violent nuclear spasm of 2001 that was the bitter outcome of a struggle for global dominance.

There is no real escape from this shockscape where life always hangs in the balance, vulnerable to newly demonic nature, barbarism, lawlessness.

But they are the warrior survivalists, and they endure—in the way of the lion, the hawk and the tiger, true to nature's heart despite its ruination.

Ryan Cawdor: The privileged son of an East Coast baron. Acquainted with betrayal from a tender age, he is a master of the hard realities.

Krysty Wroth: Harmony ville's own Titian-haired beauty, a woman with the strength of tempered steel. Her premonitions and Gaia powers have been fostered by her Mother Sonja.

J. B. Dix, the Armorer: Weapons master and Ryan's close ally, he, too, honed his skills traversing the Deathlands with the legendary Trader.

Doctor Theophilus Tanner: Torn from his family and a gentler life in 1896, Doc has been thrown into a future he couldn't have imagined.

Dr. Mildred Wyeth: Her father was killed by the Ku Klux Klan, but her fate is not much lighter. Restored from pre-dark cryogenic suspension, she brings twentieth-century healing skills to a nightmare.

Jak Lauren: A true child of the wastelands, reared on adversity, loss and danger, the albino teenager is a fierce fighter and loyal friend.

Dean Cawdor: Ryan's young son by Sharona accepts the only world he knows, and yet he is the seedling bearing the promise of tomorrow.

In a world where all was lost, they are humanity's last hope....

Chapter One

"Ryan! Wake up! We've got a problem!"

Mildred Wyeth's urgent voice cut through the dreadful jump disorientation and summoned Ryan Cawdor's soul back to his pain-racked body. His stomach felt as if it had been wrenched inside out.

Bad one, he thought. Been through worse.

When he opened his eye, he was already being helped up by a firm, dry grip on his forearm. That would be J. B. Dix, Ryan's chief lieutenant, best friend and the armorer of the small group of companions who traveled the Deathlands.

"Tell me something new," Ryan said, slurring his words. He swayed as he got to his feet and was steadied by J.B. "Is everyone else awake?"

J.B. didn't have time to answer the question.

"Muties!" Ricky Morales screamed. There was no mistaking the hideous shapes visible through the opaque armaglass walls of the mat-trans unit.

Ryan was back in command of his body, and he slammed the heel of his hand on the big red button by the keypad that controlled the workings of the gateway. The LD button was a fail-safe designed to transfer the companions back to their last destination.

No one had a desire to return to what remained of the ville of Progress, but that was the least of their worries.

Nothing happened.

"So we're stuck here," Mildred said after several moments.

The stocky black woman, her hair in beaded plaits, didn't even flinch as a face pressed itself against the glass, becoming nearly visible through the opaque wall. Its nose was two holes above a wide-open mouth full of jagged teeth. Its eyes, though unnaturally round, were disconcertingly humanlike. Enough to show an almost intolerable rage.

"RYAN," KRYSTY WORTH CALLED. The statuesque beauty was staring at the base of the armaglass walls. Her sentient red hair was still coiled tightly to her scalp, as it tended to do in times of severe stress. "Water's building up in here."

"Great," Mildred moaned. "Isn't this a bit coincidental? I mean muties, yeah. Muties are everywhere. But we jump in here and the place decides to flood right now?"

"With the chamber door closed securely, that should be nearly impossible," said a tall, silver-haired man. He shot the cuffs of the dingy white shirt he wore beneath his black frock coat with an elegance that belied the shabbiness of the garment. Doc Tanner knew a little about the workings of the network—and the white coats who built them—because they'd trawled him out of his own time in the 1890s to use and abuse as a subject for their experiments in time. And when Doc proved to be a most unwilling subject, he was sent into the future to what was now the Deathlands. Their experiments had prematurely aged him. Although he appeared to be a man in his late sixties, Doc was really in his thirties.

Ryan drew his SIG Sauer P226 handblaster with his right hand and his panga with his left.

"Get ready to blast out of here," he said. "J.B., you do the honors."

The one-eyed man took in his little group with a sweeping glance. Krysty stood resolutely at his right shoulder, gripping her Smith & Wesson snub-nosed .38 revolver in both hands. Mildred stood just behind her, holding her more substantial .38 ZKR target revolver at the ready. Doc had drawn both his LeMat replica handgun, with the stubby shotgun barrel beneath its immense cylinder holding nine rounds of .44 Special, and the blade concealed in his ebony sword stick with the silver lion's head. Ricky held his Webley top-break .45 revolver.

Ryan stood right behind J.B.'s left shoulder. The Armorer had his Uzi slung muzzle down over his shoulder and his Smith & Wesson M4000 riot shotgun held level. Jak Lauren stood at J.B.'s right.

"Ready?" Ryan asked. More muties seemed to be crowding into the anteroom.

"Ready as we're going to be," Mildred said. The others voiced their agreement.

"Hit it," Ryan told J.B.

He maneuvered the lever that opened the door, and water swirled in, almost to the tops of Ryan's boots. With it came stink of sewage so thick the one-eyed man almost choked.

J.B. was already striding forward through the anteroom with his scattergun held level. The mutie that had pressed its hideous face against the armaglass swung a black-taloned hand at the Armorer.

He blasted it in the belly with a charge of #4 buckshot. The weapon's report almost imploded Ryan's eardrums in the walled confines of the jump chamber. The mutie vented a high-pitched squeal and doubled over, clutching its ruptured gut with three-fingered hands.

The Armorer dealt it an uppercut with the butt of his longblaster. Its round head snapped up on its stalk neck and it fell over backward. It raised a splash of foul-smelling water that was already up to the tops of J.B.'s ankles. By now the rest of the companions had left the jump chamber and were all through the anteroom and into the control room.

The other muties closed in as Ryan and Jak fanned out to the sides. Ryan stepped forward to close with a mutie slashing overhand at him. He blocked with his left forearm and hacked at the creature's upper arm with the panga.

It felt more as though the weapon was hitting dense mud or clay rather than flesh, but it struck bone. The mutie keened and struck with its left claw. Ryan kicked it in the belly, and it staggered back with thick blood oozing from the gash in its arm.

A mutie attacked from Ryan's left. Doc stepped forward and thrust his sword through the creature's head. It fell.

Four of the muties were down. The other four hung back as if uncertain. Unfortunately, they were between Ryan's group and the door.

A loud *crack* almost like thunder echoed through the facility. The floor shook once, hard, beneath Ryan's boot. Raw sewage sloshed up the walls and on the inert, dark comp stations that lined them.

A grinding squeal sounded behind Ryan's left shoulder. He snapped his head around. A section of concrete wall as high as his head split open, and a sheet of greenish-brown water shot into the control room. It splashed down.

"Aah, shit!" Mildred exclaimed as a wave of water broke as high as her waist. Ryan set his jaw against the stench. It wouldn't kill him. The muties—or drowning in shit— might.

The long-armed muties dithered as if unsure whether to fight or flee. In other circumstances Ryan would have been glad to have his friends hold off, saving their energy, and ammo, to see if the creatures decided to bolt.

Unfortunately, the sewage was rising rapidly now. The sulfurous smell made Ryan's eye water and his head swim.

"Power on through!" he shouted.

Following his own command, he charged ahead. He swatted a mutie in his path in the side of the head with the wide flat blade of the panga. Not because he was feeling unduly merciful, but because he didn't want the knife getting stuck.

The door leading into the corridor was jammed open. Raising a brown wave from water already up to his thighs, Ryan sloshed down the hall, beating J.B. to a staircase and pounding upward. A mutie shambled down the steps toward him from the landing above. The one-eyed man gave the trigger a double tap, and both shots hit in the creature's chest. It coughed in a very human-sounding way and fell against the wall. Ryan raced past. It didn't even try to swipe at him with its claws. Just as he reached the landing, he heard the cry from below. "Ryan!"

He stopped and looked back. J.B., Doc and Jak were all on the stairs right behind him. Mildred and Krysty stood farther down with the foul water swirling around them, trying to drag Ricky up out of the sewage. Apparently it had either knocked him down or floated him off his feet. Muties were clinging to the youth with their long arms, holding him back from escaping the flooding corridor.

Chapter Two

Ryan realized that the muties seemed to be using Ricky as a flotation device rather than trying to drag him to his doom.

"I have had enough of this shit," Mildred declared. She drew her ZKR 551 handblaster, which she'd holstered to try to help Ricky. Aiming quickly, she shot both muties through their round heads. One uttered a croak of dismay as it let go and floundered back into the eddying sewage. The other threw up its arms and sank without a sound.

Ryan turned back and started moving again as the women got Ricky onto the steps. The water was following more rapidly now.

As Ryan turned on the landing to head up the next flight, Jak eeled past J.B., who halted, holding his shotgun muzzle up.

"More muties," said the albino, who'd obviously slipped ahead to scout the next floor when Ryan paused.

"Waiting for us?" Ryan asked.

Jak shook his head.

"Most sleeping," he said. "Some awake. Starting move this way."

"Push on, J.B.," Ryan said. "We can't stay here."

"On my way."

He headed up, shotgun at the ready. Ryan bulled past Jak, intent on being right on J.B.'s heels when the little

man hit the next level. Jak faded back against the wall to
let Ryan pass, then followed close behind.

The next level was open space. The ceiling lighting had
malfunctioned, leaving alternating areas of light and dark,
interspersed with a few patches of flashing illumination.
The stairwell itself was unenclosed. The open space was
wide enough that its actual size was indeterminate in the
shadows. It suggested a parking garage, though Ryan registered quickly that that was mainly because the sturdy
structural columns were exposed to view.

The air was thick, barely stirred by the redoubt's venti-
lation system. It smelled heavily of stale urine, feces, mil-
dew and not-quite-human sweat.

Around him muties were stirring from what he could
only think of as nests: little rough enclosures improvised
of broken furniture and random scavenged material, with
moldering cushions and bits of cloth for padding from the
hard, bare concrete floor. Some muties began to shamble
toward them, waving their arms menacingly, from a nest
not twenty feet away.

J.B. raked them with two quick bursts from his Uzi,
the copper-jacketed 9 mm slugs slamming the muties to
the floor, where they lay clutching their guts and squalling piteously.

The noise roused the others, who came out of the well
as J.B. headed up the exposed stairs.

Ryan followed J.B. tightly. He heard shots from behind.

"We're fine!" Krysty shouted as the cracking concrete
echoed through the vast empty space. "Keep moving! Water's rising fast!"

Ryan moved. They hit the next landing and kept on
going. A mutie turned onto the stairs from the floor above,
silhouetting itself against a flickering glow from more mal-

functioning overheads. It started down before registering norms were charging up.

J.B. slashed the creature with the butt of his M4000. It released an ear-splitting squeal and fell against the steel railing to the Armorer's right. J.B. raced past.

Ryan split its teardrop-shaped head with an overhand stroke of his panga in passing and never even slowed. The creature toppled backward over the railing and plummeted to the floor.

The distinctive boom of the shotgun mounted on Doc's LeMat echoed up the stairs at a volume that seemed to make the wall ripple. Ryan didn't glance back.

"No more stairs!" J.B. called out as he reached the top of the flight.

"Find us a way out, J.B.," Ryan said.

The Armorer let the M4000 fall to hang by its sling over one shoulder and scooped up the Uzi on the sling on the other. He hastily fired a short burst over the handrail. Ryan joined him.

This level was divided into rooms. A corridor ran along the near wall, while another stretched away from them at a T junction. As on the floor below, the lighting here was patchy.

By the flickering light and alternating patches of shine and shadow J.B. had just blasted a trio of muties coming at them along the corridor running away from the wall. One of them went down thrashing at the half-rotted rubber floor runners, spraying thick green blood everywhere. The others ran off twittering.

The bad news was they ducked into one of the doors standing open to both sides of the corridor.

Ryan took quick stock of their situation. They had three choices of which way to go from here—other than back down, which wasn't happening. The corridor looked to move on to more lateral passages at either end. It was clear both ways for the moment.

"Gotta move!" Mildred's voice boomed up from the stairs beneath Ryan. "Crap's still coming. As well as a whole boatload of more muties!"

"Where is all this pressure coming from?" asked J.B. He swiveled his head constantly to make sure no new threats caught them unawares.

"Clearly, the sewage floats on water coming from a substantial body of it, whether lake, river or even ocean," Doc called up.

He punctuated his statement with two quick, echoing blasts of his .44 blaster. Then he continued unperturbedly. "Quite nearby. Possibly above us."

"Above us?" Mildred repeated. "That's great. So what if there's no way out?"

"They didn't build this place with no exit other than the mat-trans," Ryan said. "There's a way out."

"Also a way in," J.B. added. "Unless they bred those muties here. And unless they don't have to eat."

"Got too many pointy teeth for that," Ryan growled.

"Look!" Jak pointed along the corridor where the death throes of the mutie J.B. had shot were subsiding to chirps and twitches. An overhead light had come on at the far end, revealing a door with a grated window that looked suspiciously as if it led to another set of stairs.

"Go," Ryan said as another pair of shots boomed out from just below. He recognized the sound of his lover's Smith & Wesson 640. Its short barrel produced more noise than muzzle energy. If Krysty was blasting, it meant the muties were getting close.

Jak was usually a master of stealth, but he set off running at full speed. His long white hair streamed out behind his head like the neck cloth of a cap.

J.B. took off after him at a trot. He'd already swapped the Uzi for the M4000.

Ryan followed, panga and SIG Sauer at the ready. Jak was clearly bent on reaching the possible exit—at least from this level—as fast as possible. His companions had to keep the muties from the side rooms off his back and away from themselves. And above all, they had to keep moving.

There would be no room-by-room sweep, despite the fact it was safer, to say nothing of the possible scavvy awaiting them. Right then the only thing that gave them a chance at surviving another ten minutes was speed, speed and more speed.

For a moment, Ryan thought Jak was going to run the gauntlet of open doors unscathed. Then a mutie popped out of a room to the right, just at the end.

Jak punched it across the face with the knuckleduster hilt of the trench knife he carried and never slowed. The creature reeled back out of sight, clutching itself and keening in anguish.

Jak sped to the other end of the corridor, the open doorways to either side spewing claw-waving muties in his wake.

"Fireblast!" Ryan exclaimed. "We can't shoot or we might hit him!"

He and J.B. kept charging ahead regardless. There was nothing else to do.

But Jak had grown up fighting. He knew he was in his friends' line of fire as well as they did. Through the crowd of fluting, growling, arm-waving muties blocking their way, Ryan saw the slim white figure slip aside, out of his line of sight. A moment later the boom of his .357 Magnum Colt Python reverberated down the hallway, muted only slightly by the dropped ceiling.

J.B. promptly snagged the grip of his Uzi in his left

hand, rotated the muzzle upward and fired a quick blast into the mutie mob. Apparently oblivious to Jak's passage, or just attracted by the more target-rich environment the other way, they had surged toward him and Ryan.

As before, the front rank of creatures staggered back. One fell backward, flailing its long arms. Others tried to bolt back—into the faces of their fellows.

The Armorer charged into that ball of confusion. He let the Uzi drop to the end of its sling and grabbed the fore-grip of his M4000 shotgun.

He fired two quick blasts into the mass. Green ichor flew. Muties bleated and shrilled in pain and fear.

Then J.B. was into them like a buzz saw. His scattergun was designed and built to be used as a riot baton as much as a blaster. There was nothing delicate about the weapon.

J.B. made full use of it. He jabbed the muzzle into the sunken chest of a mutie that was trying to hold in its guts and pushed it out of the way. A high-pitched scream issued from the mutie as the still-hot steel branded its chest.

J.B. flung it to the left, knocking an apparently un-wounded mutie into the wall along with it. Then he broke a second's spindly neck with a backstroke of the butt plate.

These things aren't so tough, Ryan thought as he followed hard behind J.B. So far things had gone the way of his friends and himself.

The mutie J.B. had forced out of his path with the dying body of its comrade caught Ryan across the cheek with a swipe of its long black talons.

That was his blind side. He yanked his panga free of the mutie he'd just dispatched and, turning his head that way, slashed savagely in reprisal. He caught a look of round-eyed surprise. The eyes were big and blue and altogether human—too human. The monster yelped and flung up its arm protectively.

A pulse of viscous green mutie blood gushed toward Ryan as the claw-tipped arm was slashed below the wrist.

The mutie howled. It grabbed its hosing stump with its remaining hand and slid down the wall.

Ryan turned his face the other way in time to intercept another claw coming for his good eye. Blue-gray fingers flew into the air. Ryan raised the SIG Sauer in his left hand and fired a shot into the open saw-toothed mouth. Brains splattered across the bare wall behind the mutie's head. Behind him he heard a mutie squeak in alarm, then a wet sound, followed by Doc crowing triumph. "Be gone, brigand!"

Apparently the old man had chosen to wade in close behind Ryan, as Ryan had done with J.B. That put the three with the most effective melee weapons in the lead, leaving the women and Ricky to guard their backs. For all his occasional mental deficiency and frail demeanor, Doc was as seasoned and formidable a fighter as any of them.

Unlike some muties, these weird, long-armed creatures with their rubbery flesh were total berserk diehards who kept attacking regardless of how many were killed. Their wailing and chirping changed pitch, taking on a frantic tone. They began to jostle and fall across one another in their haste to dive back into the rooms they'd just left.

Ryan was fairly sure they ate humans. Those pointed teeth were meant to rip flesh, and the instantaneous eagerness with which the muties attacked them on sight suggested appetite was a strong motivating factor. Although they could simply be outraged homeowners defending their violated castle, he supposed. Cannies usually were norms.

No reason they can't be both, he thought. Doesn't matter much. We'll be done with them in a few minutes, anyway. One way or another.

"Don't slow down to admire your handiwork!" Mildred

yelled from the rear by the door at the last set of stairs. "A whole bunch is coming right after us!"

That warning was punctuated by the characteristic bark of her ZKR 551.

Jak stood with his back to the wall by the handle side of the heavy door with the grated window. He had his trench knife in one hand and his Colt Python in the other. His white hair flew as he swiveled his head sharply left and right to look both ways down the corridor that ran along that wall perpendicular to the one his friends were running down.

A pair of muties lay still at his feet.

"Clear?" J.B. called to him.

"Clear!"

"Secure the stairs," Ryan commanded.

The corridor had emptied miraculously ahead of them. As Jak yanked on the door and rushed through the opening, J.B. increased his pace to full speed. Such as it was. Ryan had to keep his own steps throttled back to keep from overrunning his friend with his much longer legs.

"Be careful passing the open doors," he yelled for the benefit of his friends behind him.

"We know that, Ryan!" Krysty called back. She sounded exasperated. "Just go, all right?"

He followed his own advice, cranking his head rapidly left and right to check each yawning door as he passed to make sure none of the muties had become emboldened enough to join the attack. He caught glimpses of knots of the creatures huddled back as far from the door as possible. Clearly they'd had enough of fighting for now.

They'll be on our heels quick enough when the sewage starts to gurgle up around those black-nailed toes of theirs, Ryan thought.

J.B. reached the end of the corridor. He stopped and

turned briskly left to peer that way with the longblaster presented at his shoulder. "Clear," he called, then looked back over his shoulder.

He repeated his assurance.

"Move!" Ryan yelled to him.

He did. He flashed across the crossing corridor, hauled open the door Jak had disappeared through and followed.

Ryan barely broke stride to check the cross passage was still empty of threats. He caught the heavy door as it closed and threw it wide. A long arm in a black coat sleeve reached out to catch it and hold it.

"Ladies first," Doc announced as Ryan dashed in to turn to look up the next stairs.

"Your ass, old man!" Mildred shouted. "Just keep moving!"

Ryan pounded up the steps to the landing. Jak was crouched at the next level, which Ryan could see was the top. Of this stairwell, anyway. J.B. stood on the steps right behind him, shotgun ready.

"Way out," Jak said. "Clear."

"Go," Ryan ordered. It was getting repetitive. But it was still needed. Just because the situation they'd been dropped face-first into kept hitting them with simple yes-or-no choices didn't mean the answer was ever clear. And as lead wolf in the pack, it was Ryan's call to try to guess which alternative was bad and which was worse, every time, with no time to think.

He smiled, briefly and grimly, as he remembered a pre-dark phrase Mildred sometimes used: "That's why I get paid the big bucks."

Jak popped out the door with J.B. right behind him. Ryan hastily followed.

As he did, he heard Krysty shout, "All the muties in the world are coming up after us!"

The first thing Ryan saw when he emerged from the open door to the stairwell was sunlight streaming in from tall, narrow, broken windows onto a concrete floor littered with fragments of tables and chairs and, incongruously, a scattering of dry, gray leaves.

He stepped quickly to one side. A doorway was a bad place to linger. It was set flush to the back wall of what had obviously been a store or restaurant, as if it gave onto a utility closet. There was no front door. The light was that of morning by color alone. He saw surprisingly lush trees across the street. Through the leaves he glimpsed yellow stone and a hint of some kind of tracery of stone or metal. It reminded him of the leading used to hold stained glass in predark churches.

J.B. had taken a position on the other side of the door to the hidden stair. Finding the room empty, he had switched to his Uzi. Jak slipped cautiously toward the window.

"No time!" Mildred yelled as she came bursting out the door on Doc's heels. "They're right behind us!"

Ryan heard the boom of Ricky's Webley handblaster echo out of the stairwell and started moving toward the window.

"Looks clear," Jak said, peering around the edge of the empty window. He promptly slipped around and onto the street.

Deciding that securing escape was more important than helping discourage the long-armed muties from following too fast, he went for the front door. The others came hot behind, starting with J.B.

Ryan burst out onto the street. The first thing he noticed was the humidity that hit him in the face like a wool blanket soaked in hot water. The second was how profuse the vegetation was—grass and flowers were pushing up through big cracks heaved in the pavement, and there were trees all down the block that extended to his left.

The third thing he noticed was a tall, skeletally thin woman with an electric-green Mohawk casually strolling around the corner of the building across the street to his right.

But there was nothing casual about the way she whipped up the M16 she'd been carrying in patrol position and aimed it at Ryan.

Chapter Three

"Get down!" Ryan shouted to his companions. He snapped off a shot and threw himself back toward the door to the redoubt.

He bumped into Doc. That had been half his intention—to keep those behind from blundering out into the unexpected enemy's field of fire. The other half was to try to back out of it himself.

The black longblaster snarled out a burst of full-auto fire. Ryan didn't know where the bullets hit. He only knew they didn't hit *him*.

Then J.B., who had come out right behind Ryan and taken a reflex step to his right, ripped off a short burst of his own. The woman dropped onto her buttocks. The front of her grimy gray T-shirt was already showing darker, redder stains overwhelming the old ones.

"More!" Jak yelled from his position crouched before the window to Ryan's right.

Ryan had caught himself on one knee in the doorway. Now he saw more men and women fanning out diagonally across the street. They sported variations of partially shaved heads and spiked, outlandishly colored hair. And a nasty assortment of weapons.

"Pull back!" he yelled. He turned and scrambled into the cool dimness of the derelict room.

"But, Ryan—" Mildred began.

"Shut it! Get back in the corner." He gestured toward the far rear corner where they'd come out. "Now!"

Shots were crackling outside with a sound like a big, dry tumbleweed going up in flames. By sheer bad luck the companions had come up against a sizable local faction. One with itchy trigger fingers—and the blasters and bullets to give them a hearty scratching. Bullets clattered off the stone exterior and whizzed through the vacant windows or snapped with tiny sonic booms. They ricocheted off the back wall and tumbled, whining, in random directions.

J.B. hunkered just inside the doorway, leaning out—randomly varying high, middle and low—to rip off quick rounds, two-shot bursts and singletons. It took a good blaster man to make the Uzi do that. J.B. was the best—a master. Ryan snapped a shot from his own 9 mm handblaster at a figure with a black leather vest open to show a fish-belly-white washboard torso, aiming a sawed-off double-barreled scattergun. Fortunately it was clear across the street and unlikely to hit much at that range. Or not with many pellets, anyway. Though as Ryan knew well, they all hurt.

He never saw whether he hit the dude or not. He was already turning away to follow his advice and sprint to the rear corner of the dimly lit room, well back in the shadows. He heard Jak's big Python crack. The albino had simply jumped back in through the window and was crouching to shoot out over the sill.

"Tables!" Ryan yelled. He sheathed his panga. "J.B., come on! Give me a hand."

J.B. loosed a lengthy burst out the door as he wheeled away to obey. Then he and Ryan were each manhandling a pair of tables with tops a yard or so square toward their friends, who were already hunkered down in the corner.

Jak joined them dragging a detached tabletop. Ryan decided the place had to have been an eatery of some sort.

"Hoist them up!" Ryan yelled. "Barricade yourselves behind them!"

He hurried into the corner with the others, right next to Krysty. She helped him shift the table so that one edge rested on the floor, whose covering had long since eroded to bare concrete, with the legs pointing into the room. His other friends did likewise.

Not an eyeblink too soon. The door to the secret stair puked muties. They gushed out in a blue-gray, squalling, whistling horde, waving their long-taloned arms in the air. At once they made for the open front door.

It took a moment before any even noticed the norms, huddled off in the shadows as they were. A pair turned toward them menacingly. Since that had been expected— he'd wanted the improvised tabletop barricades for cover— Ryan wasn't too worried. He fired a couple shots from his SIG into one mutie. Krysty and Mildred blasted the other. One fell on its face. The other staggered back into the violent flow of its companions.

They flung it ruthlessly aside. Whether they were especially squeamish about getting soaked in the sewage, or just concerned with not drowning, Ryan couldn't know and couldn't care less.

The rest of the stream of oddly rubbery-fleshed muties shot straight out into the street. And into the faces of the gang of locals, who had deployed into a skirmish line and were advancing on the diner to mop up the intruders.

Through a window Ryan saw their jaws drop and their eyes widen in shock. "Fuck us," somebody yelled. "It's clayboys!"

The muties ran right into them and commenced to rip at them with their claws. Blood and bits of flesh and guts flew. Blasters roared. Men, women and muties screamed and flailed at one another. The locals who weren't instantly overrun or caught up in the wild melee pulled back to fire into the geyser of panicked muties. Ryan saw a couple turn tail and run.

Though muties were still coming out of the stairwell, Ryan stood up from behind the table. None of the muties so much as glanced his way. Clearly they had something more urgent on their minds. The sulfurous stench that suddenly filled the room gave him a good clue as to what that was.

"Let's power out of here," he ordered. "Out the window and left down the street."

Krysty jumped up. The table fell with a slam.

Ryan let her go out first. She was his woman after all— though as capable as a man in a fight and better than most. He followed, darting a few steps to the left as soon as he cleared the opening, then turning back to cover his friends' escape.

They came popping out in surprisingly good order. Beyond them a pitched battle between locals and muties filled the street and claimed everybody else's attention.

"You'd better move, Ryan!" Mildred called as she raced past.

Ricky was last out the window. He stumbled and almost fell on his face getting out. The youth caught himself, picked himself up and started running up the block away from the scrum. As he passed, Ryan did likewise.

The others sprinted past an alley and rounded the corner of the next building. As he flashed past the alley mouth, some instinct made Ryan glance over his shoulder—just in time to see a green-brown gusher of sewage blast out the door and windows of the redoubt's surface false front and swamp the battling humans and muties in a reeking torrent.

"That's not something you see every day," J.B. remarked as Ryan reached the others.

"Keep going," the one-eyed man said. "Unless you want to get wet again. We don't know how far that stuff's going to flood."

They trotted down the cross street. From the angle of the sun and the time of year, Ryan knew they were heading southwest. What mattered most now was that they were heading away from the shit-flooded death trap the redoubt had become.

Turned out, the sewage didn't reach far at all. Glancing back from a block or so away, Ryan saw a brown puddle flow out into the intersection and then stop. Apparently the pressure had finally equalized.

Which was a good thing. The very next block up the street from the hidden redoubt was effectively dammed by a skyscraper that had fallen to the east, knocking down the opposing building like a giant domino. Had the sewage continued to rise, things might've gotten way too interesting in a hurry.

"I don't think they're following us," Krysty said.

Mildred laughed. "Understatement of the day."

Ryan directed the group into a gutted corner building on the right side of the street. Its interior showed sign of a major fire, but from the lack of smell or even soot, it had burned out long ago. There was no furniture or serious trash buildup in the corners. Everybody sat on the floor to take a breather and a pull from their water bottles.

"I know where we are," J.B. said as he stepped into the shade. As hot as it was inside it was still a relief after the blast of sunlight. He was tucking away his minisextant. "Detroit."

"Outstanding," Mildred said. "I've been here. It was crappy *before* the balloon went up."

"Did you check your rad counter, J.B.?" Krysty asked. "Something busted the ville up pretty well."

"Already on it," Ryan said, looking down at the small rad counter pinned to the lapel of his coat. "Rad levels are high, but not enough to be a real problem in the short run. We'll just have to keep our eyes skinned for fallout hot spots."

Mildred shrugged. "Somehow the idea of dying of cancer in thirty years doesn't really terrify me," she said.

"I daresay that when you visited Detroit before," Doc said, looking out a window to the southwest, "it looked substantially different from this. And I do not refer to the obvious damage."

"I didn't expect it to be this overgrown," Mildred said. "I mean, it's pretty humid here. This is Great Lakes country after all. There's a river not far south and a smaller lake somewhere not too far east. But usually urban desolation is more, uh, *desolate*."

"That may suggest where the water pressure came from to drive the flooding of the late redoubt," Doc said.

"What could've cracked its shell like that?" Ricky asked.

"Mebbe shockwave from a ground burst," J.B. said. "Or some of those big earthquakes they had everywhere before the bombs even stopped falling."

"Been over a hundred years of hardship and bad times since," Ryan added. "A lot can happen in that time. Even to a redoubt."

He gestured out the window Doc had been gazing through. "And I don't know if you've noticed. It's not all just overgrowth busting up through the pavement and whatnot. That's an actual open field right there next to us, though it's a small one. And that's not random weeds and brush, either."

"By the Three Kennedys!" Doc exclaimed. "It's a truck garden! They even have growing frames."

"Well, we know people are here," Mildred said. "They have to eat. It makes sense they'd grow food where they could." She laughed. "So that gives us an idea where all that poop came from. But why so much of it?"

"Mebbe a lot of people live in these ruins," Krysty said. "Might be plots like this all over the place."

"But why would they all be pooping into the old sewer system?" Mildred demanded. "I mean, I know gravity still works. Without power to pump it to treatment plants, it'll all just flow down to the river. And God help the poor bastards downstream. But why do they bother?"

Ryan scratched an ear with his forefinger.

"Mebbe we don't live as refined as people did back in your time, Mildred," Ryan said, "but we still remember the old saying, 'Don't shit where you eat.' And why bother digging latrines if you got sewers?"

"You're right, Ryan," Mildred said, instantly contrite. "I didn't mean to imply everybody these days is a barbarian."

Ryan chuckled. "Mostly we are. Just not that kind."

"So where do we go from here, lover?" Krysty asked.

"There's a big structure another few blocks, the way we were going," J. B. said. "Looks half-trashed. You could still fit a respectable ville's worth of folks inside by the looks of things."

"Downtown seems to be behind us," Ryan said. "And to the north from what I could see as we were leaving the redoubt. Not that I looked hard at anything but a way out of there."

"Do we *want* to potentially meet a whole ville's worth of people?" Mildred asked. "That first bunch seemed anything but friendly, and I'm not even counting the muties. What'd they call them again?"

"Clayboys," Ricky said. He had taken up station beside a front window, keeping an eye on the way they'd come. He had his DeLisle unslung. Jak crouched by the southwest window like an alert dog.

"Yeah. Look," Mildred added, "if I recall correctly, Windsor's right across the river. It used to be part of Canada. The only part of Canada south of a big U.S. city, at least in the old lower forty-eight, I think. And if we're south of downtown, or close to it, we're near the river. Maybe we should head that way."

"Mebbe not everybody's as hostile as that first crew," J.B. said.

"And here I thought you were the reliably paranoid one, John," she replied.

"I just reckon that if we took people by surprise in their own backyard, naturally they're gonna react."

"Who's growing the food?" Krysty asked suddenly. "Those punk types didn't strike me as the farming sort."

"More like enforcers," Ryan said. "Or raiders."

He rubbed his jaw. Quick-growing stubble rasped his palm.

"Why did we want to be in a hurry to shake the dust of this place off our boot heels?" he asked.

Everybody looked at him.

"I presume that was not a rhetorical question," Doc said slowly. "Inasmuch as you have notoriously little patience with such."

"No. Practical. Why do we think we'd get a better reception in this Windsor ville, anyway? Seems like they're in pretty much the same boat as Detroit. And let me remind everybody, although we've got lots of ammo at the moment, we're starting to run low on rations."

"Then what's your plan?" Mildred asked. "It doesn't

look as if the beans and corn across the street are near ready to be picked and eaten."

"Not to mention they'll be guarded," Krysty said. "Either by the bunch with the pink Mohawks or those against them."

"And that's it," Ryan said. "You got food here. You got people growing the food. You got people with blasters. That means you got trouble."

J.B. shrugged. "Could have stood pat with just, 'You got people,'" he said.

"Yeah. Well. What I'm saying is, there's trouble for us to fix. And food to pay us with for fixing it. I'm not sure a better deal's liable to just come strolling along."

"It's a big city, Ryan," Krysty said. "Isn't that kind of a tall order?"

He grinned.

"When isn't it?"

THEY HEADED OUT. Ryan decided to keep going the way they had been, southwest, in the general direction of the immense half-collapsed rectangular structure.

Krysty had misgivings about that. She was in her own way even more attuned to the natural world than their former wild child Jak, who was now ranging out in front of the rest scouting for danger—a job he insisted on doing despite his discomfort in urban surroundings. Being in the middle of the steel-and-concrete corpse of a great predark city felt unnerving enough, though the greenery bursting out through cracks in the rubble as if to reclaim it in so many places kept her from feeling cut off from Gaia.

The corner they approached was apparently an entrance. It consisted of blocky shapes tiered outward and upward from a corner cut out of the giant building. The doors had once held glass, long since blown out, leaving rusting metal frames like cage walls.

A colonnade ran down the building face along the street to their left. The street itself remained more or less intact. It was still passable, anyway, in spite of being heaved and broken in a crazy quilt of angled planes. And still passed, she reckoned, to judge by the fact that little more than sprouts and tufts showed through the network of innumerable cracks.

The space between it and the facade had obviously been a broad walkway. Now the pavement was gone, replaced by neat rows of cultivated plants—potatoes, beans twining up stakes, green vegetables, rows of shoulder-high corn along the edge closer to the structure where they wouldn't deny the other crops light. It all looked terribly vulnerable to Krysty.

"I wonder where everybody is," Ricky said from behind her.

As they approached the vast derelict—or *ruin,* she corrected herself, because somebody pretty evidently still occupied it—they had fanned out into a V formation, with Ryan at the point, Krysty at his left side and J.B. to his right. Mildred walked just behind J.B. Doc followed Krysty. Jak zigzagged cautiously ten yards ahead of Ryan. Ricky brought up the rear in a line behind Ryan.

"Somebody's spent a lot of time tending that garden," he said. "Like the one behind us. And somebody keeps the junk from building up in that place we took our break. So where are they?"

"Laying low," J.B. said. "They likely heard blasters. Decided to duck and cover until whoever was having the disagreement sorted things out."

"Think they're inside that thing?" Mildred asked uneasily.

"Seems likely," Ryan said.

Jak crouched up the concrete steps to the entrance, well over to the right so he wasn't walking right up to the open, Cubist cave mouth. He glanced inside.

"See nothing," he called back softly.

"Ryan?" Krysty asked.

"Drive on," he said firmly.

"You sure that's wise?" Mildred asked.

"No. If we were wise, we wouldn't be here."

"Where else would we be, then, Ryan?" Doc asked.

"If I knew that," Ryan gritted, "we'd be there. Right. We walk in like we own the place."

"Won't somebody spot us?" Ricky squeaked.

"Son," J.B. said, "somebody has. You don't think people survive in a place like this without keeping close watch on everything that goes on in their immediate area? *Especially* intruders coming into it."

Ryan led the way boldly up the steps. Jak slipped around and inside the building, trusting his superior senses and reflexes to alert him to any lurking dangers—especially ambushers—and get him out of the jaws of any trap before they slammed shut.

Inside was cool and dark, especially after the hot dazzle of the downtown street. Coils of razor wire were positioned at both sides of the entrance, at angles to leave the way in and out clear.

"Looks like somebody likes to be able to shut the place up tight," J.B. remarked. "Keep unwanted guests out."

"It is not working on us," Doc said.

J.B. shrugged. "Mebbe we're not what they had in mind."

"Huh," Mildred said, sniffing the air. "It doesn't smell like sewage. Much. Other than us, I mean. We have *got* to get cleaned up. I know everybody these days has a super immune system, but if we don't want any little scratch to give us *pseudomonas,* so that our legs swell up and go gangrenous and have to be cut off—"

"Enough," Ryan said. He halted them just inside the lobby.

"Anyway, it seems like a good sign," she finished.

"People live," Jak said. He crouched in an area right of the entrance, where a picnic table and some chairs had been set in what might have once been a kiosk. Its enclosure was now just metal uprights to hold long-vanished glass.

"Yep, they do," Mildred said. "Somewhere. The question is, do any live here?"

"They do," Krysty said. "I smell food cooking. With onion, garlic and basil."

Her stomach rumbled as she said it.

"Mebbe they'll invite us to join them for lunch," Ricky said.

"Or to be lunch," J.B. suggested.

Other tables and chairs sat on a tile floor, dark gray on lighter gray down the central strip that ran from the door, mixed shades of blue and gray to the sides. It looked as if the area was used for socializing. A dead escalator rose at the far end to a second story surrounded by a rail.

"Ryan, look," Krysty said as they advanced. She pointed at a giant square doorway that opened to their right.

Like several others, it spilled yellow daylight onto the floor tiles. Through it they could see what looked to be another farm or garden. A hole in the roof—or a roof that was missing entirely—allowed the life-giving sunlight in.

"Huh," Ryan said.

"Nobody home," Ricky stated.

"Waiting and watching to see what we do, likely," J.B. said.

"So what should we do, lover?" Krysty asked Ryan.

He had reholstered his weapons when they ducked into the building across the intersection. Now he cupped his empty hands around his mouth and hollered, "Hello! Anybody here? We've reached this ville and we're looking for work."

A blaster shot fired from the railing toward the escalator was his reply.

Chapter Four

"Mebbe they don't like outlanders," J.B. said.

"You rad-sucking fool, Tyrone!" a man's voice shouted from the gallery. "Why'd you give us away?"

"They're mercies!" another voice yelled back defensively. "We can't let Hizzoner's blasters on Angels turf!"

"Back outside!" Ryan yelled, racing toward the doors, which fortuitously were open.

As the companions turned to sprint the few steps back to the outdoors, another shot cracked out. Tile splintered to Ryan's right. Then another blaster spoke and another.

"More right!" Jak yelped. Meaning other enemies were appearing in the doorway to the odd interior garden plots.

"Hold your breath!" J.B. shouted. "Poison gas!"

Then Ryan heard a clatter and sound of something metal and weighty rolling on tile.

"Gas!" one of the ambusher screamed from the railing.

A female voice cried, "Get back!"

Ryan burst into the sunlight. He took a few steps down the steps to the street, then spun, unlimbering his Steyr and dropping to one knee. He intended to cover his friends' retreat.

He saw dirty yellow-white smoke billowing up from the middle of the wide floor. Already it rose high enough to obscure the second-story gallery from view, which meant it also obscured *them* from their enemies' view, making aimed fire impossible.

Ryan grinned as his friends came flying out of the giant half-gutted building, racing past him. He heard a rip of full-auto fire and recognized J.B.'s Uzi. The Armorer was clearly giving their attackers some additional reason not to be fast about rushing to pursue.

Of course, they would pursue. That was a given. Especially once they figured out that what J.B. had unleashed on them wasn't poison gas at all, but just one of the black-powder smoke bombs the Armorer and his apprentice, Ricky Morales, had started making in their spare time weeks ago.

Ryan was impressed by just how much smoke a bomb the size of a predark beer can produced—and how quickly.

"Best power right on," J.B. called as he trotted down the steps, holding his Uzi in his right hand and his fedora pressed to his head with his left. "They're starting to get organized, and it sounds like we got them hot well past nuke red."

Jak raced past and took off to Ryan's right to put himself in front of his companions. Everybody else was clear. Ryan had checked them off mentally as they passed him.

They headed southwest again, away from downtown—where they knew there were hostile blasters who more than likely were still keeping eyes skinned for them, even though they hadn't pursued. They wouldn't be any better disposed toward the companions after they had treated them to a faceful of mutie talons and all the accumulated sewage of some unspecified but no doubt vast swath of the great half-overgrown urban ruin-scape.

It was as good a direction as any. Ryan stood and followed.

WHEN HIS BUDDY Jak sprinted past him to take the lead in the hasty retreat, Ricky found himself half-disappointed and half-relieved. It wasn't that he was afraid to put his life on the line for his friends—he did that all the time. It was that he was a bit on the near-sighted side and hated leaving his friends' survival dependent on senses that were far less keen than the albino's.

He carried his DeLisle carbine in preference to his Webley handblaster. The big top-break, double-action revolver, converted by his uncle Benito to fire the same .45 ACP cartridges the longblaster did, was handier to use in a close-in fight, and faster, too. But he already knew the Detroit ruins hosted muties with bad attitudes toward norms. And the green growth that exploded through the broken pavement here and there, or sprouted in more or less orderly rows in the cultivated plots they sometimes passed, provided enemies with excellent cover. The sturdy, stocky DeLisle made a far better melee weapon than a handgun did.

They were running down the northwestern edge of the great half-ruined building. Even as he looked around for potential enemies, Ricky took in more of the extent of its ruination. He realized quickly why the big space they had glimpsed through the side door was full of crops and the daylight that gave them life. Something had taken off or collapsed the roof of the blocky center from twenty or thirty yards down from the entrance, all the way back to where an elevated track or walkway to a circular parking structure had been taken down by the same catastrophe. Or a similar one. The parking structure itself, mostly open, had survived intact, at least as far as Ricky could see. Open structures always seemed to have survived nuke blasts better than closed ones.

Another cultivated plot grew at the building's far end, where the elevated track had gone down. From there, several figures in dark vests jogged into the street in front of Jak and Ricky. One of them, with brown hair hanging to his shoulders, knelt and aimed a longblaster at Ricky.

A sharp *crack* punched at his left ear. He yelped and swerved.

The man with the longblaster dropped the weapon and folded over backward. What Ricky had heard, as his rational mind belatedly informed him, was the miniature sonic boom of a longblaster bullet going by him faster than the speed of sound. But it was fired from behind him. Ricky recognized the boom that reached him as the enemy gunman fell as the sound of Ryan's 7.62 mm Steyr Scout.

Not that Ricky was accustomed to hearing it from way out in front of its business end.

Jak swerved right into an intersection. Ricky followed, even as he heard Ryan yell, "Covering fire!"

Jak reached a concrete building corner. He hunkered down, leaned around and fired an ear-shattering blast from his Python.

Ricky joined him a few heartbeats later. He pressed his shoulder against the wall. Wishing he were a lefty so he could shoot without exposing almost his entire body, the youth stepped out enough to get a look at the new pack of pursuers. They seemed to be coming out of a gap in the wall of the big building. Long slabs of the fallen track lay behind them, tilted at random angles amid thick, low vegetation.

He laid his iron sights on the bare chest of the man running in the lead and pressed the trigger. His hefty longblaster fired a pistol cartridge, so it didn't have much of a kick, and the suppressed weapon barely made a sound.

The shot took the man at the upper-right top of his rib cage arch. Ricky could tell because he saw the blood splash red from beneath his target's right nipple. The man took a header, dropping his long-barreled single-action revolver and rolling over and over on the cracked blacktop.

Jak's big .357 Magnum Colt Python made more than enough noise for both weapons. When he cranked off another shot, three of the vest wearers hit the pavement. Ricky had no idea if his friend had even hit one of them. There was no way he could've nailed all three, even with the Python's tendency to overpenetrate. At least two people fired back, and Ricky and Jak had to duck hastily as chips of concrete flew from the corner.

Shots were fired from up the street, too close to be the original pursuers—they had to come from Ryan and company. Ricky bent to avoid making his head a ripe target by poking it out where it had been before and risked a quick look at the enemy.

Their pursuers were picking themselves up off the street and racing back for the far side. They left only two of their comrades lying there: the rifleman Ryan had shot and the runner Ricky got.

Their five friends pelted by, turning up the same street they had.

"Better move along," J.B. called in passing. "The first bunch got themselves sorted out, and they're not happy!"

Ricky and Jak looked at each other and grinned. Then they headed out after the others as J.B. fired a quick burst back the way he'd come, then pivoted to loose another across the street.

As RICKY AND Jak moved on, J.B. took station against the textured gray wall a few steps down the street. He held his Uzi ready. No new targets presented themselves immediately, from either the original pursuers storming out the front entrance after them or the new set from the giant building's far end. He knew they wouldn't stay out of play for long.

Ryan ran past him, turned and knelt, bringing up his Steyr.

"Into the garage!" he shouted.

J.B. promptly wheeled right and trotted toward the entrance. It was wide, meant to allow two-lane access for cars going in and out of the parking structure. He slung his Uzi and took up his shotgun.

Jak slipped in first. He still had his Python in one white fist, which looked like a child's compared to the big blaster. Concern was written all over his pinched features.

Ricky waited beside the open bay, clutching his DeLisle and peering uneasily inside. Krysty, Mildred and Doc stood in the street, out of direct line of the wide door, covering the street and the bluish building across it. They kept their handblasters ready.

Unspoken but obvious—even to J.B., who didn't take hints—was that *they* weren't any more anxious to plunge into the depths of the garage than Ricky was.

"Back me up," J.B. told his apprentice as he went by. He entered the building without waiting to see if Ricky followed. He would.

The Armorer took a step to his left to clear the fatal funnel of the doorway. Nothing good could come from standing there silhouetted by the bright daylight. While his eyes adjusted, he covered the interior with his M4000 held almost but not quite at shoulder level, ready to whip the rest of the way up at the first sign of trouble.

Jak squatted next to a thick pillar that supported the next level. In the daylight that filtered in through the building's open sides J.B. saw lots of humped shapes—cars stalled by the Big Nuke and left here to rot. Some had been torn open by scavvies. In places he could make out what looked like piles of fiberglass body panels that had been torn off by industrious scavengers looking to reclaim the metal frames.

J.B. wondered why they hadn't been far more thoroughly mined out. A colony as populous as the big ruin looked to be could always find uses for that much steel and other metal, either for itself or as valuable trade goods. They could also muster the manpower to cut up even heavy frames by hand into chunks small enough to haul away.

"Keep moving," Ryan said. "Out the other side and right."

The others were already inside the building. Ryan fired a couple quick blasts out the way they had come, though glancing back J.B. could see no targets. Evidently the one-eyed man was just reminding their pursuers of the possible consequences of sticking their noses around the corner to peer in after their prey.

J.B. doubted it would discourage them. For long, anyway. But he knew Ryan's mind and realized the idea was to keep them off everybody's asses *long enough*.

He walked forward briskly. Jak was still where he was, looking around. He clearly wasn't happy, which meant J.B. wasn't happy. He wasn't ready to charge ahead until he knew what was eating the albino.

"Not like," Jak said. "Smell…something."

J.B. had already smelled something disquieting: death. A dead creature was rotting somewhere not too far off.

That didn't mean a bent cartridge case. At any given moment, tons of dead things were rotting away around the Deathlands. Some of them once had names. No doubt plenty of various sorts of chills were decomposing away right here in the Detroit rubble.

Jak knew that as well as J.B. did. It could be a bad sign, sure. But it wasn't bad enough news to hold Jak back.

"What?" J.B. asked.

Jak shook his head. "Not tell. Something."

The death stink, somehow sweet, pervasive, infinitely horrible no matter how often you smelled it—which in all their cases had been often—could mask a host of other odors. Bad luck. But the potential dangers that smell hid were that—potential.

The pissed-off people chasing them were real. And immediate.

"Gotta go," J.B. told him. "Double fast."

Without an instant's hesitation Jak took off. He decided to run full-out, secure their way out. Speed was needed here more than caution.

J.B. followed him, less rapidly, and not just because his legs could never keep him up with Jak's even though J.B. was taller than he was. He held his shotgun across his belly, ready to blast whatever made the mistake of jumping out to challenge the intruders. He heard the footfalls of his friends pounding close behind.

When he was just past the midway point to the brightness of the far exit, a voice shouted out from behind, "There the bastards are!"

And Jak wheeled around, his face a white mask of alarm.

"Stickies!"

Chapter Five

J.B. spotted them right away, off toward a broad ramp descended from the level above.

The muties looked like tiny humans, not much smaller than Jak. They were as vicious as any creature in the Deathlands, human coldhearts included. Their noses were vertical slits, and their mouths were filled with needle teeth. They also had tough, rubbery skin, which contributed to making them double-hard to chill. Many needed a shot to the head to chill, but the companions had run across plenty who could be taken out by any kind of mortal wound.

J.B. now understood what had been tickling Jak's sensitive nostrils, despite the overlying smell of death. It was the distinctive reek of stickies. The death stink that hid theirs probably came from victims, human or animal, the muties had either not finished eating yet or got tired of and just left to rot where they lay.

He gave the muties a couple blasts of #4 buckshot without even slowing them. Unless a lucky lead ball happened to punch through one of those big, staring eyes into the malevolent inhuman brain beyond, it had little chance of killing one of them. But one stickie fell down, shrieking and slapping at its body with its sucker-tipped fingers, and the other staggered back a pace or two.

"Full speed!" Ryan yelled.

Jak stopped long enough to hold his Python out the

full length of his arm and trigger a shot. The blaster's
roar bouncing between the concrete floor and roof made
its usually unpleasant noise seem to clap the sides of J.B.'s
head like planks of wood. But that beat what happened to
the stickie's head. The 125-grain jacketed hollow-point
round imploded its right eye and blew the brains out the
back of its round skull in a black fountain.

Shooting broke out from behind J.B., more than his
friends alone could account for....

RYAN LOOKED BACK. People stood in the street behind his
companions. After just a handful of seconds inside the
darkened parking structure, they seemed to swim against
a sea of dazzle. A couple opened up with handblasters.

Ricky leaned out from around a stout concrete pillar
painted in badly flaking yellow and fired a shot from his
DeLisle. A figure went down, dropping a semiauto handblaster as it did. The other three or four pursuers continued to pop off shots into the structure.

Sooner or later, they'd catch a break and hit somebody.

Ryan rapidly holstered his SIG and unslung the Scout.
Turning and dropping to one knee, he raised the longblaster to his shoulder.

There was no time for the variable-power Leupold
scope. And at twenty, twenty-five yards max, no need.
As soon as he had a target in his ghost ring he squeezed
the trigger, sharp as he could without jerking it and pulling the shot offline.

A jeans-clad leg buckled under an enemy. The man
dropped a lever-action longblaster as he fell flat on his
face on the hot asphalt.

The other pursuers threw themselves down as well, but
they kept shooting.

"Handblaster, Ricky!" Ryan shouted to the kid. "Covering fire, but keep coming."

He turned as he straightened.

A gibbering, chittering horde of stickies was flooding the ramp now. "Run!" Ryan yelled at his companions. "Just run!"

He fired a snapshot into the mass. A couple of the muties squealed and fell as the 7.62 mm bullet punched through their torsos. It wouldn't keep them down for long. But following muties tripped over them and fell. With their bloodlust amped all the way up, the creatures began to snarl, slap and snap at each other in crazy rage.

Others came flowing around them. They fanned out to attack the encroaching norms.

Jak was already by the far exit. He emptied his blaster at the stickies. Ryan saw another go down with the back of its head blown out.

He slung his longblaster and moved forward. Krysty, Mildred and Doc had already passed him and were racing for the exit. Doc stuck out his hand and unloaded the shotgun barrel of his LeMat into the face of a charging stickie. It took out its eyes and tore off the upper side of its face. The stickie uttered a human shriek of agony and despair and fell to its knees, clutching the ruin of its face.

For a moment Ryan thought they'd make it with a few steps to spare. But that was the thing about stickies—they could move bastard fast.

One darted toward Krysty. She veered and it missed its grab at her. But the suckers on its fingers caught the right sleeve of her shirt.

She yelped; other muties closed in, chittering triumphantly.

Krysty let the mutie turn her hand toward itself. In that

hand was her Smith & Wesson 640. She emptied the five shots in its cylinder into the creature's belly.

The horror barely even flinched. It opened its mouth wide and swept its free hand up to try to rip off her face.

"Krysty!" Mildred yelled. She grabbed the taller woman by her left upper arm and yanked her away.

But it still clung to her despite the blood leaking black through the holes in its abdomen. Other muties converged on what they took for a certain chill.

Ryan waded in. He booted away one that was trying to get around behind Krysty. Then he lunged forward and severed the hand that was stuck to Krysty's sleeve just above the skinny wrist.

With Mildred's help Krysty was yanked from the cluster of stickie hands. Ryan had had to overbalance to hack through the mutie's arm. His right boot slipped on something wet and slick on the concrete beneath him. He dropped to one knee, hard enough to clack his teeth together and send a lance of pain from his kneecap up through his whole body.

But Ryan never lost his presence of mind. That was something he'd always had, that gift of constant, unswerving focus—on survival.

He batted away the grasping, suckered hands, slashing with his panga. And even as he fought desperately the awful screeching muties who swarmed around him, he was roaring, "Go! Get out of here!"

He moved his arms violently to prevent any fingertip suckers from latching on. But the stickies were cunning monsters. They adapted. One wrapped its arms around his right forearm, fouling his panga. It stretched its head out on its neck with jaws gaping wide to take a chunk out of the one-eyed man's face.

In his peripheral vision Ryan saw something dark and

slender, and yellow flame belched forth. It bathed the whole side of the stickie's head with its yawning, sharp-toothed maw in fire.

The left side of the stickie's head exploded. Its arms relaxed in death, releasing its hold.

Ryan thrust his panga into another flat stickie face, bursting a staring eyeball. The panga's blade was much too wide to pierce through to the mutie's brain, but the creature fell back shrieking.

Ryan saw a stickie head's transfixed from his left to his right with a slender steel blade. Then hands were hauling him away from the stickies as handblasters spoke shatteringly from either side of him.

He got the rest of the way to his feet on his own. He saw it was Mildred on his left who'd blasted the stickie—and left him with a ringing in his ears that would last for hours. Krysty was to his right.

A quick flurry of face shots dropped three stickies and slowed the others.

Ryan drew his SIG with his left hand and shot a fourth through its open mouth as it vaulted a scrum of writhing bodies.

"Nuke it, the stickies didn't get them!" a voice called from the street.

"Give the mutie bastards a chance," somebody else yelled back.

The stickie swarm had split the party in two. J.B. had almost reached Jak, still lurking by the exit, when the mutie caught hold of Krysty. Now the muties were surrounding everybody else, gobbling and squeaking in triumph.

"Stay behind me," Ryan yelled to Krysty and Mildred. The sickening stench of stickies was so thick now it made his head spin. The spilling of stickie blood, brain and guts didn't make them smell any sweeter. "Doc, Ricky, right and left outside them."

The women complied.

Though Ricky was the newest of the group of companions, he'd been with them for months now. He knew how they worked and how to work well with them.

Ryan led the way back for the exit away from the human pursuit, hacking with the big panga, warding off blows and attempted grabs with the SIG. He only fired when there was no other choice.

Doc, outside the two close-together women to Ryan's right rear, was stabbing mutie faces with his sword and bludgeoning the ones who got close with his massive LeMat. Ricky held his carbine by its fat sound suppresser. He hacked at the muties with the butt to keep them away, alternating baseball-bat style with ax-type overhead action. Because it had been built out of a military weapon that was intended to bust skulls as a last resort, the DeLisle could likely survive the rude treatment with little damage.

But the companions had to survive for that to matter a lick.

The muties wouldn't run, but they could be forced back. They weren't big. Ryan had no trouble bulling through them, though not as fast as he liked, by just using his size and strength. And the women, holding on to each other for support, booted any stickies who got through the rough equilateral triangle of the males.

Then a mutie right in front of Ryan had its head smashed from behind by a downward butt stroke of J.B.'s M4000 scattergun. And the one beside it pitched forward with the back of its skull staved in by a punch from the studded brass-knuckle hilt of Jak's trench knife. Ryan had to lash out with his shin to knock the creature aside and keep it

from tripping him—or latching on to his jeans-clad leg
with its suckers.

"Quit screwing around," J.B. told Ryan. Without even
seeming to look he jabbed the muzzle of his shotgun hard
to his left. A stickie reeled back into its circling, capering
buddies, wailing and clutching the spurting crater where
its left eye used to be. "We've got to get going."

The pair had waded back to help their friends. The
stickies faltered, confused rather than scared. "Power on!"
Ryan bellowed.

They all ran flat-out for the exit. Stickies that got in
their way were knocked down. Ryan trampled one that
J.B. had half spun with his shoulder. His friends ran over
it without breaking stride.

The one-eyed man heard angry shouts from behind,
then shots. A bullet cracked past his head to the right.

Then he was out into the bright, blessed sunshine of the
Detroit wasteland. His friends, all miraculously still alive,
were right on his heels. A whole pack of stickies was left
behind to keep their pursuers off their asses.

A bullet kicked up fallen leaves and some concrete dust
three feet in front of him.

Chapter Six

"Fireblast!" Ryan shouted.

He checked himself and pivoted, bringing his long-blaster to his shoulder.

A group of at least a dozen men was approaching cautiously from the direction of the big half-ruined building. They all carried longblasters and wore the distinctive dark vests of their original pursuers. They were still roughly fifty yards away.

Behind them, another garden lay past the structure's southwest end. This one was enclosed by a barbed wire fence and more rolls of razor tape. Inside it were the jumbled remnants of what Ryan realized was a raised road that had once led to the circular structure. Now it was a spiral ramp. Apparently the big building had had rooftop parking.

Ryan fired a shot at the enemy. He didn't hit anybody. They ducked anyway, a couple stretching flat on the ground.

They weren't driven off, though. They promptly opened fire.

Caught between stickies in the semidarkness and so far inaccurate blasterfire in the sunshine, he had only one choice. Fortunately, before the first shot had alerted Ryan to more trouble approaching, he'd spotted a gap between buildings across the street and not twenty yards to the right of where he and his friends emerged.

"Go, go, go!" he yelled, waving his arm at the half-overgrown entrance to a street or alley. As his friends ran by behind him, he dropped to one knee and took quick aim.

His scope happened to fall on a blond head behind the receiver of a Mini-14. It looked like a woman.

That meant nothing to Ryan. If a person pointed a weapon at him or his friends, the person would die.

No exceptions. He pulled the trigger.

The Steyr kicked his shoulder with the buttplate. He held on to the stock, rode the recoil and brought the blaster back online with practiced ease.

A pink spray blossomed behind the shooter's head when it reappeared in his telescopic sight. It plopped forward, revealing the ragged red mess where the back of the skull had been knocked out by the bullet's passage.

He heard a rippling roar of blasterfire from behind him to the right.

"Haul ass, Ryan!" J.B. shouted. "We're clear."

He sprang up and ran for safety through a barrage that crackled around him like bacon frying on a grill.

Ricky knelt among weeds at the corner of a building, laying down covering fire with his suppressed longblaster. J.B. kept stepping out to fire a quick, short burst then nip back into cover.

"Here come more of them," Ricky said as Ryan raced past him.

"Looks like the first bunch that set out after us decided not to mess with the stickies," J.B. commented, putting his back against the wall out of the line of enemy fire. "Seems like shooting some of them just made them madder."

"Happens sometimes," Ryan called.

"What do I do?" Ricky yelled.

"Try to keep up!"

HER BREATH WHISTLING in her ears, Mildred slogged heavily
through a muddy field of leafy green vegetables. The farmers who'd been tending it went flying in all directions at
the approach of a heavily armed crew of strangers, flip-
flops flopping and flat-cone straw hats falling back behind their heads to hang by chin straps.

The fact that a much bigger, just as heavily armed and
amazingly pissed-off bunch of people in leather vests was
running fifty yards behind the intruders probably didn't
reassure them.

Mildred felt bad as her boots squashed tender plants into
the carefully tended soil. She knew these people worked
hard at their plots because their survival was at stake.

But so was hers. So on she ran, heedless.

Though it couldn't have been more than a handful of
blocks, the whole flight had become a nightmare steeple-
chase in her mind: a blurred montage of cracked streets,
shattered buildings, burned-out husks, riotous under-
growth and orderly plots like the one they were so indus-
triously, if incidentally, violating.

The pursuers fired off an occasional shot. Like all the
others—so far—it didn't hit any of them. The bad guys
were shooting on the run. Whoever it was chasing them
so doggedly had discovered a few turns back that if they
actually stopped to aim, they got left behind.

As they approached a half-collapsed building, Jak suddenly appeared out of a staring, blank doorway. He gestured to his friends frantically.

The place looked trashed. Once several stories tall, the
building appeared to have mostly fallen in on and around
itself, judging from the fragmentary sheets of red stone
sticking out of the piled rubble. But the lower floor looked
intact. The place still looked anything but promising, much
less remotely safe.

Ryan headed for the door without hesitation.

The others followed. Ryan Cawdor wasn't always right, but his decisions had kept them alive so far, through some of the worst situations imaginable.

At the door he turned, shouldered his Scout longblaster and fired back at their pursuers. Mildred didn't bother glancing around. It only made her more likely to stumble or maybe twist an ankle, which would be fatal.

Anyway, there was no need. The men—and occasional woman—in vests chasing after them had had been taught caution by Ryan's and Ricky's marksmanship. They knew to duck when one or the other opened fire on them. They didn't care to come too close yet, but they showed no signs of giving up.

Ryan, Krysty and Doc entered the ruin. Jak was already inside, leading the way. Mildred followed.

As she stepped inside she heard J.B. murmur something behind her. She glanced back to see Ricky nodding and grinning.

"Best keep moving," J.B. said to Mildred.

The interior of the fallen-in building alternated shadow and shafts of sunlight from holes in the overhead. It stank worse of death than the stickies' parking structure had.

As she followed immediately behind Krysty, Mildred quickly found out why. The path Jak led them on wound down hallways and through broken walls. A bloated torso lay against a wall inside a room next to one they passed through. Mildred couldn't tell what sex it had been. A head with long, dark hair was turned away from them.

She reckoned that was fortunate. Along with being mottled red and yellow and green from rot, the chill had neither arms nor legs. The wounds visible through big tears in the gray-on-gray plaid flannel shirt gave Mildred the impression it had been partially eaten.

By something big.

To her physician's eye those marks had been inflicted postmortem. She didn't find that terribly reassuring.

To her relief she was quickly outside in the sun again. Almost immediately her relief vanished. Her group had come out on the south side of the building—meaning they were now headed back toward their pursuers.

Then she realized they were east of the street she'd last seen their enemies on. And the sight lines between were blocked by fields of high weeds. In the middle of it stood the remains of a small shantytown. The small, frail constructions, knocked together from random bits of rubble, trash and scavvy, were all the more pathetic for having obviously been trashed and abandoned. Some were no more than burned-out skeletons of charred tree limbs and twisted metal rods.

As they headed southeast, Ricky trotted out of the ruin to join them. "Did you do like I asked, Ricky?" J.B. said to him.

Ricky nodded vigorously. "Yes, sir!"

"Good man."

Jak led them through the weeds toward a dark gray building that showed them a long, blank face. No windows were visible, only some intact ducts on the level above the street.

He moved toward the northeast end of the mostly blank wall, near an abutting building that had several more stories with glass in the windows. It might have been an annex of the first one. A loading bay door stood open between shrubby trees. The albino slipped up a ramped walkway to the bay's far side. He crouched next to it and looked in.

Then he looked back at his friends and nodded. But he held up a hand in the sign for caution.

A crackle sounded from behind the companions. It

quickly expanded into a storm of gunfire. Mildred reflexively ducked, then turned back. She saw nothing but the weeds, the shantytown and the red-faced ruin.

"Fireblast!" Ryan exclaimed. "What the nuke?"

"Ricky left them one of the little surprises he's been working on," J.B. said, as proud as a new poppa.

Ricky blushed. "Nothing lethal. Just a string of black-powder firecrackers with a tripwire and a pull initiator left in the front door of the place we just left. It works just the same as a firefight simulator."

"That does not sound simulated," Doc declared as the blasterfire continued to rage from the direction of the derelict building.

"It's not," J.B. said, "now."

"Triple clever," Ryan told them. "Now get your asses in gear. That won't keep the bastards busy long."

Ryan went up the ramp to where Jak still hunkered down by the yawning bay. The albino gave way for him to take a quick look inside. Then the taller man straightened and walked in.

"Because the walk-in-like-we-own-the-place thing worked so well last time," Mildred said grumpily.

"Have some faith," Ricky said earnestly.

"Famous last words," Mildred replied. But she followed her friends into the relative darkness.

"COMPANY," JAK SAID QUIETLY.

Ryan halted a few steps inside the loading bay. As he had ascertained, not much mileage could be gained by skulking. The bay opened into a large open space two stories high, with a gallery running along the far end. The stained concrete floor had been picked bare of everything except scattered trash.

It smelled of concrete and decaying greenery. At least

it didn't smell as if any chills had decomposed in here recently, Ryan thought.

His hands were empty. As risks went, it was carefully calculated. If whoever was in here was hostile and started blasting from ambush, if they did or did not have weapons wouldn't make much difference. But whether or not they showed blasters might make a major difference as to whether anybody in here started shooting at them.

Ryan's gamble was based on a simple judgment call. Should they go into a potential hiding place where they might find trouble, or stay outside where they knew trouble was actively hunting them?

As J.B. and Krysty stepped up to flank him, a voice called down to them from the gallery.

"Well, well, well. What have we here?"

It was a man's voice, sarcastic but nonthreatening.

"Name's Cawdor," Ryan called back. "We're outlanders just looking for a place to lie up a bit."

A man stepped out of a darkened doorway on the upper level. He was average height, broad across the shoulders but not carrying much extra weight that Ryan could tell by his dark T-shirt and black cargo pants. His mustache and the shock of black hair hanging over his forehead made his face look pale. A handblaster rode in a flapped holster at his left hip. Ryan couldn't make out the kind.

"Lie up, huh?" the man said. "Sounds to me like you might have something to hide out *from*."

Ryan shrugged. "It's easy finding trouble in a ville this size. We're not looking for any."

"I think they're trying to jump our scavvy, Nikk," a second voice said.

It belonged to a woman who emerged from the doorway behind him. She was about the same height as her partner and had short brown hair sprouting from a grimy camo headband. She wore a rust-colored halter top with overstuffed cargo shorts, and an MP5-K machine pistol rested in a right-hand cross-draw holster strapped in front of them.

"Always the cynic, Patch," he said as she took her place at the railing alongside him.

She shrugged. "Realist." Her manner was as cool as it was skeptical. "Somebody's gotta be, with a dreamer like you in charge."

He chuckled indulgently. "At least they were smart enough to come in with their hands empty," he told her.

Then to Ryan he said, "We've got blasters on you."

"I figured," Ryan said. "So it doesn't look as if you've got much to fear from us, does it?"

"Could be a trick," the woman said.

Nikk laughed out loud. "It could always be a trick," he said. "That's what makes it a game."

"Razor Eddie's reporting from the rooftop, Nikk," another man's voice called out the door. The speaker didn't appear. "Says a gang is heading this way. Well armed. Thinks they're the Desolation Angels."

"Oh, shit," a man said from the blank darkness of a doorway on the ground floor, which dispelled any suspicion Ryan might have had that Nikk was bluffing about them being covered.

Not that he'd had many to begin with.

"Aren't they outside their usual range?" Patch asked. She wasn't just skeptical of Ryan and company, it appeared.

Nikk shrugged. "They've been expanding lately. Prob'ly looking to keep up with DPD."

"Who's DPD?" Ryan asked. "I don't think we've made their acquaintance yet."

"You should hope that you never do."

"They bad news?" J.B. asked.

Nikk grinned. "You really must be new in the ville," he said. "If you haven't learned yet that, here in D-Town, there are only two kinds of news. Bad news—"

Patch laid her head against his shoulder. "And worse news," she said.

"Quite the comedic duo," Doc murmured.

Nikk shook his head. "Sorry. We've got no beef with the Angels. We're not looking to start one, either. You'd best be moving on."

"And if we don't?" Ryan asked.

"Well, say what you will about the Angels," the scavvy boss said, "which is mostly that they're stoneheart bastards through and through, but they aren't sadists. So I don't reckon it makes them much, never mind whether we hand your bodies over to them still breathing or started on your way to room temperature."

Chapter Seven

Ryan hit the bay door running. Rather than take the ramp, he hopped down to the driveway.

Immediately he heard shots from the west. He ducked. Unslinging his Steyr, he lay prone on the pavement, then crawled forward. The concrete-lined side of the cut totally covered him from enemy fire and concealed him from their view. He heard some of his companions drop from the opening behind him.

As it sloped down close to sidewalk level, he stopped and raised his head to peer over it. The grass was too tall to allow him to see anything.

Cautiously he raised his body on his left arm, as though he was doing a one-armed pushup. He still couldn't see anything.

Getting uneasy at not being able to see an enemy who obviously had seen *him*—or who knew roughly where he was—he pulled his knee forward, got a boot sole on the concrete and came up into a bent-forward kneeling position.

At least he was able to glimpse their enemy over the tufted tops of the grass. The Desolation Angels were about fifty yards off. He saw a dozen or so, spread out into a creditable skirmish line, advancing with longblasters across their chests.

Since they got a notion of what kind of quarry they were dealing with, the Angels had begun displaying a degree

of professionalism. Apparently the war for dominance—
or just survival—here in the Detroit rubble was a fierce
one. Fierce enough to force the players to learn something
a little better than the usual bullying and mob tactics used
by gangs. Or even a lot of ville sec forces.

Ryan knew there were a lot more Angels after them
than the ones he could see. And they had no way to fight
them off, especially not from the loading-bay cut. And he
didn't fool himself that he could deal with Nikk and his
bunch—by either sweet-talking a way back into the big
building, or forcing their way in.

He didn't hold it against the scavvies that they'd turned
his companions out to face the Angels' wrath. He would
have done the same thing.

He raised the Steyr and looked through the scope. It had
long eye relief, meaning it was mounted farther forward
than most so that there was no danger of the eyepiece kicking back and cutting into the eye socket when it fired. It
didn't make it any harder to acquire a target or aim.

He quickly lined up a face like a sunburned fist in the
reticule. Allowing for the up-and-down bob the Angel's
trot imparted, he timed his shot and fired.

The man had already fallen out of sight beyond the grass
when he got the rifle back down and the scope lined up.

He yelled to his friends to run.

Ryan fired again. This time the target, an older-looking
man with a full beard, turned back to yell something just
as Ryan's trigger broke. The shot hit him in the left shoulder and spun him.

"Smoke bomb out!" he heard J.B. yell from right beside
him. Something arced down into Ryan's field of vision,
trailing brownish-gray smoke.

"Didn't think they'd fall for the 'poison gas' gag a second time," J.B. said. "Come on, Ryan. We've got to go."

Without a second thought Ryan jumped to his feet. He'd had no intention of sacrificing himself to hold the pursuers off while his friends escaped. For one thing, he doubted it would've worked. There were just too many of the bastards. He saw no point in risking his ass when there was no need to.

A huge cloud billowed up between him and the enemy.

"That's our last one of those for now," J.B. said. He ripped off a short burst from his Uzi into the smoke screen, just to make the Angels think twice about barging in blind through the smoke. Then he and Ryan sprinted down the block away from them, after their companions.

Though another large, cultivated field opened to the north, Jak had led them not toward it but along the street, back toward the jagged but looming ruins of downtown. Ryan understood his reasons—and knew the albino youth was right. Once the Angels had stopped shooting holes in the air in response to Ricky's makeshift firefight simulator, they almost certainly had fanned out from the fallen-in building Ryan and his team had ducked through. So they probably had men heading for the field and to the building Nikk's scavvies claimed for their own. Above all, the fugitives needed to put as much distance between them and the Angels as possible and as fast as possible.

After he'd run a couple hundred yards, Ryan stopped and turned back. Once again he dropped to one knee.

People were just starting to emerge from the yellowish cloud of smoke. The air was still, so it was still mostly intact, dissipating only slowly in the humid, heavy air. Once more he drew a quick bead on the nearest, a tall black man with the sides of his head shaved. Ryan shot him through the chest and ran after his friends as the other Angels in sight opened fire.

So far none of them had turned out to be marksmen,

which was lucky. But throw enough lead in the air, a person was bound to hit something eventually. This battle could not be allowed to go on.

At least they still had some air between themselves and the baying, blasting pack. Ryan and his crew needed to find either escape or cover to stand off the Angels until nightfall.

He ran past the exposed base of a white skyscraper. It appeared to be propped up by the remnants of a building it had crashed into. The bottom floor was an open wound of structural steel and broken concrete.

Jak had already turned the group north-northeast up the next street to take them out of their pursuers' line of fire. Ryan followed, with J.B. just ahead of him.

"Head right at the next intersection!" he called.

"Blocked!" yelled Jak, who had sprinted ahead to scout escape routes. He was ace at his job—the best, as Ryan and his friends had learned, and learned hard some weeks before, when simmering resentments between Jak and Ryan had sent the younger man heading in one direction and the rest in another. That had gone disastrously for them all.

Jak kept running the way he was going. Up ahead Ryan glimpsed what looked at first like another shantytown, but in a fairly open space between a perilously leaning skyscraper on one side and a long, low white building on the other. This one was somehow much more colorful than the sad collection of burned out and abandoned shacks they had passed before. Also it was anything but abandoned; it was occupied by a throng of people.

A few heads started to turn as someone noticed Jak running toward them, with Krysty, Doc and Mildred close behind.

"¡Nuestra, señora!" Ricky yelped. He was just crossing

the next intersection, the one with the white skyscraper toppled right across it. "Angels!"

"Bastards die hard," J.B. said.

"Just run!" Ryan yelled.

J.B. fired a burst left as he entered the intersection without even slowing. Ryan had slung his Steyr and drawn his SIG.

Sure enough, a passel of the vest-wearing coldhearts was moving fast through the shadowed canyon of the broad east-west street. The white building lay tilted at somewhere south of forty-five degrees. It had crunched into a sinister-looking brown-and-black building across from it and had domino toppled into the building north of it.

Chunks of rubble big and small had fallen from the crazy-angled building. The Angels had to slow to pick their way over, around and through that, but no more than they had to. Ryan snapped a couple shots their way.

Once again they paused to return fire. Bullets cracked through the air around Ryan. One bounced off the pavement right ahead of him and howled away in ricochet.

J.B. paused by the corner of the tilted brown-and-black skyscraper to fire a burst at the Angels under the slanted structure. Ryan saw one go down, yelling and kicking. The others dropped to take cover among the rubble.

That turned out not to be a good idea. Apparently the fallen skyscraper wasn't altogether stable. Or perhaps the earth had just shifted in a tremor Ryan was too preoccupied to feel. A block of masonry the size of one of the Motor City's most famous products—a big old gas-guzzler sedan—dropped straight down and crushed a kneeling Angel. The others cut off their assault and scuttled away like frightened quail.

"That was more luck than we deserve," J.B. commented.

He fired another burst but didn't seem to hit any of their pursuers.

Ryan raced past him. J.B. grinned as he flashed by and moved to follow.

Jak had burst in among the colorful shacks. To his surprise Ryan realized it was an active marketplace of sorts. The colors came from old scavenged signs, cracked panels of plastic and that old standby for Deathlands building and decoration both, hammered-out soda cans. The shacks themselves seemed to consist largely of nonmetallic car body panels.

The people swapping goods and gossip broke apart like a flock of pecking birds that had had an alley cat dropped in their midst. Some of them, mostly keepers of the kiosks of fresh fruits and ancient predark goods, stood their ground, shaking fists and shouting in outraged anger at the intrusion.

"We're sorry!" Krysty and Mildred shouted as they ducked between the stands. Mildred knocked over an angled rack of brightly colored garments and sent them fluttering to the ground, which was bare earth hard packed by decades of feet.

Ryan glanced back as he and J.B. came among the stands. The group of Angels that had chased them out of Nikk's domain had appeared behind them. As he watched, so did the ones the block's fall had flushed.

Shouts and shots started to fly from the two groups of Angels. Fortunately, with all the kiosks and the bodies of fleeing customers, Ryan and his friends had plenty of concealment.

Unfortunately, there wasn't much cover available. The rapidly dwindling number of incidental bodies would stop bullets much more reliably than the fiberglass panels.

"What you wanna go and bring the Angels here for?"

a sturdy-looking woman in an apron and a red bandanna shouted at Ryan as he darted around her table full of what looked to him to be fried rats on sticks.

"Didn't have much choice in the matter, lady!" he yelled back.

At that moment a wrinkly stepped from between two booths up ahead, raised a giant black single-action blaster in two palsied hands and shot Doc in the head from twenty feet away.

Chapter Eight

"Fireblast!" Mildred heard Ryan yell.

From his tone of voice she knew something bad had happened. She turned, feeling sick fear in her gut. That last shot had sounded shatteringly loud, meaning it had been fired from nearby.

Mildred stopped, turned and saw Doc reeling, a hand clapped to the side of his head. Blood flooded between his fingers and down the back of his hands, ran down his cheeks and dripped onto the lapels of his long coat. And off to her right stood an old guy, wearing nothing but a grimy loincloth stained with she didn't even want to imagine what. He held a big battered Ruger Blackhawk in both his pale, liver-spotted hands, and he was trying to crank the single-action hammer back with his thumbs.

Mildred's reaction was automatic. Inevitable. She'd taken a half step to turn her right side toward him. She raised her right arm, stiffened. Her ZKR 551 target revolver was held at the end of it. By reflex she thumbed the hammer back as she brought it up.

The blocky sights aligned on the old man's stringy-haired head, as if the upper half of it were sitting on top of the front post. At that instant she pressed the trigger.

She saw blood spray pink out the side of the elder's head. His skinny legs and grubby fish-white body folded beneath him. She had chilled him and never given it a thought.

He was just trying to defend his place in the world, she thought, then reality set in. Tough titty. Her survival, and the survival of her companions, was paramount. She had done what needed to be done.

Now, blaster still in hand, she was moving swiftly toward Doc. He was still on his feet, but barely.

"No!" Mildred heard Ricky scream from behind her.

"Come on," Krysty said firmly.

From the youth's protests Mildred guessed the redhead had grabbed his arm and was physically dragging him onward among the now almost-deserted booths and stands.

Mildred was by Doc's side. He tried to wave her off with his nonbloody hand.

"Go ahead, dear lady. I'm fine."

"You're not fine."

As if to prove the truth of her words, he reeled and toppled into her arms. Fortunately, she was professional enough a shooter to have her finger outside the trigger guard when she didn't intend to fire the weapon. His weight was considerable, more than was expected by the look of him. But it wasn't deadweight. He was still conscious. Just woozy.

"Jak!" she heard Ryan shout as she staggered back a step. For all his protestations, he hadn't been too proud to drape his free arm around her neck for support. "Find us cover *right now!*"

He and J.B. appeared, flanking Doc simultaneously. The Armorer grabbed his left elbow while Ryan grabbed the right. They hauled him out of Mildred's arms and kept running.

They scarcely even slowed.

Shouts erupted from behind them. The pack was closing in. The Angels were already among the southern booths, though fortuitously none of them had line of sight on their prey. Yet.

Without looking Ryan stretched his right arm back and cranked off two shots from his SIG. A stout black lady in a red turban scurrying for cover threw up her hands with a wail of despair and fell to the ground.

Mildred steeled her heart and turned to run after the three men. Ryan didn't like to chill without need any more than she did. But if random third parties got in the way of shots he fired in defense of himself and his friends—even just popped off to try to spook some caution into whatever happened to be chasing them—he wouldn't lose a second's sleep over it.

She doubted he'd even remember it five minutes from now.

But *she* would. And she'd likely lose the sleep for him.

"Why isn't Doc dead?" Ricky asked.

Krysty looked over the bottom of the large, empty front window, her snub-nosed .38 clutched in both hands. A large man, bent over with his big gut hanging out the front of his open vest, approached through the waist-high weeds and brush of the overgrown parking lot. She quickly lined up the sights and fired.

To her surprise the man dropped straight down out of sight, as if she'd actually hit him from fifty feet away. That was far from a given with her handblaster.

The overgrowth lit up and began to shake from multiple muzzle blasts as the Angels lying among them returned enthusiastic fire.

They ran into a former fast-food restaurant—the nearest available cover on the northwest side of a five-way intersection just north of the market. Its roof had been blown off so that its walls stood open to the sky. For what it was worth, it offered a decent field of fire in three directions. The way they had come was mostly clear for about twenty feet before the weeds kicked in. To the southwest a hundred feet of rubble-choked former parking lot—a lot of twisted ankles just waiting to happen—separated them from a stand of chest-high wheat and barley. On the northeast side, a wide, fairly intact street lay between them and a three-story red-brick building.

Ryan lifted his head cautiously above that wall and peered across the street.

"I'm not seeing any activity over there," he reported. "Yet. If they put snipers on the roof, we're going to have a long afternoon." He jerked his chin at the structure, whose rooftop gave a commanding view of the far third of the former dining area where they had gone to ground.

"Doc got shot in the head," Ricky said. He ignored the storm of bullets cracking over his head and flying over the counter into what had been the kitchen area of a derelict KFC. "Why isn't he dead?"

"It wasn't a fatal shot," Mildred replied. Doc sat with his back to a side wall near the dark-haired youth while Mildred crouched next to him. She had the lid of one eye skinned wide-open with her thumb. "He isn't going to die. Of this, anyway. But he is concussed."

"So how is he not dead?"

"A person's skull is pretty good armor, Ricky," she said. "It's possible that a handgun bullet could bounce off, even fired from point-blank range. This was just a graze. Lots of blood, but a small wound."

"Probably a .38 slug," J.B. said. He crouched beside the naked metal frame that had been the front door. "Soft lead, round nose. If the old guy had been cranking full-power .357s through that Ruger cowboy gun, we might be singing a different tune."

The Angels hadn't rushed them yet. Now the defenders were hunkered down just inside the open-to-the-air windows and doors, waiting for the inevitable assault. They had shucked their packs and left them in the back storage area where they wouldn't be underfoot.

At least we're getting a chance to drink some water and catch our breath, Krysty thought.

Mildred bandaged Doc's head quickly, using some unbleached linen strips they'd traded for at a post.

"What's our prospect of breaking out the back?" J.B. asked.

A partly collapsed building stood right behind the one they occupied, across a narrow alley. To its southwest was the rubble of a thoroughly destroyed building, a long, low mound coming up as high as Krysty's breastbone in places. The street on the other side was partially blocked a bit farther down by another tall building that had fallen east.

"Not like," Jak called. He was unseen in the back of the store, keeping an eye on the rear entrance. "No way through."

"Looked as if there's mostly more open fields off past it, anyway," Ryan said. "Be hard to get out unseen."

"There sure seems to be a lot of open space around here, for a big city and all," said Ricky, who was crouched by the southwest wall. Nothing remained of the interior furnishings but the counter. The kitchen stoves and sinks and whatnot had long since been pillaged for scrap.

"It's Detroit," Mildred said, cutting off the end of the last bandage with a pocketknife. "The Motor City. There, old man. You look as if I just treated you for toothache, but at least you won't bleed out."

She glanced over at Ricky to see him giving her a blank look. "They used to make cars here," she told him. "So they had lots of cars. I reckon a lot of that space they've got growing crops and weeds used to be parking lots. Also, every third building seems to be a parking garage."

"How you feel, Doc?" J.B. asked.

The old man shook his head. "I'll be right as rain," he said. Krysty noticed that his words were slurred. "Just let me sit here until the dizziness passes."

"Concussion," Mildred said. "That's another reason not to make a break for it. This old coot isn't fit to run any foot races. Least of all with bullets."

"Why haven't they attacked us yet, lover?" Krysty asked.

"Waiting," Ryan said. "Working their way into a position they like. Mebbe waiting on reinforcements. Then they'll rush us."

Krysty glanced over the wall. Her heart skipped a beat.

"Here they come!" she yelled.

As IF KRYSTY'S warning cry had been a signal, a furious storm of blasterfire erupted from outside.

Ryan drew his SIG, cursing himself for paying so much attention to the multiple-story building across the street. Sure, if the Angels got blasters in there, it would be triple bad, but he'd seen no sign of them even trying. And anyway, if Trader had caught him back in the day obsessing over potential danger with an obvious, actual one hanging over all their heads like an ax ready to fall, he probably would have left him high and dry in some pest-hole ville.

But regrets and reproach wouldn't put a fired bullet back in the blaster.

J.B. leaned forward to fire his Uzi left-handed out the front door. He ducked back hastily as bullets started skipping in through the opening and across the floor right next to him.

It was obvious what the Angels were trying to do. A

bunch of them were cranking shots into the former fast-food restaurant as fast as they could to keep the defenders' heads down while other Angels charged the place. They had enough blasters out there to make it work. As long as they were careful not to hit their own attacking people.

Ryan wouldn't have wanted to be one of those cold-hearts trying to storm the restaurant, caught right between blasters like that.

"Right!" he yelled as bullets zinged and screamed crazily around the roofless interior. The same stout brick walls that kept bullets out also kept bullets fired *in*. "Let the bastards come, then blast them when they try to get in."

J.B. sat on his heels with his back to the wall by the door. His right hand now held his shotgun muzzle upward by the pistol grip. His left clamped his fedora on his head as if against a high wind. He caught Ryan's eye and gave his head a quick shake.

Ryan knew what he was thinking. It was a terrible plan. And it was.

Just better than any other option they had right then.

The bullet storm slacked. "Stay low, and get ready!" Ryan gritted out. That lull almost certainly meant the charging Angels had almost reached their goal. But if one of the companions popped up to shoot now, he or she would invite a reflex shot from one of the Angels ready to lay down covering fire. Or from one of the coldhearts about to break in.

He duckwalked to the front wall to avoid extreme-angle fire from the Angels' covering force. He drew his panga in his left hand. It would be ideal to keep the bastards from getting in at all.

Real was dealing with whatever actually happened.

"Jak!" he called. "Keep an eye on that west window."

Then they hit them.

A man rushed through the door. Prepared, J.B. stuck out a leg and tripped him. The attacker fell hard on his face and skidded, his long hair flying. Then the Armorer stuck his shotgun around the doorjamb and pumped out two quick blasts.

Men screamed. Ryan shot the fallen man in the side of his head as he blearily tried to push off the concrete floor, blood streaming from his face.

He plopped back down. He had a cowboy-style hand-blaster, similar to the one the wrinkly in the market had used.

Ryan shifted back two steps along the side wall to give himself an angle on the front door and window. He was gambling that there now would be too many Angel bodies in the way for there to be much risk of somebody sniping him from out in the weeds. The men lying out there were still shooting, which put Ryan back in his earlier frame of mind about not envying the assault force.

It was time to make the ones getting shot in the backs by their buddies look like the lucky ones.

A man swung a leg over the sill between the crouching Krysty and Mildred. Krysty promptly stabbed her knife through the back of his calf above his boot. He shrieked as she forced the knife out, cutting his hamstring. The leg was sucked right back over the wall and out of sight.

More bodies suddenly appeared, clogging the window and door. The Angels were so eager to get inside they were getting in one another's way. Ryan shot a man who'd gotten stuck in the middle of the door in the belly. Nothing like having a downed comrade thrashing and howling in intolerable pain to take the rod out of an enemy's pecker.

The Angel sagged back, screeching. A wild-bearded man to his left tried to throw him out of the way and barge in. Straightening, J.B. wheeled around the doorjamb and postponed the steel-shod butt plate of his M4000 right into the middle of the angry black-fringed face.

Both of them fell back against the crowd pressing them from behind. The man who had been on the gut-shot Angel's right raised a remade 1911-model .45 blaster at Ryan. The one-eyed man shot him through the bare chest. He dropped to the floor.

Doc's under-barrel shotgun roared. A man who had dived through the window, rolled and come up with a short-barreled revolver in hand screamed as the shot charge exploded his face, ripping off the skin on the whole upper half, knocking chunks of flesh from the cheekbone and blowing open that side of his skull. An exposed blue eye rolled wildly in its socket, then rolled upward as the man fell onto his back.

Concussed or not, it seemed, the old man still could focus his mind on the task at hand when the shit and the bullets began to fly.

KRYSTY KNELT BY the wall. She and Mildred angled their fire into the bodies and faces of Angels trying to climb in the big front window. Blood fell on her face like torrential rain.

The 5-shot cylinder of her 640 was rapidly exhausted. She looked around. Several handblasters and a double-barreled sawed-off shotgun lay inside the window where their former owners had dropped them.

She grabbed the shotgun. Another man swung a leg over the sill. The scuffed cowboy boot with the badly separated sole barely missed clipping her head. She jammed the twin barrels into his gut and squeezed a single trigger.

He screamed so loud she could hear him over the shotgun's roar. His leg flew backward over the sill.

A hand appeared above her head, holding what Krysty

thought to be some sort of military-style handblaster. The wrist was bent to aim the barrel down. Its owner was obviously meaning to fire blind, hoping to hit one of the defenders beneath the sill level.

Fortunately the shooter wasn't having any luck bending his wrist far enough. The trigger finger clenched twice, causing the barrel to erupt in two stunning bursts of sound.

But Krysty was not the type to stun easily. She pivoted the short-barreled scattergun upward and pulled the other trigger.

Nothing. The Angel who'd dropped it had fired it once already.

Krysty was quick thinking and not easily deterred. She simply swung the weapon by its stock in a quick, savage arc. It caught the intruding arm right on the ulna. She heard the bone crack over all the echoing shots and shrieks.

The blaster fell from suddenly numb fingers. The arm was snatched back.

Krysty dropped the empty shotgun and grabbed for the handblaster.

Mildred, having fired her own 6-shot cylinder dry— Krysty had the impression her friend had deftly refilled the weapon with a speed loader at least once—was just grabbing for a fallen compact Glock. At some point in the past somebody with little artistic skill and less taste had painted the grip of the blocky black blaster in stripes of red, yellow and black. Not recently by the chipping and wear.

As Mildred's hand closed over the gaudy grip, another blaster appeared. This was a Ruger Mini-14, gripped two-handed with the muzzle down. Bad luck had positioned it perfectly to blast Mildred's head apart from above with a high-velocity slug.

Krysty rolled away from Mildred, trying desperately to bring up her own retrieved blaster.

She already knew she could never fire in time to save her friend.

Chapter Nine

"Mildred!"

Ricky heard Krysty cry. He crouched toward the door end of the big southwest-facing window. He had his Webley Mark VI revolver in his right hand. His left gripped the DeLisle by its fat front end. Fast as he could work the bolt action, the carbine was only a blaster of last resort at a range like this, where the smell of stale sweat and unwashed bodies was still strong enough for his flared nostrils to detect, even over the stink of burned blaster lubricant, propellant smoke and spilled blood. But he was already a seasoned enough fighter to know he was likely to have need of its useful built-in head-bashing qualities.

He was also seasoned enough to have some idea just how deep in the glowing nuke shit he and his friends were right now.

But he wasn't dead yet. So far neither were any of his friends. He would do all he could to keep things that way. As long as he could.

Meaning, likely, until he died trying.

He spun away from the window, straightening his arm and swinging up the hefty top-break Brit wheelgun. He saw a pair of brown hands holding an inverted Mini-14 right over Mildred's helpless head.

Without thinking he lined up the sights on the trigger hand and pulled the trigger. Even in the heat of dire emergency, he didn't yank the shot off. His Tío Benito had trained him better than that. And his mentor J.B., Ryan and former Olympic pistol competitor Mildred herself had all made sure he didn't forget it.

He saw the hand spill blood. Shattered, it spasmed open. Krysty lunged and grabbed the skinny black barrel, twisting the carbine deftly out of the Angel's other hand.

"Ace shot," called J.B., who stood with his back to the wall by the door and his Uzi in his hands. A crouched Ryan was cranking shots out the door as fast as he could trigger them. "But mind your own place!"

The Armorer pivoted into the doorway and unleashed a firestorm in the form of a shuddering burst of full-auto fire, right into the chests and guts of the Angels still trying to barge into the restaurant.

Eyes wide in sudden panic, Ricky started to wheel back to the giant oblong opening right over his own head.

And a weight like the world landed on his shoulders and smashed him to the floor.

As the slide of Ryan's SIG Sauer P226 locked back on an empty chamber, he saw a straw-haired Angel jump on Ricky's back. The Angel had a Bowie knife held over his head in an icepick grip.

Before he could plunge it into the youth, a shot bellowed from the rear of the restaurant. The Angel's body jerked. Blood fountained out the right side of his chest as a .357 Magnum bullet punched through him side to side. Ricky rolled over, slamming his already lolling head into the wall. He scrambled back up to a kneeling position in time to shoot another Angel trying to scramble in through the side window.

J.B. ducked back quickly as a fresh fusillade of blasterfire cracked through the door. Ryan was about to drop the spent magazine from his SIG when more men rushed forward. One fell face-first, suggesting he'd caught one of his own side's bullets in the back. Several others kept charging, one vaulting his fallen comrade.

"J.B.!" Ryan shouted. "Get back, keep low, cover!"

It was a risky move. It meant J.B. would be shooting right over his friends' heads. But if Ryan trusted his life—and the lives of his companions—to anybody's marksmanship and blaster-handling skills, it was the Armorer.

Too late. Before J.B. could respond, the room filled with angry, sweat-streaming men in brown leather vests.

Opting to free a grappling hand, Ryan jammed his SIG, still slide-locked, into its holster.

He transferred the heavy knife to his right hand and then began a sweaty, frantic, close dance with Death.

JAK FIRED HIS Python dry at Angels swarming in the southwest window.

He put the piece away. There was no point in a reload, when he didn't dare shoot into the melee for fear of hitting his friends.

Ricky was standing off the attackers by swinging his funny-looking longblaster like a baseball bat. The Angels also seemed to be concerned about hitting one another, or they just wanted to finish the assault face-to-face. Either way, shooting had stopped inside the roofless box of a building.

Jak grinned. He swapped his trench knife into his right hand as he plucked a leaf-shaped throwing knife from its special place in his jacket and threw it. An Angel reeled away from Ricky, clutching at his thick neck. His bare hand couldn't do much to keep the severed carotid from spraying out a fine crimson mist in pulsing plumes, though.

Jak whipped open a butterfly knife in his left hand.
He liked things better this way, anyway.

RYAN GRABBED THE wrist of a hand holding a short but
wicked-looking knife that was slashing for his stomach.
He gave the Angel a backhand swipe across the gullet
with his panga and laid his throat open almost to the neck
bone. The sudden red gush of blood forced the man's goateed head back.

Someone grabbed Ryan's arms from behind, pinioning
them. The one-eyed man whipped his head back hard. He
felt a nose squash beneath his skull, felt cartilage crumple.
The grip slackened.

He broke free by thrusting his arms powerfully toward
the clouded-over sky. Then he spun with a brutal overhand
strike of the panga. Its broad, heavy blade took the Angel
where his neck met his shoulders. Bone crunched as it split
collarbone, muscles and ribs to bite into the lung. The man
fell to the floor, hacking up pink froth through the mask
of blood from his shattered nose.

Why didn't he knife me? flashed through Ryan's
brain. In combat he acted, letting his senses, reflexes and
training—and decades of brutal experience—guide him.
But his keen tactical mind was always working.

For the first time he wondered if orders might have
come down for their pursuers to take them alive. That
couldn't be good.

With the senses of a feral cat, Ryan detected another
lunge coming at him from behind. He back kicked and
his boot heel caught a hipbone, stopping his attacker and
spinning him.

He turned to find another Angel, a gangly black man
with an Afro sprouting above and below a red headband
like an untrimmed bush, swinging a collapsible steel whip

at his head. He blocked with the panga, then punched the man in his prominent Adam's apple. He didn't collapse the trachea, but the man went down coughing and gagging, anyway.

A tail of a motorcycle drive chain wrapped around a meaty fist slashed Ryan's right cheek, just missing his good eye. He countered that with a thrust of the panga that smashed the Angel's upper-right teeth and gashed open his brown-bearded cheek to the jaw hinge.

He got flash impressions of how his friends were faring. J.B., as always, was a machine. Hand-to-hand combat was not his favored fighting mode—he was a blaster man, and barring that, he preferred to let explosives and booby-trap gadgets do his fighting for him. But that didn't mean he wasn't good at it. He fought as he did everything: with precision, compact efficiency and a brutality born of the will to survive. It was like fighting a threshing machine.

The women were making the exclusively male attackers pay for underestimating them. Krysty was unusually strong for a woman. Mildred was built powerfully and knew how to put her broad hips and muscular thighs into blows. Ryan noticed she had acquired an ax handle from somewhere as she ducked under a clumsy knife swipe and poked her attacker hard in the bare gut with the end of it. Meanwhile, Krysty was flipping an assailant over her shoulder to smash into two others trying to attack the shorter woman like a living, flailing meat club.

Doc was on his feet, busting heads with blows of his gigantic handblaster and delivering vicious stabs with his slim sword. Dizzy or not, he had his adrenaline up. His face was dead pale in the heat of battle.

Ricky was the weak link. He'd led a relatively sheltered life, growing up in his peaceful little seaport ville of Nuestra Señora—though his uncle, the black sheep of the family, had taught him the ways of blasters and booby traps, and he had taught him well. But he'd learned much more in the time he'd spent with his companions. And he had his friend Jak, pale blood whirlwind, slashing and gashing, darting and ducking, to come to the rescue when Ricky's vigorously swung blaster wasn't standing off the enemy.

These Angels were coldhearts. They knew their way around a rumble. Whether they were primarily bullies of the weaker peasant type, or protectors, or, most likely, a combo of both, they hadn't gotten to be such a big and powerful gang by looking for trouble. That wasn't how it worked. They just made sure they ended it, hard and fast, when it happened.

Ryan knew they could hold off the horde. As the realization hit him, a straight razor slashed open his coat, shirtsleeve and the skin of his right biceps. He delivered a side-thrust kick to the razor man and sat him down hard on the concrete floor.

Enough.

"Everybody down!" Ryan bellowed, his voice rising above the din of angry voices and fearsome impacts of hard objects on flesh. *"Blast them!"*

He was obeying his own order even as it left his mouth, dropping to the hard, blood-slicked floor. As he did, he drew his SIG. Taking the risk of leaving the panga on the concrete for a moment, he dropped the spent mag, transferred the blaster to his right hand and drove home a fresh one.

J.B.'s Uzi began to chatter. Its noise was stupefying inside the four brick walls, even with all the open windows and no roof and plenty of muffling bodies. Yellow light danced, silhouetting startled Angels in its muzzle-flash strobe.

His friends' other blasters joined in, firing upward where they didn't endanger one another. Only Angels.

That did it. The attackers clearly hadn't expected such a savage and effective response from their prey. They probably expected that their overwhelming numbers would stun and shock them into panic, if not outright surrender.

But their would-be victims did not overwhelm easily.

"Clear out!" a voice yelled hoarsely. And the men in vests still on their feet plowed through the doorway and threw themselves out the windows.

Some of them were helping injured buddies. Ryan marked that. That sort of loyalty wasn't common in the coldhearts they usually encountered. Where many would see that as weakness, Ryan recognized it as a source of strength for the Angels.

It was the same behavior he and his group displayed.

"Cease fire!" he yelled, as his slide locked back again. "Let them go!"

Others were hauling themselves up off the floor, dripping with blood, to crawl on hands and knees or even bellies and elbows out the door.

It wasn't mercy that moved Ryan to let them escape. Not as such. They clearly weren't going to fight again this day. And "no chilling for chilling's sake" had been one of the Trader's prime dicta.

Also, the seven companions didn't have the energy to waste thundering on already defeated foes. Much less the bullets to waste.

"Everybody fit to fight?" he called, picking himself up. His body ached from a dozen bruises, a half dozen cuts and general abuse.

The others all piped up in the affirmative, ending with Mildred's surprisingly chipper, "Amazingly, yes."

"Right. Reload. Then secure the exits again."

Having already recharged his own weapon, he grabbed the nearest body to the door and dropped it in the opening. The next attack would have to cross a rampart of their own buddies.

He noticed that the Angel casualties all had a large round badge sewn to the back of their vests. It was red, yellow and black. The word *Desolation* curved around the top and *Angels* around the bottom. In between was a buxom female angel with spread wings, a sword and a skull face. Ryan had to admit it was nicely done.

They also looked fairly uniform. He guessed they had been sewed according to a pattern.

His friends were all drenched in blood. As he knew he was. Ricky was clutching his left upper arm, but he was flexing the fingers of his left hand, meaning he could still use the limb. He could see no other obvious signs of injury to his friends beyond the same sort of thumps and scraps and slices Ryan had taken.

Mildred pitched in, helping him shift bodies to the improvised front-door barricade. Predark doctor though she was, when the shitstorm came down, she had become surprisingly ruthless. The Angels held their fire for the moment. *Now* they were concerned about hitting their own people, especially the wounded. Probably they were more than a little shocked by the outcome of the assault.

Ryan had no doubt they were still out there in the weeds and rubble. Nor did he doubt they'd make another play for their prey once they got their nerve up again.

The companions slumped where they were, regardless of the blood squishing under their cheeks. Ryan felt physical exhaustion trying to pull him down like a pack of Plains wolves. They'd been running and fighting with little respite since they'd popped into the basement of the hidden redoubt, now flooded with sewage. And it wasn't as if they had been well rested before that....

"Fabulous," Mildred said, sitting down heavily beside the door. "Now the sewage we waded through isn't the worst smell."

More than a dozen Angels remained in the erstwhile fast-food restaurant. Some of them were still breathing, though it was pretty clear most of them wouldn't be for long.

"What did we do to rile them up like this?" asked J.B., squatting next to Mildred like a tired dog. "I don't recall pissing in their boss's bathwater."

"This individual might be able to shed light on what motivates his comrades," Doc announced. He was in the far front corner, back against the wall. Sitting beside him was a young, lean Angel with blond hair plastered to his head by blood and sweat. He was wheezing, visibly losing the fight to breathe against the blood slowly flooding his lungs from the sword thrust Doc had dealt.

His blue eyes blazed with defiance, though.

"You're chills," he gasped out. Now that he had his enemies' attention, he was making the agonizing effort of forcing the words out of his gaping mouth. "We'll never stop till we drag you down and put your heads on stakes outside the Joe."

Mildred knelt beside him. She didn't touch him, just looked at him and shook her head.

"But why?" Krysty asked, wiping her forehead with the back of a white hand. The effort just smeared the gore around.

"Nuking...mercies," he said. "Coming into the Cobo, looking to chill our leader, Red Wings. Think you're the first to try to do DPD's dirty work? You think Hizzoner...

gives a fuck? Even if you did it, he'd…pay you with a knife…in the back—"

He coughed violently, blood and foam flying from his mouth. Then his body convulsed. He settled back with his head slumped to his breastbone and his eyes rolled skyward.

"Gone," Mildred said, putting her hands on her thighs and standing.

"Easy!" Ryan rapped out.

Mildred ducked again. As she did, a bullet, coming in through the front window and passing out through the side, cracked through where her hunched-over shoulders had been an eyeblink before.

"It sounds as if the blighters have rallied," Doc said with his characteristic understatement. His blue eyes, which had been drooping seriously a moment before, snapped wide.

A new wave of blasterfire erupted from outside. It came from two sides, the fields to the southeast and southwest.

Earlier Ryan had reckoned, mostly on a fighter's intuition, that at least a hundred Angels were out there. Now even after all their losses it sounded as if a hundred blasters were opening up at once.

The storming party had been routed, but the yellow-haired Angel had obviously told the truth. The survivors weren't giving up. They had just paused to get themselves ready to go again.

J.B. risked a glance around the door frame. "Dark night!" he exclaimed.

Startled by his friend's unaccustomed vehemence, Ryan risked a quick look of his own from the other side.

Instead of beans and corns and broccoli, the now-abused

fields out there were sprouting Angels, dozens of them, firing blasters from the hip and yelling in fury.

This was the all-out assault. This time they meant to chill the intruders no matter what it cost. And given the savage cost Ryan and his crew had already laid on them, he had no doubt they'd succeed this time.

And from somewhere to the west, out of sight north of the gutted fast-food restaurant, a machine gun suddenly roared to life.

Chapter Ten

"And I thought it couldn't get worse!" Ricky wailed.

"It can always get worse," Mildred muttered. "Haven't you learned that yet, kid?"

J.B. looked at the long, straight magazine in his hand. "Last one," he said thoughtfully. He clicked it decisively home in the well in the Uzi's pistol grip.

Ryan frowned and cocked his head. The machine gun snarled again, ripping out a laddered burst—three shots, four, five, three—to reduce chance of a failure to feed and eke out a little more time before the barrel overheated and had to be swapped out or shut down, or it would burn out.

The other blasterfire, from the charging mass of Angels, had seriously slacked off.

Jak put his head up. The long, lank hair hanging down to the shoulders of his jacket was more pink than white.

"Running," he said.

"By the three Kennedys!" Doc exclaimed. "The lad's right! The blackguards are fleeing!"

The machine gun was a serious boomer. Ryan recognized a 7.62 mm, shooting the same cartridges his Steyr did. It was nowhere near the blockbuster a Ma Deuce .50 caliber would be, but it offered serious firepower nonetheless. Enough to be decisive in a street fight like this one.

When Ryan looked for himself, he saw that it had. He spotted nothing but elbows and asses and brown leather vests with those jaunty round badges on them.

"The sapient Arabs have a proverb," Doc said medita-
tively. "The enemy of my enemy is my friend."

"Naw," J.B. said, hauling back the bolt handle of his
machine pistol to cock it. "Your enemy's enemy is just
that. Not another thing at all, necessarily."

Doc shrugged and sighed. "So I have often found."

He stood up and shot his cuffs. "Gentlemen and ladies, our new guests demand that we give them a proper
reception. Shall we?"

Mildred got slowly to her feet. "Yeah," she said de-
terminedly.

"Hey," Ricky said as he peered over the sill of the
southwest window. "Horses."

"Horses?" Krysty echoed.

Her green eyes caught Ryan's lone one. They shared
a shrug.

Ryan glanced out the window toward the northeast side
of the street, where not a scrap of threat had come from
that tempting tall-building-cum-sniper's-nest standing
right across it. He wondered why.

"Foot soldiers on this side," he said. "Look like...
predark riot cops." His home in Front Royale, where he
grew up as the privileged son of a baron, had a library
of sorts, and he'd spent hours looking at predark picture
books.

They were, too—men wearing black uniforms bulked
out by body armor and black helmets with clear polycarbonate visors. They carried curved shields made of
the same stuff but presumably thicker gauge. Instead of
batons, though, they carried shotguns and handblasters.
Ryan wondered where they'd gotten items in such good
condition.

He looked out the far window. Other cops in short-
sleeved uniforms and helmets without visors or patrol

caps were riding into view on horses. They advanced at a walk. One raised an M4 carbine one-handed and loosed a single blast after the fleeing Angels.

Ryan winced. The big handsome bay barely twitched its ears, despite the shattering muzzle blast of high-powered rounds fired out of a short barrel.

"Now, that's something you don't see every day," Mildred said. "They look like...mounted cops?"

"Hear engine," Jak said.

Now that the albino mentioned it, Ryan wondered how he hadn't before. He realized he'd been hearing it since sometime after the last furious Angels barrage began, preparatory to their abortive all-out assault. Or *felt* it, anyway, rumbling up through the floor through the soles of his boots. They could've been firing up a dozen sirens just out of sight and he would have had a double-hard time actually hearing it over all that blasterfire. And apparently his subconscious had adjusted to the rumble, and once the furious fusillade died down, he had better things to do than try to distract his conscious mind from more pressing issues. Such as imminent death from an unexpected direction.

But there was no mistaking the sound now—the deep growl of a diesel engine idling.

"This is the Detroit Police Department," a voice barked authoritatively. "We have you surrounded. Put down your weapons and come out with your hands up. You will not be harmed."

"Detroit Police Department," Mildred repeated, shaking her head. "Really? *Really?*"

"Can we trust them?" Ricky asked, wide-eyed.

"Of course not," Krysty replied. "The question is, do we have a choice?"

"Let's see," J.B. said, pretending to count on his fingers. "We had a hundred Angels preparing to chill us at any cost. These new boys show up, and they run like bunnies."

He looked up and grinned. "I think they win."

Ryan nodded. "Yeah."

Reluctantly, Ryan scuffed a stretch of the floor with a boot sole. Then he laid down his weapons reverently.

"I hate this," J.B. muttered as he did the exact same thing. "Blood messes with the bluing something fierce."

Krysty and Mildred had already disarmed themselves. Now they dragged the bodies away from the hastily improvised human barricade. None of them was still breathing that Ryan could tell. Not that he cared.

"Weps'll clean," Ryan said, rising. It took far more effort than he expected to get to his feet.

"Don't shoot," he called out. "We're coming out." Lacing his fingers behind his head, he walked out into the cloud-filtered early-afternoon light.

"On the ground!" another voice, this one more belligerent than authoritative, barked out. "Do it now or we'll chill you!"

"Easy," the first voice called. It was a younger man's voice, this time calming rather than cracking. But it was still firm. "No need for that, Sergeant Kurtiz. I don't think we have much to fear."

Ryan agreed with him. The riot cops had appeared in the street to his left. They promptly dropped to one knee and pointed their blasters around their shields at him. More foot soldiers—or cops—appeared around the other side of the roofless building, dressed the way the horsemen were. They pointed longblasters at Ryan.

The two groups were angled so that they could burn Ryan down where he stood without cross firing each other.

"If you say so, Lieutenant," the second voice said resentfully.

Ryan glanced toward its owner. It was one of the foot cops to the west, a bulldog of a man with a black bulldog face and hatless to show off severely cropped black hair. He was reluctantly lowering an MP5-K he'd been pointing at Ryan with his left hand gripping the foregrip beneath the abbreviated barrel. The shorty machine pistol, a compact version of the old standby Heckler & Koch MP5, was the same piece Patch the scavvy woman had sported back in the building Nikk claimed as his own. Ryan wondered if that was a coincidence, or if they were just popular here.

"I don't trust these coldheart bastards as far as I can throw them," he rumbled from deep in his chest.

"We don't need to trust them," the lieutenant said. "We have enough blasters pointed at them to vaporize them."

That man was mounted. He was tall, with a surprisingly young face under buzz-cut blond hair. He rode as if he knew how and carried, of all things, a broom-handle Mauser in his right hand.

"It's all right," Ryan called to his companions, who had prudently remained inside when the sergeant started yelling threats. "You can come out."

The others filed out to stand flanking him.

"That's all?" the lieutenant asked in surprise.

"Bullshit!" Sergeant Kurtiz yelled, warming to his theme again. Ryan was getting the impression he usually didn't talk so much as yell. "No way a measly group of seven ragged-assed Deathlands derelicts could stand off that many Angels."

"He's got us pegged right, anyway," Mildred said.

"No talking, you—"

"Sergeant, stand down." This time the fresh-faced officer put a little crack back in his voice. The sergeant stiffened.

"What were the Angels doing this far north, anyway, Loot?" asked one of the nonriot foot troopers. A pair of others went cautiously into the building, blasters ready.

"Chasing us," Ryan said.

He didn't see any profit in lying. Not about that, anyway. Although he knew better than to trust a sec man, at least the lieutenant was acting friendly. Ryan wanted to do what was reasonable to keep him that way on the off chance it wasn't an act.

The officer squinted at him. "What in the name of blessed Stephen did you do to make them so mad at you?"

"No idea," J.B. said.

"We just walked into that really huge building not far from the river," Ryan said. "The one with half the roof knocked off. They saw us, started yelling something about 'DPD mercies' and opened fire. Been chasing us like a pack of hounds ever since."

"Glowing night shit!" a voice called from inside the fast-food restaurant. "It looks like a nuking slaughterhouse in here! Blood's ankle deep, and there must be twenty Angels. All chills."

Ryan heard a loud moan from behind him. A moment later a gunshot echoed out of the roofless brick box.

"All right," the cop yelled. "All chills now."

He'd exaggerated the body count, at least by Ryan's admittedly unscientific reckoning. He felt inclined to cut the sec man some slack. What he'd found inside was enough to take anybody aback if they'd walked in on it unsuspecting.

"Blasters lying all over the place like somebody knocked over an armory," the other cop yelled. "And a bunch of backpacks stashed in the back."

"Those'd be ours," Ryan said. "Also the weps." He grinned. "Some of them, anyway."

The lieutenant stuck his Mauser C96 in a cross-draw holster in front of the clasp of his web gear. Ryan wondered if those were fashionable in the Detroit rubble, too, or it was just another coincidence.

The mounted officer pointed to several of the infantrymen in turn. "Go secure the weapons and gear," he said. "Load them in the Commando."

That had to be where the Diesel growl came from and no doubt the heavy MG fire, too. The V-100 Commando was a burly four-wheeled armored car made by Cadillac Gage, which if Ryan could trust his ancient history, had once been a proud Detroit company.

"I'm Lieutenant Mahome," the officer said, turning back to the captives.

"I'm Ryan Cawdor." Ryan named the others off in turn.

"What are you doing here?" Mahome asked. "Apart from walking into the Cobo Center and kicking the whole Angels hornet nest right the nuke over?"

"Was that their headquarters?" Ryan asked. "Cobo Center?"

"Not exactly. It's their stronghold, where a lot of their fighters and workers bunk. They actually farm the old show floor with the roof gone and all. Protects the crops from the wind."

"We saw," Ryan said.

"But their real fortress is the Joe. Old hockey stadium right near it. That's where their boss, Red Wings, hangs his hat. Vicious, crazy old bastard that he is."

"That used to be the name of the hockey team in Detroit," Mildred said.

"Is that so? Anyway, Mr. Cawdor, you were about to explain how you happened to stroll in there."

"We just arrived in the ville," Ryan said. "We're looking for work. Don't know the place, so we just started walking."

"Come across from the Windsor rubble, did you? Don't blame you for clearing out of there. Stuff happens down there that'd gag a stickie."

"Funny you should mention that, Lieutenant—"

"Oh, you ran into them, too? They got into that old parking structure right across from the Center ten years or so back. Angels get their asses handed to them whenever they try to clear them out. Makes them hotter than nuke red."

"Easy with those weps, son," J.B. called to a cop emerging from the building carrying his M4000 in one hand and Ryan's Scout longblaster in the other. "We'll be wanting those back."

"No fucking way, coldheart," Kurtiz barked. "We're confiscating them."

"Not necessarily," Mahome said.

The sergeant snapped his head around. Ryan was surprised he even could, given how little he showed by way of a neck.

"What do you mean, Lieutenant? We can't let a bunch of random assholes out of the Deathlands wander around our city! What happened to restoring law and order?"

"That remains to be seen," Mahome said evenly, "until we get them back to headquarters. Where their fates will be decided by people above your pay grade or mine."

He looked back to the prisoners. "You can put your arms down."

"Yeah!" Kurtiz shouted. For once he sounded approving, though still shouting every syllable. "That way we can secure their wrists!"

"No," Mahome said. "I don't think there's a need for

that. They're disarmed and we outnumber them. And I don't think they pose much flight risk, now that we have all their stuff. Do you, Mr. Cawdor?"

"Depends," Ryan answered. "If you're just taking us back so your bosses can chill us, I'd rather we take our chances here and now."

"We don't play that way," Mahome said. Ignoring that Kurtiz muttered "*I* would" under his breath, the lieutenant went on loudly, "As the sergeant rightly reminded us, we're the forces of law and order. We're the good guys. Anyway—" he grinned "—anybody who can make the Angels that mad, and kick their teeth in that hard, could be a useful asset. I'm not making any promises here. Because, don't get me wrong, I can't. But if you're looking for work, it just may be that the Angels' paranoid notion of you being mercies working for us might turn out to be prophetic after all."

"I don't like it, Lieutenant," Kurtiz said.

"You never do, Sergeant."

"My job."

A breeze was rising. It shifted to blow from east to west. Mahome suddenly frowned.

"What the nuke?" he demanded, sniffing hard, then making an awful face. He stared at the captives. "Did you—did you all wade in sewage?"

"Well, yes, Lieutenant, sir," Mildred said. "But it was an accident."

Farting and snorting like a rhinoceros who'd eaten more fiber than it was used to, the armored car pulled around the rubble mound to park closer to the building so the cops would be able to load the equipment recovered from the restaurant more easily. Sure enough, it was a V-100, night-black with a disk-headed battering ram sticking out from its sharply angled snout. And sure enough, it sported a mounted 7.62 mm M240 machine gun in its turret.

"Cool!" Ricky exclaimed. "Can we ride in it?"

Mahome sniffed again.

"No."

Chapter Eleven

"A remarkable story, gentlemen…ladies," His Honor Claude Michaud, mayor of Detroit, said, nodding. His hair was gleaming white, and even the retreat it was beating from his high black dome of his skull was dignified. "Don't you think so, Chief Bone?"

The tall man looming at the mayor's side at the front of the big room looked doubtful and disapproving. He was well equipped to do that, Krysty thought, and just as well named. He wore a black police uniform closely tailored to a frame that was gaunt almost to the point of skeletal. And the long, clean-shaven face looked like a bleached skull above the midnight outfit, with its flaring cheekbones, hollow cheeks and dark eyes sunk into sepulchral pits. His head was shaved up to a patch of short, ice-white hair standing up from the top.

Krysty and her companions sat in the front row of heavy pews in what had once been a chapel. Like the building itself, it was still in good shape, all golden tan and dark brown, with its round-vaulted ceiling and arched arcades down either side. It even sported second-story boxes down both sides like some kind of theater, the dark hardwood gleaming from recent oiling.

The lingering scents of mold and unwashed bodies and an indefinable smell of rot undermined the overall impressive effect of the place. She was able to notice that because Lieutenant Mahome had allowed them to change into different clothes from their packs before locking up their gear in a separate closet and sending what they had been wearing off with a distinctly unhappy-looking patrol officer to be washed. He'd been quite insistent on the point.

"If they're telling the truth, Your Honor," the sec boss said. "It's a far-fetched story, if you ask me."

"You're too cynical by far, Chief," Hizzoner said. "Your young Lieutenant Mahome vouches for the veracity of their account. Or at least its gory aftermath. And you assure me he's a reliable officer, do you not?"

The skull visage nodded. "He is. But naive."

Michaud chuckled indulgently. "He'll learn."

"I guarantee it."

MAYOR MICHAUD'S CITY HALL may have been provisional, but it was certainly impressive, even though Krysty had so far seen no sign it was anything but the headquarters for the self-proclaimed Detroit Police Department.

It lay a surprisingly, and blessedly, short walk from the gutted restaurant where they'd made their final stand against the Angels. Krysty judged it to be no more than a half mile, if that.

Mahome had had the column assemble on the street that ran past the derelict restaurant to the east. Ryan had pointed up to the three-story red-stone building across from it.

"So how come the Angels didn't climb high up there and shoot us to pieces?" he asked one of the foot patrolmen who'd hemmed them warily in. "I kept thinking they were going to do that. We would have been cold meat."

The officer, a slight black man, laughed incredulously. "That's Rock City turf. Not even the Angels want to mess with *them*."

They set out along the street to the northwest. Though

Mahome claimed not to regard them as either threats or flight risks, he did make sure the seven outlanders were surrounded by his forces. His ten mounted officers, two of whom turned out to be women, rode in the lead. Then Krysty, Ryan and the others followed, with the lieutenant riding alongside and chatting amiably with them. The couple dozen regular patrolmen walked flanking the companions. Twenty sec men in full riot gear followed them, and bringing up the rear rumbled the armored car, its turret turned so that its powerful automatic blaster could cover their back trail.

"How'd you happen along when you did?" Ryan asked the young officer. "Got to say it was pretty lucky, your turning up right about then. We were in deep rad dust."

Krysty walked alongside Ryan, holding his hand. They were passing through the mostly clear area Ryan had spoken of when they were considering their options to escape. To their right were extensive fields, and off to the northeast, a stand of forest, all interspersed with the occasional ruined building. To the left lay industrial-looking buildings, some mostly intact, interspersed with wide, weedchoked rubble fields.

She reckoned Ryan was right. They never would have reached the more substantial standing structure before the Angels ran them down. Or just ran out of patience and blasted them.

"We got reports of a big commotion going on south of the Seven-Five," the young officer said. "The brass thought the Angels might be staging a raid. So they threw together a scratch force to come down and see what was what, and if it turned out the Angels had gotten big ideas, to beat them out of them."

"This is a scratch force?" J.B. asked from right behind.

Mahome laughed. "We have a lot of officers," he said,

"but we also have a triple-big amount of ground to cover. And we still don't hold much beyond the south end of Midtown. Though Hizzoner hopes to change that soon."

"Don't give 'em all our secrets," Kurtiz growled.

The burly sergeant was trudging behind Krysty's group. He actually had a baton, which he beat disconsolately against his palm. He seemed to be doing a slow burn.

It seemed insubordinate to Krysty, who admittedly didn't have a good feel for the ways of authority. But the young officer—who was quite handsome in a juvenile sort of way, she had to admit—just laughed again.

"Don't mind the sergeant," he said. "He's a good man. Just case-hardened by a long life on the streets."

Krysty frowned. To her he was just another sec man, a bully with a bludgeon and a blaster and license to use both liberally. The fact they wore uniforms and called themselves "police" didn't change what they were.

As always, there were exceptions. Lieutenant Mahome seemed unusually humane for a sec man. He even laughed a lot.

They crossed a broad freeway that was surprisingly intact. It looked as if the wreckage of the collapsed overpasses in view to the east and west had been cleared enough to offer passage for two-way wag traffic. No one was moving along it at the moment.

The area on the far side was also a mix of buildings and open spaces, some cultivated, some riotously overgrown. These buildings were mostly of a more modest scale than skyscraper-heavy downtown, which might have had something to do with the fact that they remained more intact, and only one or two they passed had completely collapsed.

Then they came upon a structure that was anything but modest: a big tan limestone building with what looked like a medieval French cathedral at one end of it. From all the black uniforms going in and out of it—and the young phalanx of riot-armored sec men standing guard—it had to be their destination.

The horse riders veered off to the left—all except Lieutenant Mahome, who dismounted and handed his bay off to a female trooper to lead. He ordered a pair of the infantrymen to escort him and the strangers, then dismissed the rest. He also had a thoroughly grumpy-looking Sergeant Kurtiz accompany them, possibly as a conciliatory gesture. The bulldog sergeant looked as if he was scandalized past the point of words.

"Where'd all the ace weps come from?" J.B. asked as Mahome headed them up broad steps to the arched entrance of the cathedral-type place.

"Same place the snappy uniforms did," the lieutenant said with a broad smile. "And the armored car. We found an armory a couple years back."

J.B. looked at Ryan, then nodded and whistled approvingly.

"Now that's some scavvy," he said.

"So," MAYOR MICHAUD SAID, pacing at the head of the converted chapel. "You made the Desolation Angels look like monkeys. Just the seven of you."

"I wouldn't say that," Ryan said in what Krysty realized was his best studiedly neutral voice. He sat next to her with his long legs crossed. He might have been the third son of a baron before he was half blinded and chased into exile by a brother's treachery, but growing up he'd learned a few things about diplomacy and negotiation.

And a lot more since.

"They're a determined bunch," he said. "We hit them hard and they just kept coming. And they do have skills."

"Then why are you still alive?" Chief Bone asked.

Ryan looked him in the eye. "We have more."

"They once were a great deal more formidable," Michaud said. "Time was, they were the biggest power not just in downtown, but in all Detroit. And it looked as if they'd manage to get their boots on the neck of the whole rubble, from the Detroit River to 8 Mile Road. They were still just a gang of common coldhearts, you understand. Criminal scum to the core. But a mighty gang."

"What happened?" Krysty asked.

She wasn't sure how they'd wound up here, sitting comfortably in this elegant place, instead of being thrown into a jail cell. But however temporary it was likely to be, she was fine with it.

And although Ryan did have definite diplomatic skills, they weren't the ones he exercised most frequently. She figured he might find a little of her help useful here. And the fact that he didn't instantly snap at her to shut it bore her out.

Hizzoner beamed and nodded. Clearly, that was the question he'd been hoping for. Although equally clearly, he was prepared to go charging on without it.

"They lost their grip," he said. "Thirty years ago there was a succession struggle for the post of president—what they call their baron. It got ugly, as such things do. The first incident was that various factions took over various sections of their domain and began fighting one another. The second was a bunch of uprisings by their subjects.

"For a time it appeared the Angels would be destroyed, either by their civil war or by insurrection. By the time things settled back down, their little rubble empire had broken down into gangs controlling neighborhoods, blocks— even individual buildings. Some of them were ruled by former Angel faction leaders, some by successful rebels. The once-proud Desolation Angels were reduced to clinging to just the Cobo Convention Center and the Joe Louis Arena."

Ryan glanced at Krysty. His lips twitched slightly in a smile.

"But they came back, didn't they?"

"You could say that," Bone said drily.

"So they did." Michaud nodded. "So they did. About twenty years ago they were being hit hard by raids and attacks. Their strongholds were strong, they grew a lot of their own food and the water table's high enough that close to the river that they got all they needed from wells. But any wall will crack if you pound on it enough.

"Their president had a son and heir who was both charismatic and capable. He earned his wings leading counterattacks to hit their biggest enemies—gangs like the Penobscot Punks, Rock City and the Felonious Monks—where they lived. He had some nasty setbacks at first, but he learned and followed them with a string of victories that soon convinced the Angels' enemies to pick on easier targets.

"The aging president got jealous of his son. He imprisoned him, but the young man broke free and supplanted his father, who soon died in questionable circumstances."

"Might actually not have been murder," Bone said. "Old man was a blackout drunk. His kid's following his footsteps."

"Who's telling this story, Raymond, you or me?"

"You are," the sec boss said. "But you're starting to walk all around the blaster instead of getting to the trigger."

"And *you're* getting ahead of the story. The new Angels boss, who took the ancient and revered name Red Wings as his own, started out as a wise and capable baron. Yes, even criminals can display such traits—although as my esteemed chief of police has so pithily reminded us, the criminal nature will always come out. He acquired trade relationships and even alliances with the Angels' former enemies—they had no friends. And he built up his people.

"However. In recent years Red Wings has become more heavy-handed and belligerent—despotic with his own people, aggressive toward others. The Angels have begun trying to expand again, but they're finding it no easy task. Many of the myriad rival gangs that sprang up during their initial collapse retain memories of what life was like when the Angels held the whip. Nonetheless, they have become a definite threat. Specifically to this, the duly constituted government of the City of Detroit and our own efforts to return the rule of law to these nuke-blighted ruins."

Ryan and Krysty exchanged looks. Ricky, who sat behind Ryan and J.B., made a skeptical sound, quickly stifled. They'd had a recent run-in with another man who'd claimed to be trying to restore rightful government and the rule of law, in the form of the mad Hanging Judge Santee in his ville of Second Chance, in the midst of the vast mutie thicket known as the Wild. It had not ended well. Though much the worse for the late, and little lamented, Judge.

"If I may be permitted to ask, Your Honor," Doc said, "what about your own government during the years of Angel ascendancy?"

Michaud stopped before them. He looked at the old man, smiled and nodded benignly, as if he was bestowing gifts. Krysty knew he'd been dying to get asked just that. She also knew Doc knew it, too. For all his ancient, befuddled appearance—and despite the fact that he spent plenty of time actually befuddled—he had the keen mind of a scholar to go along with his courtly old-days manners.

"Since the dark days of the Big Nuke, and the literally and in some way figuratively darker days of skydark, the rightful government of the City of Detroit has continued to exist and survive. Even though for more than a century—and even still today—we have served in effect as a government in exile within our own domain. But from that day to this, the torch of legitimacy has been passed from hand to committed and caring hand."

"A likely story," Bone said.

Michaud chuckled indulgently. "Well, it's the story that was passed onto me. And it's not as if we have evidence to the contrary, now do we?"

"No," the skeletal man admitted without apparent rancor or reluctance.

"So, for the past three generations, at least, we have persisted. For decades our only holding lay far away in the North End. That's how dominant the Angels were in downtown and its surroundings. And even after the catastrophic collapse of their rule, the gangs that sprang up in their place were too powerful to challenge.

"But even as the Angels turned their fortunes around a generation ago, so a great and wise leader, my august predecessor, Mayor Reginald arose—"

"Your dad," Bone said.

"Reginald Michaud. Yes, my father. He arose and revitalized the City of Detroit and began the march that led us here, to our current headquarters in what once was the Detroit Masonic Temple."

He finished, holding his arms out and turning in a happy, proprietary circle.

"Which, as you see, the previous tenants, the Cass Conquerors, kept in surprisingly ace conditions for a gang of degenerate coldhearts."

"Where are they now?" J.B. asked.

"Alas, they proved unable to adapt to changing conditions and so became extinct."

Bone smirked. He seemed to have happy memories of the Conquerors' extinction.

Krysty decided she didn't like him.

Hizzoner was certainly turning out to be a well-educated man. Though that was hardly typical of contemporary Deathlands barons, many of whom were illiterate brutes, it was far from uncommon. Ryan's late father had seen to his offspring receiving a good education. "So let me get this straight," Mildred said.

Ryan's head didn't turn, but Krysty felt him stiffen. His eye flicked to the healer, who sat on the other side of Krysty. Like Krysty, he knew all too well what that tone of voice meant.

"The mayoralty is hereditary. You're not democratically elected."

Bone actually growled at that, but Michaud merely laughed.

"Dear lady, of course we are. Indeed, we hold annual elections to choose who will preside over the resurgence of our city to its former greatness."

"Just nobody ever stands against you," Bone said.

"Well, as for that," Michaud replied, shrugging, "it's admittedly hard to find candidates worthy enough to pass our exhaustive nomination process. But moving right along—my father led us here. Not quite to the true core of the city's power, the Coleman A. Young Municipal Center. But on the very verge of crossing the Seven-Five and once more occupying our rightful place.

"And I have done my modest best to continue his great work. Of course, it was substantially aided by the discovery of a most remarkable trove of equipment meant for the use of the very Detroit Police Department, including weps and even a pair of armored vehicles. Our brilliant techs, in the grand tradition of what was once, after all, the automotive capital of the entire world, have converted them to run on biodiesel. The fuel is abundant, given the wide and numerous areas of cultivation here in the rubble. Also, they have fitted out several ancillary police wags with arms and armor."

"Yeah," J.B. said. "We saw one of your war wags in action."

"It was cool!" Ricky said.

Michaud nodded. Even Bone flickered a smile. Or something a lot like one.

"So equipped, we have begun our final push to reclaim the city from the anarchy under which it has suffered for so long. We will subdue the many gangs remaining in the city despite their stubborn insistence on clinging to their independence. And we shall break the last vestiges of Desolation Angel power."

He finished in the manner of a preacher concluding a sermon. Krysty half expected him to call for an amen. She wondered if she should applaud.

She decided not to. He was just a baron after all.

Ryan uncrossed his right leg from the left, then crossed left over right. He rubbed at his chin. Krysty heard his salt-and-pepper beard bristle crackle on his palm.

"Not to look a gift horse in the mouth or anything, Mr. Mayor," he said, "but why are you telling us this? More to the point—why are you even talking to us at all? As your…police chief pointed out, we're nothing more than a scrubby bunch of outlanders."

Slowly, Michaud's smile winched itself back, revealing teeth that were even but yellow, until it was a big grin. "I need some extra sec, blasters, as it were…."

Chapter Twelve

"Looks tough," Mildred said.

"*Double* tough," Ricky said.

Jak snickered.

They lay up in the ruins of a town house a mile or so west of the subterranean redoubt from which they'd emerged. It was late afternoon of the day after they'd arrived at DPD HQ.

A hundred yards west stood a mansion that looked as if it had already been old when the Big Nuke hit. It was, they had been told, a stronghold of the Corktown Dragons, a gang recently allied to the Desolation Angels. It was a solid square structure of what looked to Mildred, when she took a turn peering through J.B.'s minibinocs, as if it had been made out of the same yellow-tan limestone so many older buildings in the area were. It had four stories, each marked by an ornamental ledge, and ivy climbing thick up the walls. Its roof was flat but built up into ramparts at the corners.

Guards armed with longblasters patrolled up there. Others prowled through the knee-high weeds of the spacious lawn. Mildred didn't see any more gang members among the town houses and detached dwellings, some damaged, some obviously patched and inhabited, that clustered around the formerly stately house at respectful distances. At least none openly toting weapons. But more blaster-carrying Dragons were keeping watch on the cone-hatted farmers working the broad fields north of their fortress. Whether they were guards or overseers or both, Mildred couldn't tell.

"Piece of cake," J.B. stated.

"Wait," Mildred said. "What do you mean, 'piece of cake'? Are you feeling well, J.B.? Usually you're Captain Bringdown. You're all, 'This'll never work because X, Y, Z, and also it's stupe.'"

"Am not," J.B. said. "Anyway, not this time. This one is a piece of cake."

"Aren't those famous last words?"

"Yeah," Ryan said. "Not this time."

"Not see?" Jak said. "Really?"

Mildred looked at Krysty, who shook her head.

"No," she said. "So, okay, I'll bite. It doesn't look promising to me at all. They've got a dozen men and women with longblasters out in the open, and they're just the ones we can see. What am I missing?"

Ryan showed her a twisted grin.

"Don't worry," he said. "We already know how we're playing this one."

Mildred narrowed her eyes.

"This isn't going to involve Krysty and me flashing our tits, is it?"

"Again," Krysty added.

Ryan shrugged. "Only if you want to."

RICKY LAY ON his belly on the roof of the town house nearest the Dragon stronghold with his carbine by his side. The building had sustained some obvious damage, including fire. Sections of the interior floors had collapsed, though the stairwell was intact. Mostly. But the far third of the flat roof was also gone, meaning the whole structure wasn't very stable.

He wasn't sure if he could actually feel it yielding and flexing shakily beneath him at every breath or had just imagined it.

But for all of that, what really gave him a nervous feeling in the pit of his stomach was watching Ryan and J.B. scale the nearest wall of the mansion.

The guards prowling around the rooftop didn't particularly worry him. The roofline also had a slight projection to it. To actually see the intrepid climbers, they'd have to lean out far and look down in the right place. Neither of them had shown any inclination to do so, so far.

Nor did the pair standing guard on the steps up to the elevated front door. Ryan and J.B. had picked the nearer wall because it was out of their sight but still gave direct access to their objective. Anyway, even though the lantern light wasn't very bright, it would make it hard to see anything out in the darkness if the door guards did happen to glance skyward at the same time one of the climbers for some reason strayed into their field of view.

Ricky's breath caught in his throat. Two men appeared around the far corner. Strolling among the weeds in the front yard, they held longblasters at the ready. If they spotted Ricky's friends, right out there in plain sight, the climbers were certain chills.

His tension mounted as they approached the corner and then went around it—walking directly beneath Ryan and J.B. Both men had reassured Ricky that people generally didn't look up unless they had a compelling reason to do so. But Ricky was still terrified the patrol might spot them in their peripheral vision.

But they walked on, oblivious to what was occurring twenty feet above their heads. Ricky exhaled. He knew he'd do the same thing on their next circuit. And the next, until his companions got away clear. Or the unthinkable happened.

Light showed through the mansion's front windows, though fortunately not from those on the side facing Ricky. The sounds of partying drifted sporadically to his ears: the clink of glasses, harsh voices, harsher laughter. The occasional bellow of rage or female scream of...whatever. Ricky didn't like to think too much about that. He knew that, like the Angels, the Dragons had a minority of female fighters. Somehow he doubted any of them were doing the screaming.

Somewhere down there Jak lurked unseen, as was his wont, ready to move in and do his work when the time came. Ricky wasn't even tempted to worry about him. His part was easy. If you were Jak Lauren.

Krysty, Mildred and Doc were stationed under cover nearby, where they could provide fire support to their comrades if anything went wrong. Krysty had Ryan's Scout longblaster; Doc had J.B.'s Uzi. But if that support was needed, the trio would also have to fight off a passel of pissed-off Dragons spilling out of nearby buildings looking to deal some swift, hard justice to any intruders. Having seen a lot of armed gang members during the course of their surveillance, Ricky wasn't too optimistic about that.

Not to mention the fact that Ricky's own position wasn't all that secure. The town house was a whole story lower than the gang leader's mansion. He didn't worry much about the roof guards spotting him. He could blend in to the piles of debris up here, enough to escape casual detection. The two guards on top of the building had spared scarcely a glance his way in the hours since he'd crept into position, which he'd done sixty minutes after the sun had gone down. They seemed concerned exclusively with watching the streets and the fields nearby.

His problems would start, and get triple bad triple fast, if they did spot him. They had a clear line of fire at him, and they could lie behind the low rampart that ran around the whole part, or even stand or kneel behind the higher ones at the nearest corner.

There was nothing he could do about it. Ricky focused on peering at the lit window on the top floor instead.

UP UNTIL HALF an hour ago Ryan had shared the rooftop with him, watching the top-floor rooms and occasionally using his big Navy longeyes. Their target was the Dragon leader, who called himself Tommy Ten-Inch. When Ricky asked what that meant, the adults just stared at him until he blushed in comprehension. Tommy Ten-Inch was known to be a drunkard with a bad temper, which Ricky thought all gang leaders probably were, so he reckoned Tommy had to be really good at both.

Then lanterns had been lit inside the room on the nearest corner. Ryan had grunted and grabbed up the longeyes and peered intently at his target.

"Looks like the man we're here for," he said. "But he's got somebody with him."

Ricky tried not to squirm too visibly. He *really* wanted to ask if he could see, too. But he was too scared to do that. Ryan could be gruff when he was focused this intently. And especially when he was bothered by requests or questions he deemed wastes of his time.

"Huh," Ryan said softly. "Couple of girls with him. Don't look happy about it."

Ricky was naive. He knew that. But he wasn't that naive. He knew what a drunk, cranky gang leader most likely had in mind taking a couple girls up to his room late at night, especially if they weren't exactly volunteers. He felt bad about the girls' plight. But sheer adolescent hormones overpowered both that and his fear of annoying Ryan.

"Let me see," he said. *"Please."*

Ryan turned his face toward Ricky. He was frowning, but even as Ricky's heart skipped a bit he realized that Ryan's expression didn't look angry. The man was close enough he could tell that just by the starlight. But he had no idea out what the look might mean instead.

"Here," Ryan had said, thrusting the longeyes toward him. "I don't think you're going to like what you see."

Ricky held the longeyes firmly. He didn't want to think how Ryan would react if he dropped the device off the roof.

He pressed them to his eye. The yellow patch of the window swung blurrily in them, and he adjusted the focus.

"Wait," he said instantly. "They're, like, *twelve.*"

"It's how I figured it, yeah."

Ricky handed the longeyes back.

"You'd better hang on to them. You might need to take a peek."

Then Ryan left.

RICKY HAD TO force himself to breathe as he watched through the longeyes as Ryan reached the narrow ledge that ran around the base of the top floor. The stone protrusions weren't enough to stand on, but the thick ivy growing up the wall gave sufficient handholds and support for both men. And the ledge did give a little extra purchase beneath the toes of Ryan's boots.

He waited, out of sight of the window, while J.B. came up on the far side.

Both men froze.

For a moment, Ricky frowned through the binoculars, not comprehending. Then he thought, oh, shit.

He raised his head to look over the longeyes. The two

roof guards had come to a stop directly over where Ryan and J.B. clung to the wall not six feet below them. One of them leaned out slightly.

Ricky set down the device as carefully as he could while being damn quick about it, caught up his DeLisle and propped in on the wall, aiming at the men. In this light it was a tricky shot, even though it was only a fifty-yarder or so. He just had to not miss....

The guard straightened. He turned back to his partner. The two walked on around the roof.

Ricky relaxed. He felt as limp as a wrung-out bar rag.

Across the weed-grown intersection Ryan and J.B. entered the bedroom.

As quiet as he and J.B. were, the first thing Ryan saw when he stuck his head above the level of the sill was two sets of huge, frightened eyes staring at him.

The girls, both still dressed, were lying on a bed that appeared to be a stack of ancient mattresses. In a well-stained jumble of blankets between them, a figure with a pair of long, pale, skinny legs sticking out from under a blood-colored silk robe lay on its belly snoring, with its head turned to one side. Ryan guessed the coldheart boss had passed out as soon as he'd laid down on the bed.

Hard man though he was, Ryan was glad of the fact.

He held his finger to his lips. The two girls nodded.

He looked back down at J.B., who was crouched with his feet sideways, one before the other, on the skinny ledge. He nodded.

They moved.

Tommy Ten-Inch, undisputed warlord of the Dragon Clan, was roused from his righteous slumber by a hard prod in the ribs.

As he came muzzily awake, he realized he hadn't yet poked his little bed warmers tonight. That pissed him off even more than the fact that they had the nerve to wake him up.

"Cassie, Allisun, you little bitches," he snarled as he rolled over on his back. "I'm gonna give it to you both extra hard tonight."

"I love it when you talk to me like that," a deep voice said.

A deep, unmistakably male voice that, to the best of his admittedly impaired recollection, Tommy Ten-Inch had never heard before in his life.

His eyes were open, but it took them a moment to focus.

Then it hit him like a bucket of cold water. The two faces looking down at him from close range were not young and—relatively—unspoiled. Nor was one black and one pale. They were older, tanned but white, beat hard by wind and weather. And…only had three eyes between them. One actually wore an eye patch.

Both, though, sported big grins.

"Wakey-wakey," said the one in the hat.

As sloshed as he was, Tommy Ten-Inch wasn't soft. You didn't get, much less hold on to, top spot in a snarling, vicious pack like the Dragons by being anything less than cement hard, brutal and triple good at it. He inched his right hand up toward the blaster he'd hidden under the cushion beneath his head. His bedmates knew better than to try to get at it, no matter how dead asleep he seemed. He'd feel it—and hurt them. And they both had families among the subject farm workers to think about.

Something gray and metallic slammed down like a wall right next to his head, cutting off his view of Cassie's wide-eyed face. Low amber lamplight glittered, revealing it to be a wide, hefty knife blade. Its tip was sunk deep in the purple satin cover. Down floated like moats in the air.

The two girls gasped.

"All right, girls," the man with the eye patch said. He was also the one on the other end of the huge knife. "You can move now."

The frozen gang lord felt his mattress-heap bed bounce as the two bodies hopped off it.

Tommy Ten-Inch felt something hard and cold dig into his left cheek. He recognized the feel of a blaster muzzle, a double-wide one. Shotgun. He rolled his eyes left to look up its length at the man who held it. He was the one in the hat. His eyes were invisible beneath the dull orange flame-reflecting disks of his eyeglasses.

The shotgun dug into his cheek right below the bone, urging him to turn his face back upright. He didn't. The blaster was withdrawn.

"You going to behave?" its holder asked.

He had a mild voice and sounded like a wimp. Tommy started gathering tension, slowly, to spring. He'd found the weak link. Time to snap it.

The scattergun barrel stabbed down into his groin. He gasped as he felt the cold kiss of the ring of steel on his cock and balls right through the thin fabric of his robe. He groaned as it dug in.

"If you don't behave," the little man said, still in that same calm, conversational voice, "we're not going to chill you—right away."

RYAN FINISHED TYING their captive's wrists behind him, then straightened. He looked down at their captive where he lay on his belly in the rumpled nest of his bed. It stank of sweat and grease and booze.

J.B. had tied a gag like a bandage behind Tommy Ten-

Inch's head of long black greasy hair. DPD Captain Morgan, who was overseeing this grab, had provided them with special equipment, all nice and neatly prepared.

The Armorer finished tying the man's bare ankles together. They were pale beneath a coating of grime. J.B. stood up and rubbed his hands together as if to clean off some of the filth.

"Here's how it goes down, coldheart," Ryan said to their prostrate captive. "The DPD is going to be mighty generous when we bring your sorry ass back to DPD headquarters. We get a bonus if you haven't sprung any major leaks."

With the tip of his panga Ryan reached down to jab the man's buttocks, fortunately covered by the red silk robe—which was badly embroidered in gold with dragons and what Ryan knew to be Chinese writing.

"But no reward means a spent shell case if we're too dead to spend it. So if we *do* attract any attention, I'll slash your belly open and leave you with your guts spilling on the street. Nod if you understand. Do anything else and I'll just cut the damn thing off and carry it back to Hizzoner in this handy black bag he gave us."

"He means your head," J.B. added helpfully. He stood to one side, his shotgun in the crook of his arm pointed toward the door. He was mostly keeping an eye on the two girls, shivering by the window in thin soiled shifts that barely covered their skinny bodies. "Mebbe."

Tommy Ten-Inch's neck bones cracked with the speed and forcefulness of his assent.

"Smart choice."

Ryan rolled him onto his back, grabbed him by the hair and forcibly sat him up. J.B. stepped forward and briskly and with no wasted motion pulled the black cloth bag down over Tommy's head.

"Neat," he remarked as he pulled the bag closed around the captive's neck. They were not carrying his nasty ass back to DPD HQ.

J.B. looked at Ryan and adjusted his glasses.

"Right size, all set up with a drawstring and everything. Seems like they've done this sort of thing before."

Ryan shrugged. "They're sec men," he said, as if that explained everything.

And it did.

He went to one of the two coils of strong, light nylon rope they'd carried looped over their shoulders and picked it up. He looked at the gang boss's erstwhile bedmates.

"You girls up for a little climb?"

Chapter Thirteen

Ricky went rigid when he saw the flame flick alive in the window. Small and brief though the predark lighter flame was, it was distinct even against the soft yellow glow of the oil lamp inside the boss's bedroom.

It meant the first phase of the op was a success. And now the scary part began.

After J.B. and Ryan had entered the bedroom, Ricky had placed his DeLisle beside him. If he left the weapon sticking out over the edge of the roof there was a chance one of the coldhearts would notice it. And he was also ever fearful that he might accidently drop it to the cracked, frost-covered sidewalk three stories below. He knew he had a regrettable tendency to be clumsy when he wasn't immediately and actively engaged in some task. Like fixing a broken blaster.

Or keeping himself and his friends alive.

His motions were precise, even assured, as he took up the carbine. He didn't hurry, even though the pair of coldhearts on foot patrol had already appeared at the far end of the front of the old mansion.

Haste missed. He couldn't afford to. Especially not now.

Ricky slid the thick barrel with its enclosing sound-suppresser shroud over the low parapet and snugged the butt to his shoulder. The illumination from the big lanterns flanking the doors cast a bright enough light for him to sight properly by. He hoped.

The sentries strolled around the near corner of the stone building. They seemed unsuspecting. Actually casual. And why wouldn't they be? Who'd dare challenge the might of the Dragons here in the heart of their domain? They had sentries out at the borders, watching for an attack in force. And the beaten-down peasants who grew their food knew better than to lift a hand against their overlords.

Ricky lined up on them. He led them slightly, by just the right amount for range and their walking speed. He knew the drill. He saw the sights fine—with almost unnatural clarity now. His early hours of fearful anticipation were gone, leaving only a sense of complete calm.

He knew that was what confidence felt like.

The guards passed beneath the lit top window, which currently showed nothing at all unusual to the outer world. From the lower floors came the sound of shattering glass. It jabbed Ricky like an ice-cold bayonet to his well-clenched sphincter. A roar of outrage was followed by general uproarious laughter.

But despite his sudden terror, neither sentry so much as flinched. They'd heard it all before.

A shadow rose from the weeds a short distance from the house. It was a curious shadow, dark in body and legs but as pale as the moon in head and hands. Making no more noise than you'd expect a shadow to make, it stole up to the front of the house.

Ricky drew in a deep breath. He let half of it out, caught it, held it. His finger exerted gentle but definite pressure on the trigger.

Suddenly Jak Lauren rose behind the man walking closer to the wall. Ricky saw a flash of white as his hand slipped under the guard's chin from behind to yank his head up and back, readying the man's throat to receive the blade.

Ricky focused his vision, his entire being, on the other sentry. The man stopped as he realized his partner was no longer keeping pace with him. Possibly he'd heard a noise, as Jak punched his trench-knife blade through the first man's neck from side to side.

Or maybe drops of blood, scalding in their unexpectedness, had sprayed him as Jak pushed the blade outward, cutting the sentry's throat and drowning his cry of pain and alarm in a gush of jugular blood down the airway.

The sentry started to turn. It was the instant Ricky had been waiting for. His finger tightened. Decisively, but not jerking.

The DeLisle bucked. Not much; it was a chunky, hefty little piece and designed to shoot a high-powered rifle bullet. The pistol cartridge barely registered against its mass.

The 230-grain copper-jacketed .45 round had a trajectory at this range approximating that of a thrown rock. But it was a predictable trajectory. And Ricky knew it well.

He saw his target jerk as the bullet hit him in the back. His legs folded instantly beneath him. Ricky already had cranked the bolt action and chambered another stubby round.

When the guard hit his knees and paused, Ricky gave him a second bullet through the back of the head. Just to make sure. Immediately he switched his aim to the door. The two guards there showed no awareness of anything unusual. They seemed to be conversing as they shared a cigarette. Smoking and joking, J.B. would have called that—in tones of stern disapproval.

But now their slack habits were good for Ricky and his friends. And for them. If they just kept hanging out, oblivious, they might get through this night alive.

He heard a chirp like a night bird's cry.

Instantly the two ends of a length of rope came snaking

out the window and slithered down to the ground. Almost
at once a dark, compact shape appeared, half climbing
down, half sliding, using gloves to protect his hands
against rope burns. Even without the shotgun strapped
across the jacketed back and the trademark fedora, Ricky
would have recognized his mentor, J. B. Dix.

Jak had quickly and professionally shaken down the two
chills. Now he crouched in the weeds with his trench knife
in his hand, scanning the surroundings. He didn't draw
his Python, Ricky suspected, because if trouble started
and it wasn't finished silently, it would likely end up fin-
ishing *them*.

J.B. hit the ground. He gave another birdcall. If the door
guards heard it over the party racket from inside, it evidently didn't strike them as unusual.

Which meant no unexpected 230-grain messengers
from the darkness struck *them*. Ryan had impressed on
Ricky he wanted to leave as small a footprint as possible.
Not because the Dragons wouldn't find out what happened,
but to delay that inevitable moment until, hopefully, they
and their prize were long gone from their range.

Now it appeared as if a sack were exiting the window,
but a sack with long, pale legs protruding from its bottom.
They began to kick back and forth—together, since they
seemed to be joined at the ankles.

Then they stopped. Ricky wasn't sure how Ryan, unseen inside the room lowering what Ricky had to surmise
was the Dragon leader by a rope tied under his arms, had
got the message across to keep the nuke still. But he knew
Ryan had his ways. And in this case they were probably
even less gentle than usual.

His heart in his throat, the young sniper watched the
hooded captive bump his way down the ivy-covered wall.
Fortunately the party noises were getting louder, as the

partiers got, presumably, drunker. So they covered whatever sounds their hapless leader may have caused on his way to the ground.

J.B. grabbed hold of the man's bare legs and helped ease him to the ground. Not, of course, to make things easier on him. But to make sure things stayed quiet.

Another shape appeared in the window. To Ricky's surprise it wasn't Ryan, but the dark-skinned girl with the pigtails he'd seen earlier through the longeyes—one of Tommy Ten-Inch's unwilling companions for the night. Without hesitation she climbed down the rope. Her blonde companion did show some fear but quickly overcame it and started down behind her.

Meanwhile J.B. had the captive pulled to one side and lying on his sack-covered face in the weeds. The Armorer had his hat at a jaunty angle, his M4000 shotgun in his hands and his right boot planted firmly beneath the Dragon lord's shoulder blades. He seemed quietly pleased with a job well done.

Though he was not complacent. J. B. Dix did not do complacent.

The girl with the pigtails helped the other one, and they made it down without visible trouble or any fuss Ricky could detect. Neither J.B. nor Jak moved to help them. They were too busy keeping watch for trouble. The girls seemed to be doing remarkably well, considering what they'd been through.

Which was lucky for them. Had they started raising any ruckus Jak would have cut their throats without hesitation. Jak was a good man and Ricky's closest friend. But in some ways, deep down, he was still the ruthless predator who'd grown up wild in the Gulf Coast bayous, chilling men and animals as needed to survive. He could be cold-blooded, even by Ryan's exacting standards.

Ryan came down last, sliding fast, barely bothering to brake his descent with occasional clutches of his leather-gloved hands.

But not fast enough that he was down before something alerted the two men guarding the mansion's front door.

Ricky was watching them over the sights of his long-blaster. The one nearer to him, a skinny guy with a brush of blond or light brown hair, actually jumped and looked around. He said something to his companion, who was fat and struck Ricky as younger, despite the dark beard fringing his moon-pie face. Then, clutching their own longblasters in both hands, they set off at a determined pace toward the corner of the building nearest Ricky.

His mind instantly went to war with itself. He had a clear shot at either man, and though both were moving, they were moving toward him—not straight, but the angle cut down the effects of their forward motion on his aim. He was as confident he could chill one with one shot, even with a pistol round and open sights, as he was of making any shot ever. He was good with the DeLisle, and he knew it. Though he might doubt everything else about himself—and frequently did—he knew that.

But he'd had some tactical sense beaten into his head in the months since Ryan Cawdor and his companions had taken him from the burning ruin of his home ville, which had been ravaged by the coldheart minions of the self-proclaimed general El Guapo. And it urgently reminded him of two things now.

First, although the Enfield the DeLisle was built from had a notably fast and easy action, and Ricky could throw it with a smooth mechanical precision that even impressed J.B., it was still a bolt-action blaster. There was a chance the second guard would be so stunned or confused by his partner's sudden collapse that he would just stand there and not start yelling his fool head off or blazing away at random into the night with his AR-15.

Yeah, right.

Ricky wasn't inclined to risk the lives of his friends to that distant possibility.

The other problem was that the absence of the door guards would probably not cause any immediate alarm when it got noticed. Although he was sure the penalties for straying from your appointed post were pretty tough and possibly awful in a stoneheart crew like the Dragons—he'd spent much of the afternoon biting his lip as he watched Dragon overseers beat workers down into the very soil they were working with brutal blows of hardwood clubs on apparently any provocation at all, and probably sometimes just for the fun of it—he doubted it was a rare occurrence. The Dragons were scum, bullies, and he couldn't imagine the sort of dogged persistence the Angels had displayed in their pursuit of the companions coming from them. Lax guard discipline was only to be expected.

But if somebody glanced out a window and noticed a chill sprawled in the weeds—that would give the whole hornet's nest a hearty kick.

All those thoughts flashed through Ricky's head, almost between one beat of his hammering heart and the next.

And—he waited. He had to trust his and his friends' reflexes and their razor-keen senses.

The two guards clearly didn't expect any serious threat. They were the Dragons, undisputed masters of this part of Corktown. Who'd dare challenge them? They walked right around the corner without a pause or even a preliminary glance.

Ricky promptly put a bullet into the hole of the fat dude's ear, as if he'd placed it there with thumb and forefinger. He was like Doc that way; no matter how doubtful he might be any other time, when the shit hammer came down, he was as steady as an anvil.

So was Jak, who had somehow heard the two sentries start to move above the festive racket from inside. Or maybe his hunter's instincts had warned him.

No sooner had the two Dragons appeared around the corner of the building than he sprang, knife first, at the light-haired man nearer the limestone wall. His aim was as unerring as his instincts. The trench knife stabbed its point straight through the man's Adam's apple. Ricky saw the albino hand savagely twist it, literally cutting off any warning scream, as Ryan stepped up to grab the stricken man and help guide him down to the weeds, where he could stare at the stars without troubling anyone at all.

Ricky watched, almost trembling with reaction, trying not to holding his blaster in a drowner's grip. But no more threats appeared from inside the Dragon mansion.

The party just rolled on.

"RIGHT," RYAN SAID, as J.B. helped him haul the kidnapped Dragon chieftain to his bare, white feet.

J.B. had just cut the rope that held his ankles together to keep him from kicking too much on his way out the window and down. "Best power out of here before somebody notices the bastard's missing."

He turned to Cassie and Allisun. The girls stood clinging to each other and shivering. Their bare legs showed goose bumps despite the fact it was a warm night.

"You two best get back to your families," he said firmly but not unkindly. "You'll be all right."

"No way," the blonde girl, Allisun, said.

"We're coming with you," Cassie added.

"No way," Ryan responded.

"Way," Allisun said.

He frowned. "Listen. We've got to move, right now and fast. We can't wait up for you. And we can't have you slowing us down."

"Watch us," Allisun said, raising herself to her full height.

"Bet we run faster than you."

"Ryan," J.B. said, holding up his hand. "Wait. Hear them out."

Ryan was so surprised that he did. If anything, his best friend and right-hand man was usually more ruthlessly efficient than he was. If he thought the two girls, innocent victims though they were, posed the least threat he'd chill them himself and lose no sleep.

"We can't stay," Cassie said. "They know who we are, and they'll blame us for all this."

"That doesn't even make—"

J.B. gave his old friend a look. Ryan shut up. Of course the Dragons would blame the girls. And their families. Or at least take their fury out on them. They were handy.

"Yeah," Allisun said. "Look, thanks and everything, but we can't stay. You have to take us with you."

"We can show you where the lookouts are and everything," Cassie added.

"We know," Ryan said. "But thanks."

"Back to Hizzoner?" J.B. asked.

The freed captives looked at each other.

"I know!" Allisun said. "Get us to Angel territory. We'll, like, throw ourselves on their mercy!"

"Seriously?" Ryan said.

"Well—Leto's mercy."

"Yeah!"

"Who's Leto?" Ryan asked.

"Red Wings's son," Cassie said.

"Everybody in downtown loves him," Allisun said. "Even his enemies. He'll take care of us."

"He's dreamy," Cassie said. "Not like Tommy Two-Inch here." Cassie spit on the Dragon leader's bare feet.

Ryan looked to J.B. The Armorer just grinned.

"Right," Ryan said. "Enough talk. We go. And don't cause us problems, or we'll all regret it."

Chapter Fourteen

Sitting in the partially ruined apartment building like a spider waiting on a fly, J.B. watched the street outside through shabby, makeshift curtains stirring feebly over a glassless window. He was content, happy even.

He paid so little mind to feelings, he wasn't sure he remembered what happy was anymore. But he had a sense of a job well done, like any craftsman.

Twenty men swaggered into the morning sunshine. These were no ordinary gangbangers, these were the Felonious Monks, the downtown rubble's second most-feared gang after the Desolation Angels.

They were all dressed in homemade blue-gray jackets over black T-shirts, black trousers, black shoes and dark shades. The leader wore expensive scavvy. J.B. wondered where they got the shoes—if they were all scavvied, or if the Monks had unusually skilled cobblers.

They walked with arrogant assurance. Most carried long hardwood sticks or truncheons in their hands. A couple carried longblasters. Most of the rest showed the telltale bulges of handblasters holstered beneath their natty duds.

More unusual than their near-uniform clothing and disciplined manner was the fact that every one was black. That sort of racial selection wasn't common these days, although Mildred had pointed out that a large part of Detroit's population predark had been black.

A sort of market was set up out on the cul-de-sac that

led to the partially fallen down but by no means uninhabited apartment where J.B. sat on an old chair. Dwellings had been made out of the town houses and apartments along the block, and rough-and-ready huts had been constructed of scavenged materials. People haggled with operators of booths and kiosks. Dogs and chickens wandered among their mostly bare feet.

The Monks had come here from their stronghold in the western part of downtown to exact a tax or tribute from the people of this ville. Just by looking at them, a person could tell that, though they were far from well-off, the folks here weren't scuffling for survival.

They didn't have enough surplus, though, to meet the Monks' demands for payment with open hands and open hearts. Especially since the Felonious Monks were not above conscripting some of them to haul their own plundered goods back to the Monks' core realm on carts or their own bent backs.

People scattered where the Monks advanced, silent, grim, certain. Some snagged up chickens and barking dogs before scuttling to safety. The ville folk would not refuse the interlopers' demands. They didn't dare even think of resisting them. They lacked substantial weapons or the skill to use them.

Nor was it easy or wise to fight the Monks. They were well equipped for the task themselves, experienced, tough and brave. They were known for following a code of honor as stringent as the Angels' own. And like their rivals, they refused to indulge in cruelty for its own sake.

But that didn't mean they treated enemies or resisters with studied kindness. They made it a practice to treat others as sternly and uncompromisingly as they were said to treat themselves. They might not be sadistic. But they believed in being *decisive*.

That the hagglers and vendors abandoned their tasks, and their wares, to run for cover didn't seem to surprise the Monks. If they noticed there were far fewer people abroad in the makeshift market this morning than usual, their impassive faces showed no sign.

They strode on, toward the head-woman's residence, not far from where J.B. waited.

Right into the kill zone.

J.B. held an initiator in his right hand. It had been provided by the DPD, along with certain other gear. He clicked open the cover and pressed the button with his thumb.

The room immediately to the right of him, separated by an intact and solid brick wall, erupted in noise, a flash and a billow of smoke as a pound of black powder lit off. It blew a couple of pounds of random scrap metal, like bent screws and old nails, with some busted glass thrown in for good measure, into the faces of the Felonious Monks.

Before the smoke obscured his vision, J.B. caught a glimpse of the men reeling back, throwing up their hands against an onslaught they were already too late to defend against. As if hands could do so.

From the right he saw another yellow flash. Ears that were ringing from the first blast were slammed by another as Ricky triggered a second makeshift Claymore mine, improvised out of a large, crudely made clay jug, as the device J.B. had set off was. It was emplaced to fire into the Monks at a forty-five-degree angle so as not to endanger J.B., the rest of the companions or any of the ville folk.

Some of the Monks, spared by the first gigantic shotgun blast, had already begun diving for cover to J.B.'s left. The shrapnel shot out by the second charge missed them, too.

In his left hand, J.B. held a second initiator. He opened the safety case with his thumb and pressed the button.

A blast of flame and flying metal caught the Monks in midair and tore them to shreds.

For a moment all was boiling smoke, falling, flaming wreckage and the ringing in J.B.'s ears. The kiosks and booths were mostly write-offs, but the "goods" the people had been haggling over were just bits of junk and trash they'd scraped together. The Monks might have spotted that had they looked closely, but they had been too intent on their task of intimidation.

The smoke began to dissipate into swirls and eddies. Wisps of cloth, blackening in flames, flew like autumn leaves around it. Through the thinning cloud J.B. saw several Monks running away as fast as their legs could carry them.

The rest were down. All except the leader, who somehow remained standing. His clothes had mostly been torn from his body. What was left was smoking. One of the lenses of his sunglasses was gone, as was the eye behind, to judge by the extra flow of red from the socket to join the sheets and rivulets of blood that covered his face and torso and legs.

But he not only stood, he also had a Beretta extended in his right hand and was firing. At what, J.B. couldn't tell. He had to admire the man for sheer grit and balls.

But it was futile. He was an enemy, still on his feet and shooting. So Ryan, set up on a floor of the ruined apartment building behind this block that stood higher than the ones in front of it, simply shot him through the chest with his Steyr Scout. Blood sprayed out behind him. He toppled to the street among the ruined bodies of his men and did not stir.

Slowly the ville folk began to emerge from hiding. Some were weeping openly in shock.

Ryan's companions came out of where they had laid or

crouched in ambush. They'd been ready to blast the Felonious Monks, but there was no need.

J.B. gathered the initiators. Either the DPD armorer would demand them back and make trouble for the outlanders if they weren't promptly delivered, or maybe, just maybe, he might forget they had them. In which case J.B. and Ricky could certainly find uses for them.

And even if the Detroit sec men wanted their fancy electronic initiators back, J.B. had helped himself to several extra pounds of Hizzoner's finest black powder.

J.B. went out through the front door. From his right, on the far side of the unused room that had housed the first Claymore, stepped Mildred. She looked at the fallen Monks. Some of them were groaning and stirring feebly. Most just lay there. Some smoldered. All leaked.

She shook her head. "That's what I call overkill, J.B."

He shrugged. "In a case like this, a job worth doing is worth overdoing."

Mildred made no move to tend the wounded Monks. Instead she turned to the ville's head-woman.

"What do you want to do about the injured ones?" she asked.

"We'll send them back to their people, if you permit," the woman said in a hushed voice. "These, at least, will do us no more harm."

Ricky was practically bouncing with elation. "Yes," he cried, pumping his fist in the air.

Then he noticed his companions were quiet. He looked at them, puzzled.

"What?"

"Shut it," Mildred growled.

THE STREET LOOKED like a butcher shop when Ryan came down from his perch, his longblaster in one hand.

He felt a stab of annoyance at his companions for letting their guard down so quickly, but he suppressed it at once. He'd seen the surviving Felonious Monks run off. They hadn't looked like men who intended to come back soon for more.

If they'd brought backup, they didn't seem inclined to step up. Why would they, when they were off on an errand they'd carried out dozens of times before, probably without incident except the odd unwise protest? Which they likely looked forward to, so they could deliver a hearty beat down to encourage the others. They might not be sadists, but they got just as bored as the next bunch of guys.

The ville people seemed especially shocked by the noise and violence. And the blood. And the smell, which was already getting thick as the morning heated up. A couple puked noisily. A couple more wept.

His companions seemed subdued. Krysty came over to him and put her arm around his waist. He hugged her around the shoulders.

"Glad it was them and not us," he said. She nodded.

The ville boss approached him. Though her brown face and dark eyes showed fear, her back was straight and her gaze was direct. She was a well-preserved woman in middle age, fairly trim, with a red turban wound around her head and copper bangles dangling from her ears.

"What is to become of us now, after this, Ryan Cawdor?" she asked. "The Monks will not be pleased with us when they learn of this."

"Like I told you," Ryan said. "The mayor will extend the protection of the Detroit Police Department to you, if you'll take it."

Which he knew full well meant taking the "guidance" of Hizzoner and his sec men. He didn't doubt the headwoman knew it, too. The pain in her eyes wasn't all regret for the bloodshed and suffering she had allowed to come into her ville. Nor dread of Monk reprisals.

Their contact, DPD Captain Morgan, a big, burly, loud man with a red face and a blond buzz cut, had explained the strategy when he briefed them beforehand. Though the Felonious Monks were no friends of the Desolation Angels, they liked Hizzoner and DPD a nukeload less. So DPD was running a flanking maneuver on them, cutting into the villes to their west that they didn't outright control but intimidated into paying them off. If DPD could get a nice, secure base of operations in that territory, they could put pressure on the Monks from a whole new direction. More to the point, the threat of attack from the west would make the gang think twice about trying to hit DPD in its flank when the self-proclaimed City of Detroit made the major move everybody in the rubble knew was coming against the Desolation Angels.

Ryan had no clue why the sec captain would bother explaining the Big Picture to a bunch of outlanders. Maybe he just wanted to brag, impress them with how smart he was. Or his boss, Chief Bone, anyway.

"We hear DPD can be worse than the Monks," a woman stated.

"Yeah," a man said. "A lot of those sec men, they get off on beating down poor folks like us just for the fun of it."

"You didn't raise any of these objections when we came to you with the plan earlier," Ryan said.

"We thank you for your help," the head-woman said. "It doesn't mean we do not fear the consequences. If we had been able to spare what the Monks demanded of us, we would never have agreed to let you do this thing."

She looked at the carnage, the blood pools, the tattered and shattered figures, some still smoking, the moaning, bloody rags of survivors being loaded into carts.

"And now," she said, not looking at Ryan, "we have no choice but to accept the mayor's offer." She shook her head. "I knew what this would mean when you came to me last night to propose this plan. But only now do I feel the full import of what you have done—and what I have done."

"You do what you need to survive," Ryan said. "Same as we do."

She turned eyes that glittered with tears to him. "This? This is what you must do to live?"

He nodded.

Chapter Fifteen

"Look," Ricky whispered as they walked into the grand front entrance of the former Masonic temple where Hizzoner hung his hat. "In that big room, there!"

Ryan frowned, then glanced down the hallway toward the enormous chapel where they'd had their first—and only—interview with their new employers, Mayor Michaud and Chief Bone.

The same two stood near the door in the aisle between the empty pews. Hizzoner had his hand on a man's shoulder. Bone stood by with his face showing the same expression it normally did, what a person would expect from the skull it resembled.

Except not grinning.

"Shit," Mildred said under his breath. "That's Tommy the Dragon lord."

"Don't stare," J.B. said softly.

"Why? Because it's impolite?"

"Because pissing off the big bosses is not the smartest thing to do when we've just walked unarmed into their fortress," Ryan said. Hired hands or not, they still had to check their weapons before being allowed inside the headquarters building. "And are surrounded by dozens of their sec men." Who did *not* have to check their blasters.

"Oh, right," Mildred said.

She didn't sound contrite, and Ryan didn't really blame her. He was only bothered by the fact of her outburst, not what it was over. He wished they could have taken down the bastard, too.

But Mildred wasn't ready to let it go.

"I've never been a fan of the third degree," she muttered, "ever since I was a black woman living in twentieth-century America. So I hate to admit I was hoping they planned to sweat him real hard. They'd have a real job ahead of them doing anything to him he doesn't deserve."

"Yet now they appear to be as thick as thieves," Doc said. "Perhaps that was the goal all along."

Ricky and Jak stood a little ways down the side corridor to the meeting room they were heading toward to debrief Captain Morgan in the wake of yet another successful foray. Ricky looked guilty. Jak was shifting from one foot to another as if he urgently needed to go pee. He was just uncomfortable being hemmed in.

"Not our problem," Ryan said. "We haven't been chilled by Hizzoner's men, and we have jack in our pockets. We get to live another day. End of story."

"Best move along soon," J.B. said. "Sec men are starting to give us the hard eye. Harder than usual, I mean."

The Armorer stood to one side polishing his glasses. He didn't appear to be looking close enough to the two riot-armored cops who stood flanking the chapel entrance for even his peripheral vision to pick them up.

"Yeah," Ryan said. "We don't want Morgan getting impatient. He's enough of an asshole as it is."

"I don't like it either, Ryan," Krysty added as they set off toward their goal.

"We work for a baron and his sec boss," Ryan said. "Which part were you expecting to like?"

They started passing more and more patrol officers. Some of them smiled and nodded and one said, "Ace job."

One fresh-faced Asian-looking man, who couldn't be

older than Jak, insisted on stopping and shaking everybody's hands.

"Thanks for helping out our guys out there," he said.

"Yeah," Ryan said, nodding. "It's what we do."

"Imagine that," Mildred commented as the young patrolman strode on. "Us saving sec men's asses."

Ryan shrugged. "It's the gig. Some of them aren't bad."

"Then there's our current boss man," Mildred said.

Ryan grunted. Morgan acted angry and contemptuous all the time—about the world in general, but them in particular. Still, the intel he'd given them on their various targets had been first-rate. He might not have liked the companions any more than they liked him, but he used them like valuable tools, not cheap throwaways.

Not that I trust him to keep doing that indefinitely, Ryan thought.

"Speaking of which," J.B. said. "Reckon he's not getting any more patient."

They picked up the pace along the fancy marble floor. As they approached the door beyond which the belligerent and overbearing Captain Morgan waited like a cranky bear in his cave, a familiar voice called to them from behind.

"Ryan! Krysty! So good to see you all!"

It was Lieutenant Mahome, striding toward them along the corridor. His blond head was bare, and he had a dark smudge across one cheek.

Ryan nodded.

The officer came up and shook Ryan's hand, then each of the others' in turn.

"You really did a great thing for us out there yesterday," he said, "saving our boys and girls from those Rock City enforcers."

"Freaking Juggalos," Mildred muttered. "I hate Juggalos."

Mahome frowned at her. Obviously the word didn't mean any more to him than it did to Ryan.

"She's not from these parts," Ryan explained.

"You're looking good these days," Krysty told the lieutenant.

"They tell me I'm in line for a promotion," Mahome said. "Right after the big push that's supposed to be secret but everyone in the department knows about."

"Try everyone in Detroit," Ricky said.

Mahome shrugged. "As long as nobody outside the department knows the details, it's all ace."

Krysty gave him a brief hug. "It's good to see you, too. You take care out there."

He blushed, thanked her and headed on his way. He seemed to be stepping out even more briskly than before.

"You getting a soft heart?" Ryan asked with a grin. "Developing a taste for handsome young sec men?"

She shook her head of glorious red hair. "He's a good boy," she said. "I can tell. They're rare, especially among sec men."

"Seems to be," Ryan replied without sarcasm.

"Let's hope he survives the fact," J.B. said.

"THAT'S A PRETTY impressive piece of construction," J.B. stated.

"Yeah," Ryan said.

He was impressed, too. Even at that early hour it was a hell of a sight, silhouetted against the unfeeling glow of the Milky Way. It looked like a weird giant mushroom, with a flat-topped funnel-shaped head unfolding from the top of a squat cylinder perhaps thirty feet in diameter.

"Rainwater collector," J.B. said. "Up on top of their storage tank. Wonder what it's made of?"

"We'll never know," Ryan said. "We weren't asked to build one of the nuking things. We're here to break it."

"Shame."

The companions lay spread out on their bellies on a slope choked with low weeds and head-size concrete rubble, looking across a narrow gully at the big, bizarre structure. Downhill to their left a few stray gleams of light showed from the usual crude shanties of a little ville, and beyond them shone the sporadic lights of midtown and downtown. To their right, up the slope, rose vast abandoned buildings, their looming walls blank and sinister.

Morgan had sent them farther afield than they'd ever been, a couple miles to the north and west of Hizzoner's HQ. The city as a whole inclined gradually upward from the river in the southeast. Their current lie up, and their target, stood on a butte or hill that stuck out of the main slope.

That location was high enough to make digging wells difficult. Plus, they had been informed that other factors precluded that option. Morgan hadn't bothered elaborating on what they were, and nobody had asked. Doc had cleared his throat suggestively, but Ryan had turned and glared him into silence.

The key was, this storage-tank-cum-collector represented most or all of the water supply that supported what Morgan said was a belligerent gang called the Jokers. They had been conducting increasingly bold and brutal raids against villes and neighborhoods loyal to Michaud's self-styled City of Detroit.

Depriving the Jokers of their water should make them a lot more amenable to listening to reason, as preached by Hizzoner and his sec boss, Bone. Or barring that, to being knocked flat by them.

The whole thing sounded sketchy to Ryan, but it wasn't

really his place to care if the plan made sense. He and his friends had to take care of business until they had an opportunity to get out of there. A pair of Jokers patrolled around the tank's base. One had a pump shotgun, the other a hunting-style bolt-action longblaster sans scope. They acted tired and bored, beyond the point of even smoking and joking to pass the watch.

Ryan checked his chron. Getting the sentries in this condition was a powerful reason to wait as late as possible before making their move, little as he liked to be crowded for time. Two and a half hours into a four-hour stint that began after midnight did the trick nicely.

"Right," he said. "Got an hour to sunup. You sure you and the kid got enough time to do the deed?"

J.B. chuckled. "No problem with that part," he said.

That kind of went down Ryan's spine, as undoubtedly his best friend and right-hand man had intended. Everything they'd done so far for DPD had gone remarkably well. Not always according to plan, but never seriously off the rails. They'd been in control throughout.

Ryan wasn't superstitious. He didn't believe some magic hex was attendant to such a run of lucky strikes that would suddenly bring the whole entire world of hurt down on their necks to compensate. He knew very well there was no kind of magic force that balanced things out. If there were, half the barons on Earth would be staring at the stars right this moment, and all the rest would be a day or two behind them.

But he also knew the odds were very strongly against the forays continuing to go well, even though they weren't terribly high risk—at least compared to what he and his friends were used to. This job looked less challenging than their usual daily life. What they mostly had been were tasks that required more flexibility and lateral thinking than was common in the regimented ranks of DPD. And probably more than was permitted.

Still, J B. was also right that the demo phase was the simplest and lowest-risk part of the entire plan. If the world of hurt was going to land, it would likely hit at a different time.

"You sure you've got enough explosives to do the job?" Ryan asked.

"Sure," J.B. said. "It's not like we have to knock the whole thing down. Just put a big enough hole to let all the water out before they can patch it. They'll get thirsty in a hurry."

"I was being sarcastic," Ryan said. "You two took enough C-4 and blasting caps to level Hizzoner's whole palace."

J.B. and Ricky exchanged grins.

"Did we now?" the Armorer asked.

Ryan chuckled.

"Jak," he said softly, "move out. I'm right behind you."

The albino youth didn't acknowledge Ryan in any way. He was like a cat that way; he just rose from where he lay in the weeds and artificial breccia and ghosted forward. He vanished into the arroyo as if phasing out of existence. Ryan started to follow.

"I still say I could take them from here," Ricky said.

"Noted," Ryan replied. Really, there was no overpowering reason not to play this the way they had the snatch-and-grab they'd put on Tommy Ten-Inch. Ricky *could* have sniped one down and Jak throat-cut the other.

But Ryan felt a need to keep his own hand in.

"Here," Krysty said. She grabbed Ryan's long hair and cranked his face around toward hers. Then she planted a fast but firm kiss on his lips.

"For luck," she said.

He nodded and was gone.

THE HUMAN BODY, allegedly, reached a sort of low ebb in its circadian rhythm at around half an hour before dawn. So did a person's mental state and morale. At least, that's what Ryan had heard, and nothing in his experience had given him reason to doubt it.

Also, half an hour before sunup—or after sunset—was said by combat types he'd encountered to be the worst time for visibility. The human eye supposedly had more trouble resolving images and making visual sense of them with a little light to work with than in total darkness. Ryan had no idea if that was really true, but he'd never come across any reason to doubt it.

Both of those facts were why that period was favored for sneak attacks.

When Ryan came up out of the brush-choked cut in the slope with his panga in his hand, it was still well shy of that golden time. The sky was still dead black. The night was quiet but for some crickets singing and some sleepy voices that occasionally drifted up from someplace downhill, not too close.

But that was what the timetable given them called for. They were to blast the water tank fifteen minutes before the sun came up. Ryan wanted to leave the actual move, starting with the sentry takedown, as late as possible to reduce the chances of detection. Their briefing said the Jokers were pretty punctual in their changes of watch, and their own observation from shortly after last night fell tended to confirm it.

But of course, a person could never tell. Some early-rising body might think to bring the watchmen coffee or some other hot drink to help keep them awake for the crucial final half hour before they were relieved of duty. Or somebody's squeeze might sneak up for a little illicit nooky—something Ryan had personally known to happen. The point was, he wanted to cut it as fine as possible.

The sentries passed by, not thirty feet away. They carried their blasters in their hands, not slung, which meant they hadn't gone completely slack. But they hung their heads and seemed to be dozing from the way they shuffled their feet.

Ryan sprinted forward as fast as he could and still keep quiet. Jak seemed to materialize in front of him, running full out without generating any noise.

Jak slowed as he reached the tank, then flashed a grin at Ryan.

The one-eyed man slowed, too. Jak would take the man nearer the rusty steel wall of the tank. Ryan would get the outside man. The sentries were wearing rough clothes, sturdy but shabby shirts and trousers—new manufacture, not scavvy. They looked more like everyday working men than gang members. Maybe this was shit detail for the junior Jokers, Ryan thought, or the ones not fit for serious fighting.

They struck. Ryan banished all awareness of Jak and his target and let his predatory senses take over. Jak's man was the albino's problem, not Ryan's.

Ryan would have sworn he made no noise as he sprinted toward his prey, but even as he reached to grab his man by the bearded chin, the sentry suddenly whipped around.

Through the dark Ryan saw the scuffed steel buttplate of the bolt-action blaster right before his eye.

Chapter Sixteen

Ryan threw himself onto the ground, tamped hard and worn bare of grass by the feet of many sentries. He had no choice; a crack on the head from the longblaster's butt would make things go bad triple fast.

The Joker was as fast as he was alert—or lucky. As he spun violently clockwise, the longblaster's butt passed mere inches above Ryan's head.

But Ryan wasn't merely ducking for his life. As he went down, he kicked hard with his right leg, scything from the left. The back of his calf caught the guard's left leg right below the knee and swept both feet right out from under him.

The Joker landed on his back almost beside Ryan.

Before the sentry could suck in enough breath to yell or do more than turn a wild eye toward his attacker, Ryan swung the panga across his body and down with frantic, vengeful fury.

The thick but keen blade cut through skin, cartilage, veins and muscles—and right on through the bones of the man's neck. The dark-bearded head rolled away from its neck as if propelled by a final gush of blood as his heart gave one last convulsive pump.

Jak was crouched over the headless body. He held his trench knife poised to strike.

"Noisy old man," he said.

"Fuck you," Ryan told him. "And thanks."

But he refused Jak's offer of a hand to help him up. He wasn't a man who stood on pride often. But now was definitely one of those times.

"I DON'T THINK I'm comfortable with this," Mildred said.

Mildred was just talking to distract herself from how nervous she felt for J.B. The Armorer and his shadow, Ricky, were hunched down at the base of the tank on the side closest to the ville it served, laying their explosive charges. The fact that the two guards lay near the pair, cooling down to air temperature, did nothing to reassure her. Their presence emphasized the risk that somebody could come up out of the ville and blow their surprise. A risk that she felt increasing with every beat of her hyperkinetic heart.

"What's not to be comfortable with?" Ryan growled.

"The men you and Jak killed," she said. She didn't feel like using euphemisms such as "took out." She was more acutely aware than usual of the fact that what they were doing was pure murder for hire, something they had always avoided, no matter how richly the victims might deserve it. Sure, they had done security work in the past for money, but they weren't "mercies." They drew the line at that. She knew that they had to do what was necessary to survive, but now they had crossed the line and she didn't like it.

"They didn't look like gangers," she said. "Not to me. Did they look like it to you?"

"No," Krysty replied.

"What are you talking about?" Ryan asked.

"They look like just, you know, working stiffs."

"Well, what do gangers look like?"

"Not like them," Krysty said. "In a place like this people usually join gangs so they won't have to do hard manual labor."

"So what—do they have uniforms?" Ryan asked.

Mildred and Krysty exchanged glances.

"Is this just a girl thing?" Mildred said. "Can it possibly be a girl thing?"

"Of course they have uniforms, Ryan," Krysty stated.

Silence. Mildred glanced across the shallow ravine. J.B. and Ricky were still busy.

Still exposed to danger.

"What are you talking about?" Ryan asked. For the first time he sounded less annoyed and more honestly confused.

"Think about the ones we've taken on," Mildred said. "The Penobscot Punks right when we came popping out of that redoubt like so many corks from a bunch of bottles of shit. The Angels and their colors. The Dragons with their tacky Chinese dragon badges. The Felonious Monks. Those assholes with their lame face paint and Mad Max spikes and hockey pads."

"The Gentleman Junkies," Krysty recited. "The Cubbies."

"Yeah. Who even puts on crappy homemade baseball jerseys and goes to battle with bats? And why the Cubbies? They weren't even an American League team."

Ryan's eye narrowed dangerously.

"Okay," Mildred said. "Point made."

"That being—?"

"They, well, have uniforms."

"Mebbe not what you'd consider uniforms," Krysty said. "Not like DPD. Except for the Monks. But still, they all had distinctive looks."

"Perhaps that is the object," Doc said thoughtfully. He had decided to return to the present after several hours of wandering the corridors of time and memory inside his abused mind. "After all, is that not the purpose of wearing uniforms? To differentiate one's comrades from one's enemies in the heat of action?"

"I see that," Ryan said. "What I don't see is what that has to do with the price of ammunition."

"So wouldn't a gang called the Jokers have their own trademark style, too?" Krysty asked.

"And wouldn't that most likely be something that differentiated them from common laborers as well as rival gangs?" Mildred said. "I mean, I'd expect the Jokers to pick something stylish. It's not like they call themselves the Red Guards or anything proletarian like that."

Ryan sighed.

"Ace. So mebbe those weren't Jokers. So?"

"Well, why wouldn't the Jokers be guarding the vital water tank? If anything happens to it, they're all in deep rad dust and in pretty short order."

"Such guard duty is boring and not widely desired," Doc said. "Perhaps they delegated it to menials."

"If they're such downtrodden menials," Mildred said, "would the Jokers give them guns?"

Ryan held up his hand.

"I don't know," he said. "Nobody knows. But the only thing that matters right now is that we've got a job to do."

A rustling in the brush in the arroyo drew everybody's attention that way.

"And speaking of which—" Ryan said.

Ricky raced out of the gully. At least the kid had sense to stay bent over to minimize the chance he'd be spotted. Especially from below, silhouetted against the stars.

"Slow down there, Snowball," Mildred said. It was another reference Ryan didn't catch, but he didn't care to bother asking for an explanation. The stocky healer seemed in a nostalgic frame of mind these days.

A beat later J.B. followed. Though he was hunched over,

too, he moved as casually as if he were walking through a well-secured campsite. Ryan was fairly sure that the Armorer was engaging in a touch of theater. He had presumably hustled through the cut. And he sure had hustled away after he and his apprentice had fixed their charges to the tank.

At least part of the way J.B. had been carefully unrolling the safety fuse behind him. He'd just taken care quickly.

He and Ricky took their places lying alongside their comrades, except for Jak, who was on the prowl, making sure nobody was creeping up on them.

J.B. snipped the fuse with his folding knife and tossed the roll to Ricky. He put the knife away and dug out an old-fashioned fuel-and-friction lighter. He offered it to Ryan.

"You light them off," J.B. said. "It's time you got to share in the fun."

"Yeah," Ryan agreed.

He took up the safety fuse with about a foot sticking out of his hand, struck a flame and applied it. He opened his hand hastily to drop the line as a glowing spot raced away along it, hissing and throwing off sparks. The flame vanished into the gully.

An eyeblink later it appeared on the far bank and streaked to the underside of the tank.

Ryan knew that J.B. and Ricky had set several charges of the moldable plas ex, sticking it to the metal at the base of the tank and squeezing it under it where possible. He never even saw the fire split into several parts before a giant white flash blanked out the whole scene.

The high-explosive detonation of about a pound of C-4 at a range of a mere forty yards or so was impressive. The rolling overpressure struck Ryan in the face like a two-by-four, and the sound was like a chop from his panga directly to his eardrums.

But even before the sound crossed that small distance his eye was able to make out water jetting out under pressure from the breaches the charges had torn in the thin-gauge steel. The floating purple blobs of dazzle afterimage made details hard to get, though.

"Well done," he said, although only he could hear his approving words.

He doubted anyone else was hearing any better than he was over the ringing in their ears, so he turned to J.B. and Ricky and gave them a wolf's grin and a thumbs-up. Ricky blushed—there was enough gray dawn light now for Ryan to make that out. J.B. just nodded. But his slight smile was the equivalent of another man's fist pump of triumph.

"Ryan," Krysty called softly but with enough of an edge to add urgency. "Down there!"

Her lover took his gaze away from the torrent of water gushing from the stricken tank and sending a substantial flood downslope to the Joker settlement to look where Krysty pointed.

Down where the foot of the butte flowed into the gentle rise from the river northwest, a pair of headlights had just glowed into life on the street that led up toward the Jokers ville several hundred yards away. The growl of a diesel engine throttling up from low idle reached their ears.

It was as if the blast that took out the water-storage tank had been a signal. A *lot* like that.

"Hizzoner's sec men," Jak pronounced.

"What's this?" Ryan asked. He looked toward J.B. as he said it but was basically asking it of the world in general.

J.B. just shrugged.

The headlights began to advance at a walking pace

upslope. Two other sets of headlights blinked open after it. They followed.

DPD had turned out in force, and they weren't making any bones about it after a surprisingly stealthy approach, given how loud their armored cars tended to be. But neither were they acting as if they intended to have to storm the ville.

"Let's swing east of the ville but get down there as fast as we can while staying low," Ryan said. "I want to find out what the story is here."

"And what if battle is joined?" Doc asked.

"One thing at a time, Doc," Ryan said.

They started to scramble down the hill but froze when lights started coming on in the ville. Between the huts Ryan could see people running to and fro, raising splashes from the ankle-deep water flowing through the settlement.

Jak, who had taken point, turned back to look at his halted friends in impatience.

"Not looking," he said.

"Reckon I wouldn't be looking anywhere but at those lights and the loud wags either, if I was them," J.B. said. "Which I am starting to be almighty glad I'm not."

The companions didn't abandon caution, but they picked up the pace. Ryan saw the lead lights come to a halt about thirty yards shy of the ville. By their backscatter and the gradually brightening dawn, Ryan could make out the distinctive humped outlines of DPD's V-100 Commando— their big armored vehicle, mounting their potent 7.62 mm M240 machine gun. Their other armored wags were a Lenco BearCat, basically an outsize, armored SUV, and two or three war wags improvised by bolting makeshift armor onto actual SUVs.

"This is Captain Morgan, Detroit Police Department SWAT," an electronically amplified voice boomed out.

"We're taking over here. Start throwing your weps in the street, or you're all gonna start getting thirsty about noon."

"Ryan," Krysty said, "this isn't right."

"No," he replied. "It's not. Let's go."

WHEN THEY CAME out of some ruins east of the ville, across the now wider and shallower gully, a bearded man dressed in the same sort of laborer's clothes the chilled guards wore stood midway between the first hut and the sharply angled snout of the DPD armored car.

Ryan had to admit to himself that Mildred and Krysty had a point. He didn't find it easy to envision the boss of a gang called the Jokers dressed like that. To say nothing of being barefoot, which he was, even if he'd gotten hauled out of a warm bed at the crack of sunup. And C-4.

"—have no choice," he was saying sadly. Behind him glum men and women were bringing blasters, knives and even swords out of their shanties and placing them on the street. Not one of them was wearing a scrap of anything that looked like gang colors. They all looked like people who worked hard all the time, went to bed dog tired and woke up only somewhat less tired. The kids looking fearfully out the doors or windows of some of the improvised dwellings were skinny and ragged.

"But I ask that you treat us humanely," the bearded man said. "As you see, we are complying with your demands."

"As you can feel from the mud under your dirty bare feet," Captain Morgan said in an overloud, bullying voice, "you don't have a choice."

He sat in the cupola on top of the Commando. He wore a helmet with built-in ear protection, and he seemed to be swaggering without even moving.

Ryan found himself striding openly from the ruins, right toward the riot-armored SWAT troopers debarking the two canvas-back trucks that sat behind the Commando. "What's going on here?" Ryan demanded.

Morgan turned his way. In the half light Ryan saw teeth shown in a mirthless grin.

"So it's our pet mercies," Morgan said. "Well, you did a good job. You'll be paid like we agreed. So why're you hanging around here? We got this."

"Mercies? We do what we have to when a blaster's to our heads," Ryan said through gritted teeth. He stopped. His friends had emerged from cover behind him and were coming up on both sides of him. "And just what have you got?"

Morgan laughed. "This ville."

Black armored officers carrying truncheons trotted past the V-100 and the sad, bewildered, bearded man and into the ville. They began bullying the ville folk into gathering the weapons that had been placed on the ground.

A woman said something to a SWAT trooper. She didn't seem heated or disrespectful, though she was too far away for Ryan to hear over the grumble of the now idling Commando. The black-armored man struck her backhanded across the face with his truncheon. She fell down like an empty sack.

Krysty uttered a little moan.

"Where are the Jokers?" Mildred asked. She sounded pissed. Ryan hoped she'd keep control of herself. He didn't want to have to rein her in. He was having a hard enough time keeping his own temper in check. But he was well aware that if shit started, he and his friends would be the ones taken out.

"Jokers?" the spokesman said, clearly confused. "What about the Jokers? Their turf is west of here. They don't mess with us."

He straightened slightly.

"We've taught them better."

"You can see these people have loads of weps," Morgan said to Ryan. "Dangerous weps civilians shouldn't be allowed to keep. And they're way too ready to use them to defend this piss-pot ville and their fields. Fact is, they've put a scare up the actual gangs hereabouts.

"Not that they'd be more than a speed bump to us, with the wag and our SWAT boys. But we're looking to own the ville and the labor. Not trash the one and chill the other."

"So you had us take their water supply," J.B. said.

"Hey—we're benevolently gonna provide them water. So long as they know who's in charge."

"Why here and now?" Doc asked. "The whole city knows you are prepared for a final showdown with the Desolation Angels. How can this possibly serve Mayor Michaud's ends?"

"Who said anything about Michaud?" Morgan said. "Hizzoner's had his eye on expanding this way for a long time. But these yokels stood in the way. He promised me that if I could take the ville without wasting a lot of manpower and valuable gear, he'd give it to me as my very own personal fiefdom. For me to be baron over. Subject to the mayor, of course. So I reckoned I'd show some initiative, go ahead and grab the place before the balloon goes up, give my shock troops a little warm-up exercise. After you folks did the heavy lifting, of course."

"That was what this was really about?" Ryan said in disbelief. "Making you a baron?"

"Of course. And it worked ace on the line. Which reminds me—"

He drew a handblaster from a shoulder rig strapped over his bulky body armor. It was a SIG Sauer P226 like Ryan's.

"Since this ville has a new baron, there's no need to keep you around anymore."

That was said to the bearded spokesman. He looked up at Morgan, not understanding.

The captain shot him in the face.

"Now that's not good," J.B. stated.

"You lied to us," Ryan said as the shot echoed down the hill. He didn't say it loud. He didn't have to.

Morgan just laughed. "Yeah, so I did. Rank hath its privileges and all that shit. I didn't want you getting slack thinking you were going up against a bunch of helpless scrubby-ass ville rats. You mighta screwed up."

"I don't like being lied to," Ryan said.

"Who gives a rat's ass? You're hired hands. Nothing more. Don't start getting ahead of yourselves. Unless you want to be paid in lead, instead of jack."

He shook his helmeted head.

"Walk away and I'll just forget this little incident. I can see how you might feel trust hasn't been a two-way street here. No reason to let that fuck up what's been a real ace working relationship, though. Not if you don't push it."

Ryan stared at him a moment longer. Then he turned and started to walk down the road, away from the ville and the evil bastard into whose gauntleted hands he and his friends had just delivered it, gift wrapped.

The others followed.

They walked through the usual assortment of clumped huts and reclaimed ruins, neat fields and derelict buildings. The rising day did not noticeably brighten their spirits.

"Is this starting to make anybody else wonder if we're fighting for the right side?" Mildred asked after a while.

"We're fighting for a baron who has control of this area," Ryan said in a flat voice. He wasn't feeling much. He didn't feel as if *feeling* was a luxury he could afford right now. "And I mean Michaud and Bone, not that prick Morgan who gives us our orders. Right doesn't enter into it that much, so long as Hizzoner can say if we live or die."

"How much can we trust him?" Krysty asked. "Michaud, I mean."

"Do you even need to ask?" Ryan said. "But for now—his is still the only game in town."

Chapter Seventeen

"Now," Krysty heard Ryan yell.

She turned around into the glassless window she'd been standing next to, her Smith & Wesson 640 gripped tightly in both hands. Two men in Angel colors were walking in her field of view in the bright morning sun. They carried blasters and walked in that sort of hunched-over way people often did when they were in what they understand to be a danger zone.

She bit down hard on her misgivings. After the part they'd been tricked into playing in the subjugation of the ville northwest of DPD headquarters, it was hard for her to think of the Desolation Angels as the ones most deserving of getting suddenly blasted. But she also lined up the sights and shot the nearer man, who had long, lank, light-brown hair, right through his bare left biceps. This was all-out war, and if the Angels stumbled on them, they'd certainly shoot first.

And then shoot again to make sure and move on without bothering with questions.

The man fell yelling. Krysty didn't know whether the soft .38 caliber lead slug had penetrated his torso or not. The farther Angel, a goateed black man, turned toward her, bringing up his single-shot shotgun. She quickly fired twice at him. She thought she missed both times, but he dived to the street, anyway.

To her left Mildred was banging away with her usual

precision with her ZKR target revolver. To the right, the
shotgun barrel of Doc's LeMat bellowed, eliciting a scream
followed by booming shots from the main .44 caliber barrel. At the southeast end of the roofless ruin of what J.B.
suggested had been a machine shop, Ryan cranked rounds
from his SIG at the tail end of the twelve-man Angel patrol.

A bullet cracked off the brickwork by Krysty's head,
forcing her to crouch hurriedly below the sill. A violent
fusillade burst from the survivors of the companions' first
volley, bullets snapping and whistling through the tall,
narrow windows.

The others all ducked down or sideways out of the line
of fire. Then from up the street came a snarl of full-auto
fire. J.B. and Ricky had opened up from behind piles of
rubble of the next building that had slumped into the street
and partially blocked it. Ricky was using his DeLisle,
Krysty knew, so she didn't expect to hear his shots.

Yells of alarm and cries of pain broke out from the patrol. Then J.B. called, "They're running!"

He fired another burst just to keep them headed in the
right direction.

Cautiously, Krysty straightened enough to peer out the
window. The street was littered with moaning, writhing
forms and ones that just lay still. From a quick glance she
could tell seven or eight of the Angels had been hit hard
enough to go down.

The sharp, hard stink of burned propellant and lubricant
was enough to beat down the smells of gore and voided
bowels.

From the east came the sounds of a major firefight.
Krysty was becoming aware of the noise again after totally focusing on the ambush—first the tense wait for the
enemy to walk into the kill zone, with discovery and disas-

ter a constant danger, and then the hot blood of the actual fight, brief and one-sided though it had been.

"All right, Jak," Ryan called, "head on out."

Jak was crouched by the door, which opened onto a cross street. He instantly rose and slipped out of the half-collapsed building. It was time for him to take his usual position scouting ahead of the rest.

The Angels hadn't been total stupes. While their patrol was scouting for the main force, sent out to reconnoiter the enemy's western flank, they had been smart enough to send a scout of their own ahead, working through the rubble on this side of the street. Possibly a second had worked the far side, also; Krysty had no way of knowing.

But the Angel scout who had investigated this building had been no match for Jak Lauren's stealth, nor his blade skills. He died without yelling a warning to his comrades—and also without providing the more customary heads-up a scout provided: getting blasted.

"Time to move on, everybody," Ryan called. He and the others headed for the exit Jak had taken.

THE DPD'S POORLY kept secret offensive against the Desolation Angels had begun, but it began in a way that took even J.B. and Ryan completely by surprise. And Ryan knew he wasn't flattering himself in thinking that was a hard thing to do—not because it was so wildly innovative that it was nothing even one of them would have come up with, but rather because it *was* that sort of plan.

As expected, they had invaded across the Seven-Five—the former Interstate 75—in force. As not expected, they didn't continue to drive on into Desolation Angels' territory to throw themselves against the defenses of a smart, determined enemy who had had ample time to prepare.

Rather, they grabbed a foothold—and dug in themselves.

It wasn't a direct invasion of Angel land at all. It was a challenge Red Wings could not ignore.

The Angels leader could only have had his questionable self-control sorely tested by Hizzoner's impertinence. Ryan presumed whoever had planned the offensive had hoped the alcoholic and angry Red Wings would act rashly and throw his forces willy-nilly against well-sited, well-supplied DPD blasters.

But Ryan didn't see the Angels' boss had much choice other than to respond, and as quickly as possible. If he let Michaud and Bone get away with the move, they'd strengthen their new position and use it to encroach farther into downtown, which would bring them into the turf actually claimed by the Desolation Angels.

And if the Angels let such a flaming insult and actual threat slide, the other gangs of the downtown area were liable to figure that their power had peaked and begun to decline again, just as Red Wings' mental state was said to be deteriorating. They'd turn on the Desolation Angels like a pack of armored coyotes.

So they counterattacked. Not impulsively, lashing out in their boss's vicarious blind fury, but before they had sufficient time to mount an optimal operation.

Still, the outcome wasn't guaranteed. Had the Angels been a pushover, the Detroit Police Department would have done the pushing long ago. Or at the very least not stopped their drive until they were partying down in the former hockey rink that was Red Wings' personal castle. A lot of fighting had to be done before anything was determined.

THE ANGELS POINT man made his way in a crouch through the rubble that covered the street. Weeds sprouted between blocks of masonry and chunks of concrete with jagged rebar sticking out of them. Bushes grew to the height of a person's shoulders. Some of them were covered with pretty little white flowers, lending the scene an entirely unwarranted air of harmlessness.

An Angel patrol ten strong had followed its leader in a wide V formation. Now the eight men and two women were moving in a crouch, holding blasters at the ready. Ryan had no idea what they expected might be lying in wait for them, nor why, if they feared ambush, they hadn't just picked another, safer route.

The bushes were high enough to provide excellent concealment, screening them entirely from the sight of enemies on the ground. Ryan lay on his belly at the top of a square concrete tower a couple blocks away and watched through the scope of his Steyr on highest magnification, but as far as he was concerned it did dick.

The tower had housed an external staircase for a four-story building that had fallen down completely. Ryan had no idea which of a litany of possible disasters had caused the structure to disintegrate so completely that the dense overgrowth where it had stood completely hid the mounds of its rubbled remains. Because the stairway had survived intact this long, and looked and felt solid enough, Ryan reckoned it was unlikely to implode beneath him.

The woman at the rear of the trailing right arm of the V suddenly jerked and fell on her face. Ryan wondered how Ricky was handling dropping the hammer on a woman. The kid had odd scruples. In the heat of action he pulled together and worked with an efficiency to make the exacting J. B. Dix proud of his pupil. But the patrol posed no immediate threat to Ricky or his friends.

He had taken the shot and made it. Ryan knew he'd have to talk to the youth later, to explain that, in the end, it was the survival of the group that counted. They'd have to bide their time.

Ricky lay on the second floor of a gutted factory two blocks to the west of the patrol. Ryan reckoned piles of rubble here and there occasionally blocked his shots. But the point here wasn't to slaughter the enemy to the last man or woman. It was to put the fear of the DPD into them.

J.B. and Mildred secured the lower floors of Ricky's sniper's nest. Krysty and Doc hid in the weeds at the base of the stair tower, doing the same service for Ryan. Jak patrolled somewhere, keeping his eyes skinned to prevent more enemies from stumbling onto his friends.

Ryan laid the reticule on the lead Angel and fired. The Scout roared and bucked.

When the rifle came back online, a new 7.62 mm cartridge neatly chambered, the lead man had dropped out of sight and the rest of the patrol was looking frantically around for the source of the attack.

Another man yelped and went down, struck through the breastbone by one of Ricky's big slow .45 ACP bullets, to judge by the sudden spray of red from his chest. Somebody else yelled to the others that he'd been hit. Another Angel noticed the woman at their rear had also vanished.

Ryan held off firing. He had plenty of targets, but chilling wasn't the object here.

As he sensed they might, the Angels broke and fled back to the southeast. A sniper was a terrible enemy to have to face. Ryan himself well knew the awful sense of powerlessness that came with being under the sights of somebody who could reach out and touch you—or your friends and loved ones—at will without you being able to strike back.

He fired another shot. It wasn't aimed at anyone in particular. Its purpose was to reinforce that sense of impotence and help the resultant fear blossom into full-on panic. He hated to waste a cartridge on principle.

However, the DPD had seen they had plenty of ammo. You had to give that to the bastards, too. They hadn't tried to stiff their minions, no matter how much contempt some—like Morgan—showed them.

So far.

Ryan watched the last of the patrol disappear beyond more ruins. Then he slithered back to the stairs, slung the Steyr and started down to rejoin his friends.

Chapter Eighteen

The Angel appeared in the doorway close enough for Jak to touch.

The man was brown skinned, dark haired and not much bigger than Jak himself. He had spotted the albino slipping into a block of bombed-out buildings. The Angel scout's first mistake was assuming Jak hadn't also seen him.

The gangbanger had a big-bladed hunting knife in his hand, and his young face was set in intense lines. He was intent on the hunt and primed for chilling action when he came on his unsuspecting quarry.

The Angel scout had washed within the past two days with a strong lye soap. He carried a handblaster that had been fired within the past hour. Jak had smelled him as he approached the entryway.

He was wearing some kind of soft-soled moccasins— obvious modern make, not scavvy. Jak had heard him, very faintly, as he approached across the rubble on the far side of a yellow-brown limestone wall whose top was jagged.

The man was good.

Jak was better. He was waiting and ready when the slight, stealthy man appeared close enough to touch.

And touch him he did, with the clip-pointed blade of his trench knife, delivered in a brutal uppercut that punched its clipped point through his bare solar plexus and up behind the shielding arch of his rib cage to cut his heart in two.

Jak reached out, grabbed his arm and held him as he

died, not to comfort him but to ensure he didn't make a lot of noise when he fell. The patrol he was scouting for was noisily advancing about a block away.

Jak twisted the knife inside the flaccid torso to make sure the scout was all-the-way dead and not able to empty all five rounds from the cylinder of his snub-nosed Model 36 .38 Special into Jak's back.

Then he pulled the blade out with a slight sucking sound and wiped it carefully on the man's baggy urban-camo pants. The leather vest with its colorful badge on the back would have been handier, but Jak chose not to dishonor the man's colors.

Hunter's honor. The man had been worthy game.

Then Jak turned and made his way back through the rubbled row to alert his friends to the rest of the squad's approach.

"SOUNDS LIKE A real meat grinder back there by the DPD lines," Ricky said as blasterfire to the northeast reached a fresh thundering crescendo.

The companions were passing through a cavernous, largely intact warehouse in a loose V formation, with Ryan at the tip and Jak naturally out in front. A lot of such structures, along with various factories, populated this area. They were staying off the streets to spare themselves exactly the sort of hurt they'd just laid on the Angel recon patrol.

After all, unlike the Angels, *they* were in no hurry.

"I'm glad we're not caught in the middle of that," the youth added.

"Me, too," Ryan said.

Because the Angels were good enough at their peculiar brand of war that even an arrogant man like Morgan had to acknowledge it, DPD's planners presumed they'd be sending scouts out around the flanks of both forces to get the lay of the land and look for weaknesses in the invaders' lines—and quite possibly try to work their way into the DPD rear where they could do disproportionate damage themselves. Possibly that could influence the battle's outcome.

That was a long shot, of course, but not so long that it could safely be ignored. Despite himself, Ryan had been impressed that the captain-who-would-be-baron had the professional skill and savvy to realize he needed to do something to minimize that risk, as minor as it already was.

"I want you to go out there, hunt those assholes down and ruin their shit" was how he'd put it in their behind-the-lines briefing before daybreak that morning.

"This is still outside Angels territory, from the maps we were shown," Mildred said. "I wonder what the gangs whose turf the Angels are tromping through to get to Hizzoner's boys think about it."

"It would appear they are opting to lie low and await events," Doc said.

"They probably don't feel like paying the price of resisting the mighty Angels and getting beaten down for their troubles," Ryan added.

"Maybe they're hoping both sides will be too worn out and worn down to look for vengeance on those who didn't actively help them out," Mildred suggested as they walked down a ramp from an elevated loading area.

"They may be a little green if they're counting on that to avoid payback," J.B. said.

"Could happen," Ryan said. "Payback's probably going to be a lot lighter for not lending a hand than fighting against them—either side."

"No doubt the more ambitious among them hope for the chance to seize new territory for themselves," Doc said.

"As long as they're lying low," Ryan said, "they're staying out of our way. And not jumping on our backs."

Jak waited just inside the far door. He was barely visible in the shadowed gloom, clear of the yellow bars of light, swimming with dust motes like clouds of gnats, that streamed in through windows set high on the northeast wall. He was hard to make out against the relative dazzle from the empty doorway.

"Close Angels," he called softly.

"Need more words here, Jak," Mildred complained.

But Ryan grunted. "I know what he means. We're getting close to actual Angel territory. Things could get tricky fast."

"Won't they be throwing everything they have at the DPD?" Krysty asked.

"Care to bet your life on that?"

"Well—"

J.B. scratched under his hat.

"We getting paid to invade?" he asked mildly.

"Point taken," Krysty said.

"Let's swing wide west and head back toward the Seven-Five," Ryan said. "Then start another sweep closer to the action." He shrugged. "I wouldn't mind seeing what's going on. Wouldn't really care to get stuck down here if the sec men break and run."

"Do you think they might, Ryan?" Krysty asked. "Hizzoner's forces are so strong."

"You've seen the Angels in action. They may be coldhearts, but they're tough."

"Sec boss doesn't usually get cagey and start using strategy and tactics if he thinks he can get what he wants by just bulling in and busting heads," J.B. observed.

"I'm convinced," Mildred said firmly. "But why circle wide? Aren't we more likely to run into more Angel patrols if we move in closer now?"

"But that's the point, Mildred," J.B. said. "We don't want those bad boys running up on us from behind, do we?"

"Oh."

THE CACOPHONY OF blasterfire, interspersed with occasionally audible screams, got louder. It wasn't, Ryan thought, just because they were getting closer.

Part of the reason was that a distinctive blaster had joined the fight. It was clearly a machine gun, and from the higher pitch and faster cyclic rate of its shots, not the burly M240 mounted on the equally burly Commando. It was a 5.56 mm, making it one of several M249 squad Automatic Weapons he knew the DPD had in its armory. That in turn meant it was mounted to one of the lesser war wags.

They cut east toward the looming, bizarrely cubist sculpture garden of downtown, with its crazily leaning skyscrapers, jagged stumped and occasional intact towers.

The companions took turns covering one another to reach a building whose southwestern-facing walls were completely gone, as were most of the top two of its three floors. Chunks of the other three walls and much of the top of the first floor remained, upheld by stout rectangular-section columns. The sun had risen high enough so that the interior was mostly shaded.

When they joined Jak, who had gone ahead to make sure the place was clear, they quickly saw the source of the machine-gun fire and the focus of most of the action, it seemed, on this end of the battle lines.

The twenty-foot-long BearCat was rolling slowly forward across a broad expanse of weeds and neglected crops.

The M249 was spitting fire and noise from the rotating roof hatch. Twenty riot-armored SWAT troopers carrying carbines, submachine guns and shotguns trotted in a skirmish line to both sides and slightly behind the car with their clear, curved shields held in front of them. About thirty uniformed cops followed ten or fifteen yards behind.

The machine gun seemed to be concentrating its fire on a cluster of three buildings in varying stages of having been smashed to rubble a couple hundred yards to the right of Ryan and friends. Looking that way, he saw muzzle-flashes flickering from windows and broken walls, from ground level to a scrap of remaining third floor at the far end.

As he swiveled his head back to look at the armored wag, he heard a rushing sound like a quick, violent burst of wind from the Angel strongpoint. Something flashed through his field of view, making a sizzling, popping sound like bacon frying on a griddle, unreeling a thin, bluish corkscrew of smoke behind it. He caught a flash impression of blue lights flickering at its trailing end.

Then the big BearCat vanished in a sheet of blinding white light.

Chapter Nineteen

"Black dust!" J.B. exclaimed. "That was a Dragon wag chiller!"

Mildred barely heard him. The thunderclap that had followed the blinding white flash by a heartbeat had been like steel spikes being shot into both her eardrums simultaneously. She had felt the explosion like a slap in her face, leaving her eyes watering.

The line of riot cops in their tinted visors and black armor faltered. A horde of fighters rose from the weed field. Some were as close as twenty yards to the stricken vehicle, which was already vomiting orange flames and greasy black smoke from all its windows. They charged, whooping their battle cries.

Mildred didn't want to think about the fate of the BearCat's crew.

"Anybody see where that missile came from?" Ryan asked, as always focused on what counted most.

"I did!" Ricky yelled, throwing out an arm as if forgetting the possibility somebody might spot the violent motion. "It came from the near end of those buildings!"

They were smack in the middle of a massive urban concentration, so from any direction you cared to look you could see what were by definition "those buildings," even if half of them had been blown up or beaten down. But Mildred knew before she looked what the overexcited kid was pointing at.

It was the Angels' strongpoint. Of course.

Unnerved by the explosive fate of one of their heavy-hitter war wags and the sudden human wave attack rising right in their faces, the black-armored SWAT troops turned and ran. Seeing their elite—and better-protected—comrades running right at them, the uniform division cops behind them promptly routed, too.

A lone officer, bareheaded and clinging to the reins of a rearing, neighing bay horse, waved a handblaster and evidently shouted at the running men, though Mildred couldn't hear him. They flowed around him and his panicked mount like water and kept running.

"Isn't that Lieutenant—" Krysty began.

Blood fountained from his neck. He fell over the saddle's cantle and vanished in the weeds. His horse bolted straight away from the blazing wreck.

"—Mahome," the redhead finished.

"Yeah," Ryan said.

Little flashes began to blossom inside the armored wag, accompanied by loud pops, as the heat of the inferno cooked off various munitions.

"Did it look to anybody else like he got hit from behind?" Mildred asked.

"Mebbe," Ryan said.

"I don't think those are all Angels," Ricky said. He transferred her pointing finger to the figures running in pursuit of the fleeing sec men. "I think I see those Punks, Rock City—"

One of the pursuers paused to strike a pose, hand on hip, right side turned toward the enemy, a big cowboy six-shooter held out straight. Just like an Olympic target-pistol shooter, realized Mildred, who had been one. He cranked the hammer back with his thumb and fired.

"And I think that one's a Dead Elvis."

Mildred saw that his face looked an unhealthy and unnaturally gray beneath his shiny black pompadour. He wore a bulky white canvas jacket with what looked like random shards of mirror and polished metal sewn onto it. Not to provide a sort of personal suit of barbed wire, like Jak's jacket, but to mimic the trademark glitter of the gang's namesake.

The awful complexion was a sign that his bunch used face paint, like Rock City, and not that he was an actual zombie. Mildred hoped.

He was too spry to be a rottie, which was the closest thing to the genuine item she and her friends had encountered in the Deathlands. Anyway, as far as they knew all of those who had been infected with the horrible sickness had been chilled for real.

"So the other gangs aren't all lying low after all," Ryan said. Mildred was starting to hear better as the ringing in her ears subsided. Also, the battle noise wasn't interfering as much with comprehension because the chase was moving away. "The Rock City bunch must be heated up way past nuke red at Hizzoner if they're allying with the Angels. Plus, they say the Elvises don't like anybody."

"It would appear that they dislike the Detroit Police Department more than anybody," Doc said. "At least for the day."

"Right," Ryan said. "Let's go."

"Where to, fearless leader?" Mildred asked.

Ryan jerked his chin toward the Angel strongpoint. "There. Wag-chiller rocket's a high-value wep. You're not going to entrust one to a random numb nut. That means whoever fired it is a high-value target himself."

"How do we know he's still there?" Krysty asked.

"We don't," Ryan said. "For sure. But nobody's come out of those ruins to join in the chase, have they?"

Krysty gave a look of green-eyed surprise to Mildred. "No, not that I've seen."

"They may be concerned about the whole rest of the DPD line," J.B. pointed out. "*They* haven't gone anywhere."

If anything, the shooting from farther east had increased in volume. It was still nowhere near as loud as the recent battle close by.

"Enough jawing," Ryan said. He turned and headed southeast.

JAK HELD UP a white fist. Then he opened it into five wide-spaced fingers.

Ryan and the others waited in the shell of a factory whose nature couldn't be determined or even sensibly guessed at, given that much of the three-story structure had fallen in on itself, leaving the bottom floor a perilous maze of heaps of yellow brick and other crud durable enough to survive a century of decay, if not necessarily in identifiable shape.

Jak squatted by the southwest wall of the huddle of ruins the Angels, including the rocketeer, had holed up in. It was yellow brick as well and consisted of the roofless remnant of a single story, with walls knocked into fanglike shapes, though they still mostly blocked view from without from shoulder height or more. Jak, however, had found a peephole into the interior.

No traffic from either direction was visible on the street. Leaving Ricky and Doc to cover them, Ryan led the others across it and a five-foot strip of weeds and low brush to join Jak. From inside the ruins came the sound of men conversing in normal tones. As the remaining pair joined them, Ryan moved alongside Jak.

Inside, as Jak reported, five men in Angels colors stood in what had been a corner room. The back wall, to Ryan's right, was largely gone. The far wall was largely intact, complete with a doorway. No door, unsurprisingly.

Two men stood by gaps in the front wall where they could watch for enemies approaching and fire on them as needed. Two more stood nodding and listening as the fifth pointed out something on a map he held.

Crucially, nobody was looking this way, much less guarding it. The Angels were good, remarkably organized for a street gang, but not good enough to avoid giving into the common battlefield condition of getting tunnel vision toward the most obvious threats.

Ryan pulled back.

"How many more?" he mouthed to Jak.

The albino held up five fingers, then closed his fist. A pause, then five fingers plus one from his other hand, followed with a shrug.

"Five or six is all?" Ryan mouthed.

Jak nodded.

Ryan nodded crisp acknowledgment. If there'd been more Angels in the complex huddle of buildings, they were gone now, likely to join the fight that still continued along the bulk of the DPD foothold.

"Dude with blond, shaggy hair's the leader," he said quietly.

There had been no mistaking that. Aside from the deferential attitude of the Angels he was speaking to, just standing there being calm he radiated presence. Ryan could feel it, just from a glance. Could he be the famous Leto? he wondered.

One way to tell.

"Take him alive, no more damage than necessary. Don't chill the others unless you have to. Self-defense only."

That wasn't mercy, but because Ryan's ever-probing mind was considering the possibility that diplomacy might come in handy at some point. He wasn't sure how, but if this was the son of the Angels' boss, slaughtering all his comrades out of hand wouldn't be the prime way of opening the conversation.

The others nodded. Not even Mildred gave him any back chat. There was too much chance of being overheard, despite the talking and the rattle of battle to the east.

"Got a little surprise for them," J.B. said, holding up a gray object roughly the size and shape of a golf ball.

"Ace," Ryan said.

J.B. REARED UP in a gap in the wall, just far enough to chuck his little lumpy ball inside. The carefully measured length of safety fuse was sputtering viciously. He deliberately pitched it to land in the far front corner of the room. It wasn't designed to chill, as such, but you couldn't be too careful with plas ex.

The man up front who was nearer to the plas ex turned his head to look, then took a step toward it as J.B. ducked.

Even with a wall between J.B. and the minibomb, and J.B. prepared for it, the explosion of the little C-4 ball was savagely loud. He grinned. That was the whole point.

"Go!" Ryan shouted.

Chapter Twenty

Ryan sprang through the gap, his panga in hand. Jak was already inside. That was a calculated risk on Ryan's part—the little albino was not so good at *not* chilling people. But since the dust-up of a few months back that had temporarily split him off from the rest, he and Ryan had seemed tighter than ever. The one-eyed man had told his friends to chill in self-defense only. Jak would do his best to do what Ryan said, even if his definition of self-defense was broad even by the standards of his companions.

Holding his shotgun in his right hand, J.B. used his left to vault through the gap in the wall he'd been hunkered near. As he did, he saw Jak rabbit punch an Angel with the studded brass-knuckle guard of his trench knife. He was the most immediate threat, by way of the Mini-14 he held ready.

The dude on watch was…not so much. He had incautiously taken a step toward the flash bang J.B. had improvised from some of the C-4 they'd happened to have left over and a blasting cap. And it had ripped his leg right off at the hip.

Could have used a trifle less, I guess, J.B. thought in passing.

His partner's head was turned to stare at him, which was what gave Jak a free shot at the guy's nape. J.B. noted a stream of blood from the Angel's right ear.

Then he was rushing the trio in the middle. They stood

blinking and clearly stunned by the blast, brutal as it was and out of nowhere.

Ryan clubbed down the nearest of the three from behind with the butt of his panga. Then he kicked the man on the far side of the evident leader beneath the cast skull buckle of his belt, throwing him back hard against the wall.

The man with the long blond hair came out of his momentary stupor and threw a punch at Ryan. The Deathlands warrior blocked with his left forearm and head butted his opponent in the bridge of his nose. The blond man staggered back with blood gushing over his mouth.

The man Ryan had clipped had gone down no farther than one knee. He started up, groping for a handblaster at his hip. J.B. slashed the butt of his M4000 behind the man's ear and he fell flat on his face.

"Boss!" an alarmed voice shouted from the doorway. "What the nuke is—! Shit, shit, shit!"

The last words came out loud but slurred. Probably from the leaf-shaped throwing knife that suddenly sprouted from his cheek and the hand he'd clapped to it. He fell back out of sight.

J.B. was still on the move. The man Ryan had kicked was struggling to his feet. His right ear was bleeding, too. It had been turned toward the flash bang.

The Armorer cracked him smartly on the side of his head with the scattergun's buttplate. He fell back down, jaw slack, eyes rolling.

The Angel named Leto had whipped out a tapering, double-edged commando-style dagger and lunged at Ryan, who grabbed his wrist with his left hand. The Angel grabbed Ryan's right wrist.

For a moment they wrestled that way. Then Ryan thrust his shin hard into Leto's nuts. It was an old trick that didn't always work.

This time it did.

J.B. knelt over the man he'd clubbed, covering the doorway and the open interior beyond with his longblaster.

"Secure your man, Jak," he called. The man in the corner was still thrashing but getting more feeble about it. The blood that had spread out over the whole corner of the room told why. He didn't have enough of a leg left to tourniquet, anyway.

"Way ahead," Jak said. J.B. turned his head just far enough to see the albino sitting on his victim's upturned butt, twisting the leather vest he'd yanked off his shoulders into a makeshift restraint, pinning his wrists at the small of his back.

Sweet trick, J.B. thought. He rolled the man he'd clubbed onto his face and started to do the same.

He heard the roar of Mildred's handblaster from the street side of the room. Somebody yelled hoarsely through the doorway.

An armed Angel appeared in the space beyond the mostly open back part of the room. The far wall was intact, the roof mostly gone. He hesitated, twitching his blaster left and right. He might not have cared about hitting his buddies, but he sure didn't want to blast his leader. J.B. had no such hesitation. He shot him in the chest. The shot column punched a big hole through his sternum and he fell backward, triggering a futile shot at the clear and merciless sky.

Ryan had the Angel leader facedown on the concrete floor and was hauling his colors down over his arms. The man he'd hit with the panga butt and J.B. had hit with his shotgun reared up roaring, raising a revolver to blast Ryan at contact range.

And promptly did the dance of death as Krysty gave him all five rounds from the cylinder of her little .38.

J.B. focused his attention on securing his own fallen
Angel. His friends were on the job.

But the Angels hadn't given up, which provided any
confirmation needed that the long-haired blond man was
a high-value target, just as Ryan had posited.

J.B. flinched as he heard the nasty crack of Jak's .357
Magnum blaster, followed almost at once by the boom of
Doc's .44.

He glanced up. Another Angel was falling to the floor
of the open space to the rear of the room. Jak was kneeling by the front wall, pointing his Python in both hands.

For a moment silence fell, punctuated by groans from
the next room.

Ryan had turned his captive sideways long enough to
fish his belt off the loops of his jeans, then used it to tie
his hands more securely behind him.

"Might as well chill me, you bastards," Leto said. "You
won't get anything out of me."

"Jak, Doc, J.B.—secure the rest of the building. Krysty,
Mildred, get in here and prepare to back them up. Ricky,
keep watch outside and don't get shot."

"You never let me have any fun!"

"Shut it."

BLASTER SHOTS CAME from the next room—Doc's LeMat.
Jak would have used his knives to finish off any wounded
who still had too much fight left in them for their own
good.

Ryan stood up cautiously. At least two of the men who'd
been in this room would survive. The obvious leader, the
real target, had pulled through with hardly a ding to speak
of.

Looking down at him, Ryan guessed this wasn't the
first time his long nose had been broken.

"Clear!" he heard J.B. call from somewhere.

He bent over, grabbed the Angel's nose with his right thumb and forefinger and torqued it back. The man bucked and yelped.

"Ow! Fuck."

"Just putting it back in place," Ryan said with a grin as he stood back up. "Don't want to spoil your good looks."

"I know what you were doing. Fuck."

Like the pros they were, Krysty and Mildred had moved immediately to cover the front windows the instant they heard J.B. pronounce the ruins free of threats.

Ryan regarded his captive. Looking past the blood beard and the two splendid black eyes he was developing, the man was good looking in a rough-hewn way. His cheekbones were a touch too prominent, his chin too long. He'd never be pretty. But he definitely had the look of a man women would want and men would want to be.

His eyes were glaring green laser death at Ryan right now.

"Who are you?" he spit.

"Ryan Cawdor," Ryan said. "You're Leto?"

"Yeah. Get a good look at me, coldheart. Because I'm the man who's going to chill you."

"Might want to watch your mouth writing checks your trigger hand can't cash," J.B. said, strolling back through the side door with his M4000 in the crook of his arm as if returning from a pleasant day hunting.

"What do you want with me? If you think you can make some kind of deal with my father, think again." He shook his head. "Nuke waste, he'd probably pay you to chill me."

"Not sure what we mean to do with you, truth to tell," Ryan said. "But you're alive, and you look likely to stay that way at least a while."

"Chill me now," the young man said, laying the back

of his head back down on the concrete and gazing upward. "That bastard Michaud will do worse than what you could think of."

"Wouldn't leap to any rash judgments there, son," J.B. said, not unkindly. "We can think of a lot of things."

"Who said anything about Michaud?" Ryan asked. "You're our prisoner. Right now that's the only sure thing."

"What do you mean?"

"That we need to have a little talk before we go making any decisions."

"I'll never—"

"Ryan," Krysty said from the front of the room, "something's happening."

From away to the north came a snarl of full-auto fire. It had a deeper tone than the machine gun that had been mounted on the BearCat.

Ryan and J.B. looked at each other. "We've heard that song before," the one-eyed man said.

He moved to the window and looked out. The war wag still had pale orange flames dancing on the inside. A round cooked off inside even as he watched.

Beyond it he could see figures running toward him across the field. Most of them wore open vests. None of the rest showed DPD black.

"Ricky, get in here," Ryan said. "Keep watch outside. J.B., Doc, hold the next room. Hold your fire unless you need to let somebody know this isn't friendly territory anymore. Jak, make sure nobody sneaks up and blasts us in the back."

He drew his SIG and turned to Leto. "And if you sing out, you're only going to get yourself stomped and anybody who tries to help chilled."

The captive stared skyward in furious silence.

Noticeably fewer gangers headed this way than had

run off south after the routed sec men. Ryan made out Penobscot Punks and Rock City members fleeing alongside the Angels. Either the Dead Elvises had fought to the last man, or they'd found their own way out of deep rad dust.

But none of them showed any interest in sheltering in the cluster of buildings where Leto had established his command post. Some headed off at an angle toward the Angel lines to the east. The rest stayed right on the street.

Behind them rolled the V-100. Black-uniformed patrolmen and a few mounted cops kept pace. They seemed to be taking their sweet time about it, and Ryan was surprised the M240 wasn't methodically mowing down the running Angels.

Then he saw a ball of fire blossom from the machine gun's barrel to his right. Apparently a few diehards were hiding in the weeds to snipe at the advancing DPD forces.

It was tense as the Angels and their allies fled past. But none tried to come in. They seemed interested only in getting back home as fast as their legs could carry them. The V-100 halted cautiously on a level with the still intact DPD lines.

What good they thought that'd do them, Ryan had no clue. Wag chillers like the one whose launcher lay discarded to one side of the room could reach out and touch them to a thousand yards and more. They were well within range. Did the Angels have any more rockets here or men to fire them?

"That's the last of them," Ricky said.

"You know you're screwed, don't you?" Leto said from the floor.

"Hush, you," Mildred admonished.

"I'm keeping my voice down," the captive said. "I don't want to bring the pigs in here faster. And neither do you."

"How do you reckon?" Ryan asked.

"Michaud's a backstabbing bastard. And mebbe a bigger sadist. Not even that taint Bone is as bad, and he's as mean as a stickie on a jolt bender."

"But he seemed so jovial," Mildred said. Ryan wasn't sure whether she was being sarcastic or not.

"Whatever reward you think you're getting, you're not," Leto said.

"We've been paid well already," Ryan said.

Leto laughed. "What is it people like you always say? 'What good is jack to a chill'? Once they're done with you, you go down hard."

"And I suppose you're totally disinterested," Mildred said.

"We'll have to watch our backs," Ryan said. "Michaud's a baron after all."

"DPD's coming," Krysty said.

The sec men had began to advance at a walk. Ryan frowned. He hadn't made up his mind what to do with their captive yet. He sure as nuke didn't want their employers clouding the issue.

"Get ready to get out of here," he directed. "We'll take our friend with us."

"Uh, Ryan—" Ricky said.

"Well, well," an all-too-familiar voice called from the street. "What do we have here?"

Ryan turned to see DPD SWAT Captain Morgan looking in at them from the back of a glossy black horse.

Chapter Twenty-One

"We secured the rocket launcher that took out your armored war wag," Ryan said, hoping to put the best face on things and encourage their immediate boss to go on about his business. Or at least elsewhere.

"Ace," the captain said.

Morgan dismounted and headed toward the building. He didn't walk toward the room directly. Apparently clambering in through gaps in the wall was beneath his dignity. Instead he headed to a door, or at least a place that was open all the way to the ground, behind the room that Ryan and his people held.

The captain appeared at the back of the room. He had on SWAT armor and a helmet with visor raised.

He stopped dead. His blue eyes bugged out of his head at Leto.

"You've got him!" he sputtered. Ryan saw flecks of saliva flying from his mouth, and the captain turned bright red. "You caught the little rad sucker!"

He grabbed for his blaster with a gauntleted hand.

"No." Ryan stepped between him and the bound, supine Angel. "He's our prisoner."

"Get out of the way."

"He's our prisoner," Ryan repeated.

"I own you, you mercie filth," Morgan screamed. "Now get out of my way, or I'll have the skin stripped off you and roll you in salt!"

"Don't—"

Morgan drew his SIG.

Ryan was faster. He drew his own and shot the DPD captain through the forehead.

Morgan's eyes bulged even farther. He fell in on himself like an imploding building.

Ryan looked around. Everyone was staring at him like an alley cat at a stickie.

"What?"

"He wasn't after you, Ryan," Mildred said.

"Do I look like I give a fuck?" Ryan said. "Do you?"

She glanced down at the SWAT captain. The color had drained from his face. His blue eyes stared up at the sky past the hole in his forehead.

"I think he looks better that way," she said.

J.B. appeared in the doorway with his Uzi in his hand. He took in the scene with a glance.

"I guess this won't help us get out of Detroit," he said.

"I—I don't think anybody else saw," Ricky said.

"The sec men are still fifty yards away," Krysty said. "They seem to be wary of approaching this place."

"Good," Ryan said. He holstered his handblaster, then turned to Leto.

The Angel was staring at him as unbelievingly as his friends had.

"You chilled him? I don't understand. Wasn't he your boss?"

"He was an asshole. Anyway, we already gave him one nice little gift we hadn't intended to. Wasn't going to do it a second time. And nobody chills someone I take prisoner."

He leaned over, grabbed Leto by the biceps and hauled him to his feet. The Angel was medium height, a few inches shorter than Ryan, but his bare shoulders were as broad. He stared at Ryan defiantly.

"What are you going to do with me now?"

Ryan turned him around and began to untie the belt he'd used to bind Leto's wrists.

"Cut you loose," he said.

"What?" Leto said.

"Ryan, what are you doing?" Krysty asked.

"Playing a hunch," Ryan said. "And that hunch is, we need a friend."

"The kid did say his dad wouldn't give a bent shell case to get him back," Mildred said.

"Who're you calling a kid?"

"Listen," Ryan said, yanking his vest back onto his shoulders and turning Leto to face him again. "This war's just begun, and you already cost Hizzoner his second-best war wag. You and him keep fighting, you're both going to just wear yourselves out. Then the rest of the gangs in the Detroit rubble will chill both of you and take over."

Leto knit his brows.

"Mebbe," he admitted.

"So I want you to go back and try your best to get your daddy to negotiate."

"What about your reward?"

"We did the job we were contracted for," Ryan said. "We get paid no matter what."

"You can't trust Michaud. I told you that."

"Our lookout."

"I can't promise I can sway my father. Fact is, I can almost promise I can't."

"Will you swear to do your best?"

"Yeah."

"Can you ride a horse?" Ryan asked.

"No."

"Best learn fast. That's your quickest ticket back home."

"Getting closer," J.B. called.

Leto ran out. Ryan heard shouts from the slowly approaching DPD forces, then shots and finally a whinny of annoyance and the sound of hooves drumming away to the southeast.

"How's he doing?" Ryan asked Ricky.

"Well, he's still in the saddle," Ricky said. "Mostly."

"Ace. Time for us to go while everybody's watching Leto."

"What about him?" Mildred asked, nodding toward Morgan.

"He died heroically cleaning out a nest of Angels," Ryan said. "The thing about sec men is, give them a story that sounds good enough, they'll swallow it so hard they'll spit it out as the truth."

"Any notion what that overly Aryan prick was doing out here all on his lonesome?" Mildred asked.

"We'll never know," Ryan said. "It doesn't matter now."

"And what about us?" Krysty asked.

"We can let ourselves out the back."

THEY HID IN the next ruin southeast, staying low and watching while the DPD patrolmen finally approached and secured Leto's former command post.

Something of a ruckus occurred when they found Morgan's body. A couple went running back across the field to the reestablished Detroit Police Department to report it. Meanwhile, the battle to the east continued unabated.

"Wonder where the Angels're getting all that ammo," J.B. said.

Ryan could only shrug.

"Mebbe they found an armory, too," Ricky suggested.

"Could be," Ryan said.

After a while the Commando came snorting and farting up, with a squad of SWAT troopers trotting behind, polycarbonate shields and all. A pair of uniforms loaded Morgan's limp body into the wag. A SWAT trooper came out with the Dragon launcher. Then the V-100 rolled back toward the DPD lines, with all the foot soldiers trooping behind.

"So that's it?" Ricky said. "They didn't even take any more territory?"

"They realized they didn't lay enough hurt on the Angels to try," Ryan said. "They don't even want to try occupying Leto's old strongpoint because they're not sure they can spare the force from the rest of the battle to hold on to it. Not with other gangs in the game."

"Perhaps Michaud and Chief Bone didn't reckon on facing anyone but the Angels alone," Doc mused.

"Probably didn't."

"So DPD lost?"

"No, son," J.B. said. "They've still got their foothold this side of the highway. Took the Angels' best shot at throwing them right back across the Seven-Five and hung on."

"They just didn't win the way they wanted," Ryan said. "No knockout punch against the Angels."

"Which was why you told Leto both sides stand to lose if the war continues," Krysty said. "But why would you try to negotiate an end to the war? I mean, I'm in favor of it. But—well, I'm more sentimental than you."

"I'm not a coldheart," Ryan said. "Well—not that cold. I don't mind chilling to stay alive or for meds or for food if we need to any more than I ever did. But this isn't just a raid or even a hit. It's war, and a lot of people are going to get hurt who mebbe don't have it coming."

"Anyway," J.B. said, "even if Hizzoner makes peace with the Angels, dozens of gangs are all over the rubble, all fighting each other. And a power of them making trouble for Michaud. We could spend the rest of our lives doing this job here."

"Not exactly what I had in mind," Krysty said wistfully.

Ryan knew what she meant. His lover had a dream of finding a safe haven—a place they could all lay down their weps, or at least get a respite from fighting, and live out peaceful lives. Building a future, rather than living day to day and just getting by.

It was a beautiful dream. He hoped they could do that, too. He just wasn't sure when or how.

But it was one of the things that kept them all putting one foot ahead of the other, day after day.

"If we can actually broker a peace deal," Ryan said, "that right there means Michaud sees the light on why he needs one. So he can also see that's a bigger service we did him than any amount of blasting bad guys and blowing stuff up."

"Lot of ifs there," J.B. said.

"Yeah. I'm not counting on it, either."

He straightened from where he knelt at a window of the small but mostly intact building. His knees creaked slightly. "But it definitely wouldn't happen if we didn't try," he said aloud. "I thought cutting Leto loose gave us the best shot. And also, like I told him, the time may come when we can use all the friends we can get."

"It's always that time," J.B. said.

"Isn't that the truth? Let's get going. Got a long walk back to HQ."

THEY WERE QUESTIONED by a weary but inexplicably nervous patrol division lieutenant named Hong. Ryan chose to tell the truth because that was always the simplest lie; he just edited parts of it.

That necessarily meant failing to claim credit for making sure the wag-chiller rocket launcher was no threat, as well as never breathing a word about capturing the heir apparent to the Angel empire. But he'd known that when he'd freed Leto.

Hong just nodded, told them "good job" and sent them on their way back toward the provisional city hall. He had orders that they report in as soon as possible, he said.

Fewer sec men than usual were in evidence when they got back late afternoon, with the shadows stretching long to the east. Ryan wasn't surprised, except perhaps by how many were still around, with a full-blown battle still going on, plus the need to secure their borders against opportunistic or even simply random attacks by other gangs.

Hizzoner had to have a lot more sec men at his disposal than Ryan had suspected.

The mood in the foyer of the former Masonic Temple was strange: half elated, half deflated. It was as if nobody was quite sure whether they'd won a great victory or had tasted bitter defeat.

Given Morgan's heroic death in action, Ryan wasn't too surprised when they were escorted back into the big chapel where they had met Michaud and his sec boss for the first and only time.

Hizzoner came up to meet them, beaming. "Well done, my friends," he said, shaking Ryan's hand and clapping him on the arm. "Well done! Come in. We have much to talk about."

Bone stood up front, by where Ryan assumed the altar would've been.

The skeletal sec boss gestured. The sergeant who had brought them back saluted and backed out, closing the doors behind him.

"I hear you all have been doing solid work," Bone said. "So good it looks as if you've put yourselves out of a job."

"What do you mean?" Ryan asked.

A dozen sec men in full SWAT riot armor emerged from pews to both sides, where they'd waited hidden from view by the pillars of the arcade. They had longblasters aimed at Ryan and his friends.

"I do hope you won't resist," Michaud said from behind. "It would be such a shame if we were forced to kill you…quickly."

Chapter Twenty-Two

"So that's how it is," Ryan said, raising his hands to clasp them behind his neck as the black-armored sec men surrounded the companions.

"That's how it is," Bone said.

"I'd say I'm sorry how this turned out," Michaud said, "but, of course, that would be a lie. I don't really like you. You're vermin from the outlands. And vermin, always, must be exterminated. Sooner or later."

"We did your dirty work," Mildred said as sec men relieved them of their gear, "and this is how you pay us back?"

Bone grinned unpleasantly. He didn't seem equipped to grin any other way.

"I told you you'd worked yourselves out of a job," he said. "We may not have the bastard Angels on the run, but we've dealt them their worst defeat in a generation. It's only a matter of time until we crack them open and suck out their life. And you did play a big role in that."

Ryan was watching like a hawk. But the sec men knew their trade. Some of them bound their captives' hands behind them, while others stood by with blasters trained on them. They seldom covered one another with their blaster barrels and gave their prisoners no chance to make a play to overpower them.

"Want me to have them chilled?" Bone asked.

Michaud frowned and pursed his lips beneath his mustache. "I think not. We can keep them awhile. We may want to blame them for something and publicly execute them." He gave a tittering laugh. "We do so much to get blamed for."

Bone was walking around the group, eyeing them appraisingly. "Is it all right if we…play with them some?" he asked.

"Why not? As long as you don't leave any marks that show."

"Excellent," the sec boss said. He fondled Krysty's right breast through her shirt. She snapped at his hand. He yanked it back, then ostentatiously slowed it once it was out of range, as if he hadn't cared.

"Spirited," he said. "Be fun breaking you."

"The women might fetch a good price," Michaud said thoughtfully, "the next time our slaver friends come around."

"Slavers?" Ricky said. "Maybe you've seen my sister, Yami? She was—"

A sec man backhanded him hard across the face with a black-gauntleted hand. He dropped to his knees.

"They don't know anything about your sister," Ryan said. "I get the feeling they sell more than buy."

"Why, yes, of course," Michaud said. "We have an ample supply of women for our own modest needs."

He gestured airily. "Chief."

"Take them out the side way," Bone directed his men. "Too many of our weak-minded rank-and-file have started looking up to these outland scum."

"And don't let anybody see them," Hizzoner said.

MILDRED CAREFULLY WATCHED where she put her feet as they reached the end of indifferently lit stairs that led to a poorly lit basement.

"Maybe it's true what they always said about the Masons," she muttered.

A truncheon gouged her in the kidneys. She just managed not to stumble.

"Shut your piehole, bitch," one of the two SWAT men escorting them snarled.

Mildred glanced back at him. "I love it when you talk rough—ugh!"

The last came out as he shoved her hard from behind. She stumbled the last few steps and slammed down on her knees on the cold concrete floor. Pain shot up through her legs. She only just managed to prevent herself from going down face-first.

Murder flared in her heart.

"Don't be a stupe," the other sec man said. "The Fat Man says he wants them kept in prime condition. These two are prime trade."

"She won't show no bruises on her legs, anyway," Mildred's guard said as he grabbed her by the arm in a thick-gloved hand and hauled her to her feet.

Which she would have taken as stone racist had he not been black. Krysty's escort was white. Mildred was tempted to see racial complexion in that but realized that was unlikely.

There's such a thing as too paranoid, she told herself. Even when everybody really *is* out to get you.

The light down there, such as it was, came from a window at the far end of the corridor. It was high up in the wall, showing that the level wasn't fully underground. Naturally, it had heavy security mesh over it—making it ideal for a prison cell.

They were taken to a room and thrust inside. It was about the size of a modest office and had solid walls, not partitions. More light, yellowed by late afternoon, came in from a window. It was barely enough by which to make out the room's contents: a pair of cots, a table, a bucket in the corner.

"Use that," the black sec man said as the white one closed the door behind them. "Hizzoner likes to keep things nice and neat."

His partner used a lighter to spark up a lantern on the table. The smell of burning kerosene filled the air.

"You trust us with a kerosene lamp?" Mildred asked.

The guards looked at each other and laughed. "You wanna check out by setting yourself on fire, feel free," the white man said.

"No one'll hear you scream," the black guard said. "Rooms are soundproof."

They stared at the captive women. Mildred did not like the way they did that. Krysty thrust her chest forward. Her large breasts bounced obligingly beneath her shirt.

"You boys don't have to run off, do you?" she said.

"Krysty!" Mildred said.

Krysty turned to her and shrugged. "Sometimes you got to go along to get along, you know?"

And with the eye turned away from the two SWAT men, she winked.

"I guess you're right," she said, forcing herself to smile as she looked back at the guards. "Anyway, we don't often get a chance to see what *real men* are like."

The black guard rubbed his cheek inside his helmet. "I dunno," he said. "Michaud says leave them in good shape."

"We don't have to leave marks," his partner said, turning and locking the door from the inside with a key from a heavy brass ring. "Unless they like it rough."

"I like it rough," the black guard said.

"Leave the face alone, then."

"No need for that," Krysty crooned. "We'll rock your world in ways you never imagined."

She ran her tongue sensuously over her full lips.

One of the guards growled low in his throat. They both started forward.

"Not so fast, boys," Krysty said. She managed to make her voice sound at once playful and commanding, like a kitten with a whip. The pair actually hesitated.

The redhead turned sideways and bent slightly, moving her hips suggestively.

"You want it from the back?" the white one asked.

"You'll see, won't you? Silly. Our hands are tied."

"What's wrong with that?" the black guard said. "You can still show us a good time like that."

"But think about how much better we can make it if we can use our hands, big boy."

I cannot believe anybody could fall for this, Mildred thought.

But Krysty's voice, her whole manner, was pure sex. And Mildred had already realized that Bone did not recruit his elite SWAT troopers on account of their big brains.

The white guard was licking his unpleasantly fleshy lips. But his black companion, who was an inch or two shorter and an inch or two wider, looked doubtful.

Krysty glanced over her shoulder at Mildred. Taking the hint—somehow—Mildred turned her more substantial buttocks toward Krysty. The two began to slide up and down each other, back to back.

"Cut us both free," Krysty purred, "and we'll put on a show for you you'll never forget."

"And we *guarantee* you'll have a happy ending," Mildred added as seductively as she could. The pure sex thing had never been her department.

"All right," the black one guard. "I'm in. Man, I'm in!"

"Good man," the other said. "What's the harm? We're Detroit SWAT. What can a couple of bitches do to us?"

THE FIVE COMPANIONS sat on the floor of the windowless cell in the light of a single kerosene lantern. The table it rested on and a bucket in the corner were the room's only furnishings. If you could call them that.

"Well," J.B. said, "it's not like Leto didn't warn us."

"Yeah," Ryan said. He could've said that clearly the captive Angels heir was self-interested and trying to sow doubt. But that would be making excuses. "I just didn't figure on the bastards turning on us quite this fast."

"So this isn't how it ends, is it?" Ricky asked. He started sounding disconsolate and passed all the way to almost giddy optimism by the end of the short sentence. Ryan marveled at his resilience sometimes.

"I mean, we've got a plan. Don't we? Don't we?"

"Nope," J.B. said. "Every line comes to an end eventually. Looks like this is the end of ours."

"Oh." Ricky hung his head. It struck Ryan as mostly an attempt to hold back tears.

"Aw, I'm just jacking with you, kid," J.B. said. "Takes more than this dreck to keep us in. These boys are double stupe."

Doc shook himself, as if shedding the internal mists that sometimes enveloped his mind.

"It is the common concomitant of arrogance," he announced. "An occupational hazard of being a powerful baron. Or his sec boss."

Ricky had perked right up at the Armorer's dry admission. Now he looked at his friend Jak, who slouched against a wall looking comfortable, which was surprising, because he tended to be claustrophobic in manmade surroundings.

"So how come they never shucked you out of that jacket?" Ricky asked. "It's, like, a lethal wep in itself."

"Not like touch," Jak said.

"Yeah, they don't like to frisk you much, either. You still got some weps concealed, I bet."

Jak just smirked.

"*I'm* not fishing for them," Ryan said. "I don't like to touch him, either. Not with those razors sewn into the collar and who knows where else."

Ryan inched across the few feet that separated him from J.B. The bare concrete floor was cold on his tailbone. Starting to feel uncomfortably hard, too. Ryan didn't have much padding down there.

J.B. obligingly turned his back toward Ryan, who pushed in close. J.B.'s hand began to fiddle with his belt buckle.

Ryan saw Ricky's eyebrows raise.

Apparently J.B. noticed, too. "You know it's not like that, kid. And Krysty would kill me," he said.

"What is with you today, J.B.?" Ryan asked. "You practicing to start up one of those predark comedy clubs I read about?"

"He is peculiarly well qualified," Doc said. "When he kills, he really kills."

"Now everybody's a comedian."

"Just circumstances, I reckon, Ryan," the Armorer said. "Gotta laugh at life sometimes."

"That is kind of a new philosophy for you."

"It's a hard old world," J.B. said. "A man's got to adapt to survive. There. Got it."

Ryan immediately scooted back away from him. Unless he had no choice whatsoever, he didn't trust any kind of blade that close to his balls. Even if it was relatively tiny, like the hidden one the Armorer had just extracted from his belt buckle.

Even a man as good as Dix needed room to work, anyhow.

Across the room Jak held his hands up before him, shook them to restore circulation and lazily stretched like a cat.

In another moment the Armorer was free and deftly snipping Ryan's bonds. "Still got the lock pick in your boot heel?"

Ryan grinned.

JAK SHIED BACK from the corridor junction. "Sec men coming," he said.

"How many," mouthed Ryan, who was right behind him with one of the albino's leaf-shaped throwing knives in his hand. Ryan was not the knife fighter Jak was, but he was skilled enough to like his chances in a scrape, even with a little knife, and especially when he had the advantage of surprise.

Jak held up two fingers. His pale skin helped Ryan make them out in the gloom. Hizzoner sure believed in sparing every expense on illumination down here in his prisoner holding area. Some light, faint and gray with the dying of the day, filtered in through the small windows at either end of the cross corridor. Otherwise, there was nothing but the odd kerosene lamp, turned low to do no more than help a body not trip on anything.

Ryan couldn't help wondering what use the original architects had had in mind for this basement. The rooms had stout walls on all sides. They made ideal cells.

He only hoped they'd find Mildred and Krysty in one of them.

He came up alongside Jak. Obligingly, the smaller man

lowered himself in a deep squat, allowing Ryan to bend above him to take a quick look.

Yeah, two of them, not that he doubted their scout. Still twenty yards away, but walking briskly, the guards wore full DPD SWAT riot armor and held side-handle batons in thickly gloved hands. One tall, one short. For some reason both had their bulletproof face shields down. How they could see through the tinted plastic to walk that fast was a mystery to Ryan.

Maybe they were just that familiar with the dungeon. It served him anyway, because it helped him avoid being spotted.

He gestured the others back so that he and Jak could press against the wall, right by the mouth of the other hallway. He took the closer spot. He'd take the taller sec man. The faster-moving Jak could handle the other.

It felt good to be striking back against the bastards.

"Don't kill yours," Ryan said from the side of his mouth. "We need help finding the women."

The steps got louder. Ryan listened carefully.

Then he struck. He flowed around the corner, grabbing the nearer guard's wrist and twisting it up behind his back as he slid behind the man. He brought the throwing knife up to the unarmored side of his captive's neck.

"No chill!" Jak whispered urgently.

Chapter Twenty-Three

Ryan froze. His nostrils dilated. He sniffed.

Now he noticed what Jak had smelled a few seconds earlier. It was a pleasant aroma well-known to him.

His heart dropped to his boots. Now he noticed the bright lock of hair escaping from beneath the black helmet. It stirred gently, as if in a breeze.

"Ryan?" Krysty's voice was muffled by the polycarbonate visor. "We've got to stop meeting like this, lover."

"Well, that's convenient," the other riot helmet said in Mildred's voice. "We were just looking for you boys."

Ryan hastily pulled the knife away from Krysty's carotid artery. She turned, flipped up her visor and planted a kiss on his lips.

J.B. stepped up to give Mildred a quick hug. Mildred gave him a quick peck on the cheek before he could escape.

"Always the romantic, John," she said. "I'll fix you later."

"How?" Ryan asked.

"You know," Krysty said with a shrug.

"Testosterone poisoning," Mildred said. "Too much tumescence drawing too much blood from too-small brains."

"So they…passed out from oxygen deprivation to the small brain and you took their shit?"

"Oh, no," Krysty said brightly. "One of them asked

what they had to fear from us bitches, so we showed them."

"Not that they'll be in position to take much advantage of the lesson," Mildred said darkly. "And we won't have to worry about them raising the alarm on us."

"You didn't—" Ryan began.

"Oh, no," Krysty said. "We just chilled them."

"Somehow I find that less disturbing than the thought of you castrating them."

"They didn't piss us off enough to even consider that," Mildred said. "Bone, however…"

"Later," Ryan said. "We've got to shake the dust of this place off our heels before somebody comes down here and finds us."

"What about our stuff?" Ricky asked.

"No time."

"But my DeLisle! My uncle—"

"Won't shoot itself if we get caught and chilled." He led off back up the corridor they'd just come down. "But how are we set for weps?"

"Krysty and I found a Remington 870 and an MP5," Mildred said. "Plus ammo."

"Great," Ryan said.

"You want them?" Krysty asked.

Ryan shook his head. "Keep them. Give the batons to J.B. and Doc, though."

The corridor ended in a stout metal door that bled the last light of day feebly in through a grimy, fly-specked window, which was naturally covered with security mesh.

Ryan reached for the push bar.

"But the sign says Emergency Exit—Alarm Will Sound If Opened!" Ricky squeaked.

Ryan turned and gave him a look.

"Oh," Ricky said. J.B. reached up from behind and gave him a brisk tap atop the head with his fingertips.

"Might it be locked?" Mildred asked.

Ryan transferred the look to her, then he grinned and pushed the bar.

The door opened. It stuck a little, from evident long disuse, but it did open. No alarm sounded, lacking power to produce one.

"This is the back way out," he said, pushing it open enough to see up the short flight of stairs and beyond, north, to where what looked like the remains of town houses a couple of hundreds yards away, past a parking lot that still seemed to serve that function for a handful of DPD.

Jak promptly peeled out. "We reach cover among the buildings and then circle south," Ryan said.

J.B. hefted the riot baton speculatively in his hands. "We could use a few more blasters," he said a bit wistfully.

Ryan grinned. "I got that covered."

THE STURDY MAN in the canvas apron and his gawky but similarly clad assistant turned suddenly away from the long table when Ryan cleared his throat.

"Good evening," Ryan said, holding his hands out to the side.

J.B. stood next to him in the outer verge of the circle of yellow lamplight in which the DPD armorers worked. He had the riot baton tucked into his belt at his side and was doing his level best to look as innocuous as possible. To Ryan that made him look even more menacing, but these two didn't know him as well as Ryan did.

The older man's shoulders dropped as tension flowed out of them. He smiled.

"Oh, it's you two," he said. "You kind of scared me there."

"Sorry," Ryan said. "You know us?"

"Who doesn't know Hizzoner's outlanders?" He adjusted his round wire-rimmed spectacles to look at the two better. The specs looked a lot like J.B.'s.

"You must be Ryan Cawdor. And you would be J. B. Dix."

"Yeah," Ryan said. The Armorer tipped his hat.

"A special pleasure to meet you, Mr. Dix. I understand you're a wep smith?"

J.B. nodded.

The man's brown, deep-seamed face beamed. "Ace," he said. "You might say I'm your opposite. I'm Dominguez, chief armorer for the Detroit Police Department. And this is my assistant, Bartoli."

"Hi," the black kid in the apron said.

"Yeah," Ryan replied.

He gestured at the tables of blasters and a few other weapons—machetes, swords and even a couple of battle axes—that formed three sides of a square around the two smiths in a field a couple hundred yards behind the DPD lines. The table they stood by had one end cleared for a work space. Ryan smelled blaster oil and the traces of burned powder.

"Are these what I think they are?" Ryan asked.

"I imagine so," Dominguez said. "If you mean weps recovered from the battlefield."

He gestured around at them with a broad, strong-looking brown hand.

"So many, as you can see." He sounded sad. From the southeast came a clatter of small-arms fire. The battle was still going on, though not at the intensity it had been. "We're inspecting their condition, to ascertain which are still functional, which need to be repaired and which can be parted out."

"Should you be telling them this, sir?" Bartoli asked.

"Why not? They already figured it out. So what can I do for you gentlemen?"

"It's not just us," Ryan said. He stuck two fingers in his mouth and whistled. It was for effect, of course. His friends were lurking out of the light in some brush not far off. They couldn't be seen outside the lamp light, not that Dominguez and his apprentice had been looking anywhere but at their work. But the other could see Ryan and the others well enough.

They came forward.

"All of you?" Dominguez asked. He picked up a rag and wiped his hands. It seemed to just redistribute the grease on them.

Ryan introduced the others quickly. Dominguez nodded knowingly, as if he'd heard of all of them by name, which he might have. Bartoli just stood looking nervous and confused, his prominent Adam's apple riding incessantly up and down.

"So again I must ask," Dominguez said when Ryan had finished. "To what do we owe the honor?"

"We need to ask a favor of you, Armorer Dominguez," Ryan said. "We need to borrow some of your weps."

"You mean requisition?"

J.B. shrugged and smiled.

"'Borrow' sounds nicer," he said.

The two nodded to each other. If they'd been any more on the same wavelength, they would've started talking in unison.

"But where are your weps?" Bartoli asked.

"We ran into a rad-dust hotspot," Ryan said. "Had to leave them at headquarters for decontamination, along with the clothes we were wearing. They lent us a couple blasters, then told us to come out here and hit you up."

Of course, no one had told Ryan any such thing. J.B. had suggested they'd find just such an operation going on behind the battle lines. And naturally, he was right.

Dominguez gestured at one table. "Those blasters there are all serviceable. Far as we can tell. Obviously we're not in a position to test fire them. Take your pick."

"Armorer," Bartoli said in alarm, "are you sure—"

"It's not as if the original owners have any need for them anymore. And they technically shouldn't have been allowed to possess them in the first place, if you go by what they call the law these days."

Mildred was already at the table, inspecting a Smith & Wesson Model 10 revolver she'd picked up.

"For a police armorer, you seem a bit skeptical about the law."

"I believe in justice," Dominguez said. "And peace and order. On the whole, my department has brought those things to the Detroit rubble and promises to expand their scope in the future. But laws—" he shrugged "—can be surprisingly flexible, when they are made by decree."

"What about regulations?" Bartoli asked.

"Much the same," his boss said calmly. "And in case I need to remind you, when it comes to the regulations concerning the maintenance, handling and issuing of weps, *I* decreed them."

"Yes, sir."

Dominguez reached out and tousled his assistant's short hair fondly. "My apprentice takes things much too earnestly. It is the way of the young. Relax, son. The armories back at HQ are packed with far more weps in mint condition than we have officers to shoot them. No one is going to go without."

He frowned. "Unless the war drags on. Then, who knows?"

"Ammo?" Jak asked. Oddly enough, he had found a Ruger Super Redhawk revolver, double action and chambered in .44 Magnum in good condition, which meant it would also fire the same .44 Special rounds as Doc's currently confiscated LeMat. He preferred knives to blasters, but he appreciated the need for them.

Dominguez pointed to a number of metal ammunition boxes and buckets set beneath one of the tables.

"Our men recovered lots of that, too. Along with a number of magazines, obviously also for a variety of blasters. Bartoli, here, spent much of the afternoon supervising several walking wounded in sorting and labeling them."

He shrugged. "I can't promise that we have abundant ammo for every blaster. You'd be surprised what's floating around out there, including personal arms carried by our officers. But as long as you can satisfy yourselves with the more conventional and common calibers and models, we can probably help you out."

That made Bartoli shift his weight from foot to moccasined foot and eye the strangers uneasily. He obviously was not happy in being included in that "we."

"Fortunately," Dominguez said with genuine pleasure, "we have turned up eighty or a hundred .44 Magnum cartridges. So you can make use of that handblaster if you wish, Mr. Lauren."

Jak looked at him as if unsure who "Mr. Lauren" was. In fact, Ryan wasn't sure he'd ever heard Jak called that before. But he smiled, nodded and went over to the ammo bins.

They all got down to rummaging through the available armament. J.B., content to let his friends pick first, stood by talking shop in low tones with the DPD weaponsmith.

Bartoli got so fascinated by their discussion he gave up watching the others as if certain they were all stickies in human-skin suits. He even quit ogling Krysty and Mildred.

"Look what I found!" Ricky exclaimed. He lifted a Husqvarna, a bolt-action blaster whose wood stock went all the way to the muzzle. It had a low-power scope mounted. "It's even .308. Or, uh, 7.62 mm."

The latter was a mil-spec variant of the former, its load optimized for the working of semi- and full-auto actions. A bolt-action blaster like this one would never notice a difference.

"So how does a sniper rifle wind up, uh, here?" he asked.

"We lost a couple of department snipers when the Angels blew up the armored wag and overran our position temporarily," Dominguez said. "We do have plenty of 7.62 mm and a couple other .308 loads. Of course, that particular longblaster lacks a detachable box magazine."

Ricky turned the blaster over in his hands almost lovingly. Then his shoulders moved in a sigh. He turned and held it out to Ryan.

"Here. You should carry this."

Ryan shook his head. "Thanks, kid. But I'm taking this."

He held up an M4 carbine. "Reckon this is best suited for the work we got ahead of us. You'll be our sniper for now."

Ricky stared at him, then smiled as if his face would split. He got down on his knees and started scooping up .308 cartridges from a tin bucket.

Though there were a number of shotguns available, Mildred wound up handing over her 870 riot shotgun to J.B. in exchange for an M16. He liked it because it had a pistol grip and synthetic furniture like his M4000. She also kept the .38 caliber Smith revolver, which, though no match for her target-model ZKR 551, was close enough for comfort. Krysty hung on to the machine pistol she'd taken from the dead SWAT cop.

Doc selected a Smith & Wesson M29 with a four-inch barrel. He managed to find a couple dozen .44 Special cartridges, which he promptly loaded into the blaster. He also took some longer Magnum cartridges, just in case. Ryan got a Beretta M9 and J.B. a Glock 17, both common designs, both in the ubiquitous 9 mm. There were more magazines available for both than either could comfortably carry.

Finally the group picked up a few odds and ends of cutlery to round things out. As Doc pointed out, a good blade never ran out of ammunition.

"I suppose the assignment you're on is strictly need to know," Dominguez said when they were done.

"We were never here," Ryan assured him.

"Armorer," Bartoli said, eyes wide. "Are you sure we're doing the right thing?"

"Absolutely," Dominguez said.

"We'll be taking our leave now, Chief Armorer, Armorer Bartoli," J.B. said, tipping his hat. "Much obliged to you both."

As they started off into the night, Ryan paused and turned back.

"Thanks," he said. "In return, let me suggest you and your assistant watch your backs extraclose the next few days. In fact, mebbe take a little bit of a furlough when you get a chance."

For the first time Dominguez frowned.

"I tell you this as a man you helped out in a major way," Ryan said. "And a man who pays his debts. And I can tell you one thing—you may not care much for some things that're about to happen. But if this plays out, you may like the way things shake overall. No guarantees."

"I can't ask for any more than that," the chief armorer said. "Go safely, my friends."

"YOU REALLY THINK there's the slightest chance that poor old Mr. Dominguez is gonna like what you have in mind?" Mildred asked Ryan as they made their way through the bizarre, colossal, derelict industrial buildings and swinging west around the reestablished flank of the DPD lines. They relied even more heavily on Jak than usual, trying to avoid lethal pitfalls and other hazards lurking in the dark, including the ever-present possibility of ambush—by humans and creatures perhaps even more unkind.

The fact that Ryan felt an indefinable need gnawing at his gut like a trapped rat to keep moving as fast as possible made the journey even more hazardous.

"Like I told him," Ryan said, "he won't like what happens next if we pull it off. But what happens after that might suit him better if he's sharp enough to follow my advice."

"You mind sharing what that might be?"

Ryan shrugged. "End the war. At least the current big one between DPD and the Angels. Same thing I told Leto."

"You still think it's possible after all that's happened?" Krysty asked.

Ryan laughed softly. "Mebbe easier now than before. Of course, the *how* is the part Dominguez is probably not going to like."

"We're going to bring down DPD?" Ricky asked eagerly from near the rear. J.B. was pulling drag, walking behind him at the very end of the line. Ryan, of course, had the front, with Jak ranging invisibly ahead and only reappearing when he needed to impart warnings and information.

"No," Ryan said. "Don't count that possible, given the resources we got available."

"What, then, lover?" Krysty asked.

"I reckon it's time the so-called City of Detroit and its police force had a change of management at the highest levels."

Krysty laughed a little ruefully. "I can't argue with that. But why us? Why are we bringing it about? I gather that's your plan."

"It's not just to get our stuff back, is it?" Mildred asked.

Ryan laughed as loudly as he dared let himself. "Not hardly. Though I intend to do that, too."

"You're not developing a social conscience at this late date, are you?" Mildred said. "You're going all soft and gooey and humanitarian on us."

"No call to be insulting, Millie," J.B. said.

"I can never tell if he's joking when he says something like that," she complained. "You've known him since Christ was a lance corporal, Ryan. Is he joking?"

"Beats me," Ryan said. "You'll have to take it up with him. And—not exactly. I'm not doing this to get anyone out from under Michaud's yoke. Although it also doesn't exactly break my heart that that is a predictable consequence of what I got in mind. I told you before that I'm not a monster."

"What, then, my dear Ryan?" Doc asked. "You may rest assured that we shall follow you, whatever your design. Yet I believe we deserve to know."

"Simple," Ryan said. "It's like I told Dominguez—I pay my debts. Everything follows from that."

Krysty came up beside him and clasped his hand. They

traveled for a time through the hot and restless night and the ruined monuments of a long-dead civilization.

And so they made their way to the Joe Louis Arena, palace and stronghold of the Angel overlord Red Wings, where they found his son, Leto, standing trial for his life.

Chapter Twenty-Four

"It doesn't look good," J.B. said as he peered out over the auditorium.

The terraced seats were packed with sweaty, shouting Angels. Giant bonfires danced on the former hockey rink floor, throwing a shifting demonic light up their faces. Highlights danced in the golden hair of the bound and kneeling captive and glittered in the brooding eyes of the giant who presided over the hellish scene like a drunken Greek god.

"Mebbe we got here too late."

"No," Ryan said.

The two men plus Doc, Krysty and Mildred stood just inside the main entrance to the cavernous, echoing space, off to one side where they weren't silhouetted against the lantern glow from outside.

Not that anybody was looking that way.

"Leto's still alive."

A SKEIN OF highways had led under the Cobo Center, as the Desolation Angels' main residential area was called. Although the lowest floor of the building had somehow survived, the roadway was littered with a nightmare tangled jumble of fallen elevated pathways, including at least one highway bridge.

Ironically, it made it easier for the companions to infiltrate through the Angels' perimeter defenses, which seemed curiously depleted, even given the fact that at least some of their forces were tied down fighting with the DPD to the north. With Jak to scout the way, they picked their way through razor-wire tangles and past a handful of drowsy sentries who seemed, Ryan thought, to be far more concerned with a full-on DPD attack force rolling down on them than the possibility of infiltration by a small, careful group.

No one seemed to be watching as they slipped up the steep, wide steps to the main entrance. The two Angels guarding the main door were standing in pools of light from a pair of oil lamps—which messed up their night vision way more than they provided useful illumination—and kept turning around to look inside at every fresh roar bellowing out the open entryway. After Ryan and Jak all but strolled openly up and choked them both out, it became apparent they couldn't see anything but the huge lobby area.

The group quickly slipped inside. The lobby was illuminated by a few oil lanterns, which mostly emphasized the shadows and made the space seem bigger and spookier than it was, but it was deserted. All the action seemed to be inside the auditorium itself, to judge by the bellowing noise and sullen orange forge light glowing out the entrances.

They found a utility closet to stash the sentries, bound and gagged with their own clothing. Ryan sent Jak and Ricky off to hunt down a way to get high up and prepare to make serious mischief.

"But what if the door to the stairs leading up is locked?" Ricky asked.

"Did you lose the lockpick kit I gave you?" J.B. asked. "Time to put all that training to use."

The young men went off. Ryan led the others to a side entrance to the auditorium and peered inside, where they saw Leto kneeling, shirtless, between two giant leaping fires while voices from the crowd of hundreds bayed for his blood.

"How do we play this?" Krysty asked. They were crouched behind the top row of seats, more out of reflex caution than any need. "It doesn't look promising."

Ryan looked at J.B. "You, Mildred and Doc go left where there are more empty seats and work your way close as you can without getting spotted. Then get ready to back our play."

"What play is that, exactly?" Mildred asked.

"Reckon we're going to do the only thing we can under the circumstances," J.B. said.

"Which is what?"

"Something ballsy and triple stupe," Ryan said. "If all else fails..."

The two women didn't try to talk them out of whatever crazy scheme they had in mind. They knew better. Krysty hugged Ryan and Mildred hugged J.B., and then Ryan watched the trio make their way off counterclockwise around the arena.

Down on the floor a tall, lanky guy with a headband and a long gray beard was presenting the case against Leto. "By his own admission, he was captured by blasters working for our enemies. Our longtime blood enemies, who had dared to threaten our sacred domain! But how could one so highly placed among us, heir to the Presidency and Maximum Leadership of all the Desolation Angels, allow mere hired blasters to take him? I ask you, brothers and sisters, how?"

He banged the six-foot wooden staff he was holding in his right hand against the floor for emphasis.

"Treason!" voices shouted from the crowd. They were few and widely scattered.

"Whoever that dude is, he's got himself a pack of shills in place," Ryan said.

"Most of the crowd doesn't seem to be buying it," J.B. said.

"Mebbe not. But people who run shows like this one don't generally rely on luck to get the results they want. They set up a machine to manufacture consensus and then crank the handle for all they're worth. Come on."

"Blasters?" J.B. asked with one brow lifted.

"Slung," Ryan decided. "They can blast us into pink mist if we try settling this with weps. So we just march right down and announce ourselves."

J.B. nodded. "You were right. Ballsy and triple stupe."

"Did you ever doubt it?"

Initially, no one even bothered glancing their way as Ryan and J.B. walked side by side down a set of stairs that would bring them to the wall around the former rink right behind the captive Leto. Whether for or against, or just enjoying the show, the Angels in their brown vests and colorful patches were totally engrossed in the spectacle and the gray-bearded man's rabble-rousing oration.

But as Ryan and J.B. continued down the concrete stairs, they started to attract looks. They continued walking as if they owned the place.

"Nobody seems too put out to see us here," J.B. said.

"They may be used to visitors," Ryan replied. "And we sure don't look like Hizzoner's sec men."

The prosecutor was spinning a loud tale about how Leto had been trying to undermine his father's manly policy for some time. Ryan heard some grumbling from the crowd as they passed. Some of the men and women here had apparently fought alongside Leto. The portrait the graybeard drew did not agree with their personal experiences.

Ryan's, either.

Ryan strode right down to the short wall that separated the concrete floor of the former rink from the stands and clambered over. J.B. followed a beat later.

The graybeard goggled at him. He had gray eyes that had a bit of a bulge to them and wet-looking lips. Possibly he was a spitter when he speechified, Ryan thought. He wore a tan canvas shirt beneath his colors and blue jeans.

"What do you think you're doing?" he demanded. "You think you can just barge in here?"

A pair of burly gang members stood flanking the throne where Red Wings lolled. Ryan could tell it was the Angel lord because, along with the fact he was sitting on a fancy elevated chair that was mostly hidden under a variety of stained cushions right at the focus of the entire big room, he had a set of spread crimson wings tattooed across his expansive chest. And even more expansive belly. The guards started to unfold their arms and step forward.

The crowd had begun to buzz with Ryan and J.B.'s unexpected move. He continued to walk toward Leto, who kept his face rigidly turned toward his father.

"I'm here to tell you," Ryan declared, making his voice ring, "that that's not the way it happened."

The orator's eyes narrowed. "Are you calling me a liar?"

"I'm saying the story you're telling isn't straight," Ryan stated. "Somebody told you wrong."

The prosecutor drew himself up to his full height. He was as thin as a rail and didn't look healthy. But he had the presence to hold center stage and was unwilling to yield it to random interlopers.

"Who are you to barge in here to our sacred ceremony

of trial and contradict me? How would you know what happened? Were you there?"

"Yes," Ryan said. "We're the people who captured him. He was in the middle of leading a battle against the Detroit Police Department that had just routed their west wing."

"You *what?*" The graybeard stuck his head forward on his scrawny neck and his eyes stood out so much they threatened to pop out of the sockets.

"We're the blasters he told you about," Ryan said, coming to a halt beside the kneeling prisoner. The heat of the fires made the already hot night and poorly ventilated auditorium uncomfortable. But at least the scent of whatever kind of wood they were burning masked the smells of several hundred impassioned and not particularly clean Angels sweating inside their vests. "That story you were thinking was far-fetched? It's the truth."

The graybeard collected his wits with visible effort, and his prosecutorial task, or nature, promptly took over.

"Blasters!" he screeched. He extended his free hand to point a trembling finger at the intruders. "They are Michaud's vile hirelings! They've come here to add their lies to the traitor Leto's. Seize them!"

Guards were stationed around the inside of the wall, presumably to keep overly agitated or drunk Angels from climbing over and horning in. In his right-side peripheral vision, which was all he owned, Ryan saw several start forward.

"Blasters now?" J.B. asked.

"Not yet," Ryan said.

"Your call."

They stood their ground as the orator yipped about their perfidy and insolence. He had a more than decent vocabulary for a random urban gang member. Then again, Leto was pretty well-spoken, more like an actual baron's son than a gang leader's.

Despite the predicament, he had to grin at himself. There was a difference?

As the Angel sec men closed in, the giant suddenly slapped a palm on the arm of his throne with a sound like a blaster shot. The whole arena fell silent.

"No," Red Wings said in a voice that sounded as loud as a wag-size boulder rolling down a granite slope.

The prosecutor spun to look at his master. "Lord Red Wings?" he asked as if he wasn't sure what he had heard.

He might have been befuddled by surprise again, or he might have been just a good actor. "Let them have their say," Red Wings said. He leaned forward. It was quite an operation, given how his astonishing belly fought back. "This is just getting fun."

He banged his drinking vessel on the other arm of his throne. A skinny young woman with lank blond hair hurried up a set of steps to refill it from a jug.

"That's a skull he's drinking from," J.B. said sidelong to Ryan. "Human, by the looks of it."

"Didn't expect him to be quite this big," Ryan said.

"What are your names?" asked the voice of the thunder.

"I'm Ryan Cawdor. This is J. B. Dix."

"Did you come here as emissaries for the bastard Michaud? That'd be ballsy. And stupe."

"That does seem to be the consensus. But no. We separated from Hizzoner's employment. Tonight, in fact. A little manner of his deciding to reward all the ace work we did for him by throwing us in cells while he figured out how he wanted to kill us."

"Lies!" screeched the prosecutor. "It's a trick! Don't listen to them!"

Red Wings turned a massive scowl on him. He wasn't

actually equipped to do much that wasn't massive, Ryan thought.

"Shut it, Kyle," Red Wings said. "This is way more entertaining than your line of bullshit. I want to hear them out. Anyway, that does sound like Michaud. Treacherous puke bag."

"But—but Lord of the Rubble and King among Angels! I— That is, may I approach and consult with you—" he glanced over his shoulder at Ryan and J.B. "—confidentially?"

"Oh, I still intend to see the little weasel chilled for good and all," Red Wings said. "But he's still my son, and an Angel, and he deserves a fair and open trial before we execute him."

He turned bloodshot eyes on Ryan. "Go the fuck on."

"Your boy here laid a whipping on the Bone's sec men. Fried their war wag with his lone missile."

"The big one?" Red Wings asked with a gleam in his little hippo eyes.

"No. Not the Commando. The smaller one. The BearCat. But it was a solid predark armored car, not one of his junkers with rusty plates bolted on. Anyway, under his command your Angels chased off a bastard number of sec men who were advancing.

"Then we crept up on his command post, took down his guards, grabbed him."

"And?"

"Don't listen to him, Lord Red Wings!" a voice sang out from off to Ryan's right. "They're still working for Bone! They're spies, sent to assassinate you!"

Up the side of Red Wings' dais strode Tommy Ten-Inch of the Dragons, resplendent in a scarlet leather vest and pants.

Chapter Twenty-Five

"That's not true," J.B. said.

"Angels! They lie!" Tommy shouted.

"They're the ones who snatched me! They're still working for that fat bastard Michaud! He sent them there to chill your Maximum Leader and sow confusion so you could be conquered!"

"That's strange," Ryan said.

He didn't shout, but he knew how to project his voice and make it ring up to the rafters with authority. "We *were* blasters for Michaud. And right before he turned on us, threw us in a cell and tried to chill us, we saw you and him looking real buddy-buddy. You weren't shaking off the hand he had on your shoulder, that's for sure."

He did feel a certain chill at his own use of the word "we." It wouldn't do any of them any good if somebody thought to start wondering where the rest of those "we" were.

He could see the color, such as it was, drop out of Tommy's already sallow face. For a moment the Dragon lord seemed struck dumb. It couldn't have helped his credibility.

But street gangs, even as powerful and relatively well-organized as the Desolation Angels, were not notorious for their sophistication. When Tommy rallied to start bleating once again that they were lying, a number of voices shouted out agreement, although many also rose to dissent or to yell, "Hear 'em out!"

Now Red Wings, who up until then had acted reasonable and almost genial, decided to flash his mean, irrational streak.

He slammed his hand on his chair arm again. "It's a lie! Do you think we're all stupes? Who'd believe a bullshit story like that? Grab 'em, boys!"

Burly Angels stationed around the inside of the fence to keep their rowdy brothers and sisters in their seats started forward. They didn't flash blasters, but some of them waved baseball bats or trailed lengths of chain wrapped around meaty fists.

"Wait!" Ryan said. Again, he didn't shout, but he said it loud, and his voice rang with command. The Angel sec men faltered in their steps. "You might want to think twice about that."

"What's there to think about, mighty Red Wings?" Tommy shrieked. "They're assassins, sent to chill you! Chill them before—"

Ryan raised his right hand, the first two fingers raised.

Tommy's head exploded in a cloud of chunky spray.

Blood and hair clumps spattered the side of Red Wings' face. His half-clad serving girl squealed and shied away.

A noise like a giant hammer hitting an anvil filled the arena. It rang the rafters like steel bells.

Still spurting arcs of blood from the lower half of his head, Tommy toppled off the dais.

Everybody in the whole Joe had frozen at the sight of Tommy getting half decapitated. The only sound was the echoes of the blaster shot, fading away overhead.

Into that ringing silence, Ryan said, "Now that we have your attention, let me point out that if we'd meant you any harm, Red Wings, you'd be cooling down to air temperature already. Also, we did think to bring insurance."

Heads started craning, looking for the sniper overhead.

Ryan couldn't afford to look, but he trusted Jak to have found a spot for Ricky to watch for Ryan's signal, and shoot appropriately from, that wouldn't easily be spotted.

Red Wings sat glaring down at him and J.B. as if he'd never seen them before this moment. The booze that was slopping unheeded out of his carelessly canted skull goblet had dulled his legendarily keen wits.

And maybe more than booze. The Angel lord's skin looked unhealthy, gray and blotchy. Rumors suggested he'd stumbled into a nuke hotspot some months back and had never been the same since. Mildred had suggested he'd picked up a dose of one or another of the hell brew of extremely toxic heavy metals that tended to find their way into fallout, some of which were known to cause mental and physical deterioration.

Taking advantage of the crowd's confusion and Red Wings' stunned inertia, Ryan stepped right up to the captive. Drawing the Bowie he'd appropriated from Chief Armorer Dominguez's stock of dead men's weps, he cut the bonds holding Leto's hands behind his back.

The tall, cadaverous prosecutor pushed himself forward with the aid of his staff. His gray beard and eyebrows bristled impressively. He pointed a trembling finger at Ryan.

"Seize the intruders!" he shouted. He had balls, Ryan had to admit, though maybe not much sense.

Leto sprang to his feet, ignoring what had to be fierce pins-and-needles sensations from his formerly pinioned arms, and shouted, "Wait!"

The Angel sec man had started moving forward again. Evidently the prosecuting Angel—or his violently capricious boss—frightened them more than a sniper hidden up in the heights. But glancing around, some of them actually looked relieved to obey the heir to the throne's voice of command.

Ryan held up his left hand, open. That was a signal for Ricky to hold his fire. For now.

"One thing I've got to say," J.B. said, taking his glasses off and polishing them with apparent calm. "You do know how to stir the shit, Ryan."

The one-eyed man shrugged. "It's a gift."

"Angels!" Leto cried. "Listen to me! We all know Tommy was a dirtbag. Why would we trust him?"

"He was our ally!" a voice cried from the crowd.

"He was a shithead," a female voice cried. "We never shoulda got tight with him."

"You all know me," Leto said. "You know that I've always lived to serve the Angels—and my father."

That stirred the old man to life.

"You ungrateful little shit," he rumbled. "You've been interfering with everything I've tried to do for years. Always want to take the pussy way out. But this is the Detroit Rubble. And the only language anybody understands here is a bullet in the gut and a boot in the face!"

"What about us?" Leto said. "Are the Angels mindless, violent stupes?"

He turned and waved an arm around. "You all know what we've built here. You all helped to build it."

"Yeah," Red Wings said, "and the bastards want to kick it all apart. Just for laughs."

He was sounding lucid again, but his flab jiggled like jelly with what Ryan couldn't tell was palsy or suppressed rage. Likely both.

He reminded Ryan of a volcano about to blow. It gave warning signs, just as the gang king was.

"If we try to fight everybody—the whole Rubble by ourselves—we lose. Anybody can see that. And it is possible to reason with them, at least some of them. We had an alliance with the Dragons, in spite of what a turd their boss was. We have a hands-off agreement with the Felonious Monks. And we had a bunch of other gangs join in to fight off the DPD invasion, don't forget. Do we want to try fighting them all, too? That's not a fight we can win. You know that plain as I do."

"What I don't get, kid," said Red Wings, almost calmly, "is why you'd let these coldheart blasters talk you into trying to get us to talk with that puke-eater Michaud and his bastard lapdog, Bone."

"Because they said to me the very things I was starting to see for myself, Father. If we and DPD continue to fight, we just wear ourselves down. And both of us lose."

"You have no right to speak!" the prosecutor shrieked. He seemed miffed at not being the center of attention anymore.

"Shut it," J.B. told him, "or I'll shut it for you."

He made no move for his Remington 870P, which, like Ryan's M4 carbine, was slung muzzle down over his back. But the graybeard's eyes widened, and his mouth shut.

Red Wings scowled as if thinking it all over. Then slowly, ponderously, he began to shake his huge head.

"You always preach the pussy way," he growled. "You're always trying to get us not to fight. You call that being a nuke-eating Desolation Angel?"

"Yes," Leto said.

But his rock-steady calm could no longer contain his father's drunkenness and rage and incipient insanity.

"You're not fit to be my son!" Red Wings roared, rising to his full impressive height.

He had to have been at least six-six, Ryan judged, and big as his belly was, his chest and shoulders were bigger. The Angels lord may have grown a few layers of lard over it, but he was still a moving mountain underneath. Looking at him standing there like a mad and raging god, Ryan didn't doubt he had the strength to take on a dozen DPD armored police—and win.

In the hot, humid, riverfront night, his enormous torso glistened like a glacier and ran visibly with sweat.

Ryan held his left hand up again. If Ricky got itchy and dropped the hammer on Red Wings, the whole arena was liable to go crazy with bloodlust for the interlopers. Leto was not likely to join in.

As calculated policy, if nothing else. What better way to cement his position, and to have all the Angels behind him, than avenge his father's treacherous murder by out-landers who admitted having worked for Hizzoner?

Red Wings was losing it completely. "Chill the little fucker!" he screeched, his voice rising to the point of ac-tual shrillness. Spittle sprayed out over his beard. "You're not my son!"

"Then fight me," Leto said, almost quietly.

Somehow that penetrated both the rising hubbub in the Joe and his father's mad fury. The bloodshot eyes blinked.

"What?" Red Wings said, his voice calm. He almost sounded reasonable again.

Ryan wasn't fooled. He'd seen how fast the Angel boss could flash from mood to mood.

Stay alert, he told himself. He didn't bother telling the man at his side. He knew there was no need.

"If we can't live together, Father," Leto said in a voice that was firm but full of regret, "then one of us has got to go. And I claim the right of trial by combat. I challenge you!"

"No need for this, Red Wings," the prosecutor stated, turning to his lord and master. "He's already on trial."

But Red Wings held up a hand. The skin was mottled with discolorations. Ryan didn't think they were all due to age.

"I accept," Red Wings said.

"At least name a champion!" the prosecutor said, almost frantic now. "No need to risk the whole succession—"

Red Wings stepped off his dais and backhanded the prosecutor across his gray-bushed mouth. The man flew backward eight feet and lay in a crumpled heap.

"Fuck that!" Red Wings bellowed. "No man fights my fights, you toad!"

He glared at his son and heir like a bull about to charge.

"Man to man, face-to-face," Red Wings said. "No blasters. No mercy."

He drew a knife from a scabbard at his hip, though the weapon was more an actual shortsword. It looked to Ryan like something an old-days gladiator would use, with a stout, two-edged tapering blade a good eighteen inches long.

In his vast paw it looked like a penknife.

"Leto," Ryan said.

The young man stood confronting his monstrous father from ten feet away. He didn't flinch from the blade any more than he had from his bellowing fury. He looked back over his shoulder at the one-eyed man.

Ryan flipped the big Bowie into the air, caught it by the tip. Then he stepped up to Leto and offered it.

"Take this," he said. "I can always get another one."

Leto looked from the knife, then up at Ryan's lone eye. He grinned and accepted the worn wooden hilt.

"Thanks," he said.

He turned to face Red Wings.

"I'm ready, Father," he said.

And from somewhere way high up behind Ryan's left shoulder, a cry rang through the steel rafters of the Joe Louis Arena.

"I found the taints who sniped Tommy! Let's get 'em!"

Chapter Twenty-Six

As the two combatants began to circle each other before
the throne and between the fires, the Angels' prosecutor
stirred. He raised his narrow head. His mustache and the
middle part of his beard were dyed pink with the blood
pouring from his flattened nose.

But he still rallied enough to yell, "Grab 'em now! Take
'em alive if you can!"

"No blasters!" Ryan shouted. "Not unless you have to!"

He still held hopes of settling this, which meant they
didn't want to go indiscriminately chilling Angels, even
to defend themselves.

With alarming alacrity Red Wings bull rushed Leto.
The younger man ducked a backhanded sword slash that
would have taken his head off his neck and danced aside.

He had a shot at his father's belly—a big target. He
didn't take it. A stab would've been more dangerous to him
than his opponent; it would never get through all that flab
and be able to penetrate the triple-tough body wall, Ryan
knew from experience. Plus it would risk tying his own
blade up long enough for Red Wings to get in a lick of his
own. Just a hammer fist from one of those ham-size hands
could compression fracture a man's neck, if not stave in his
skull. A slash would at least start him bleeding, and a knife
fight usually went to the man who weakened second....

Ryan had no chance to second-guess the blond-haired

young prince of the Desolation Angels. He and J.B. had troubles of their own.

In the form of ten or so hulking Angel sec men closing in on them with clubs ready to beat them down.

THOUGH JAK HAD warned him of Angels coming up the stairs to their platform that gave onto the catwalks criss-crossing above the arena floor, far below, the warning cry made Ricky jump.

The worst thing was, neither young man could do anything about the Angels closing in. They needed to keep their exact location secret as long as possible. Although Jak was a master of the stealthy chill, having a body tumble down the stairs with its throat cut—or just blood falling down the well like rain—would clue the other Angels pretty quick where their targets were.

The only thing they could do was stay where they were—Jak crouched inside the door, Ricky lying on his belly on the steel-mesh platform—and hope for the best.

The yell made Ricky turn reflexively. He saw a startled bearded face peering at him over the outside landing of the stairs. Then the man was whipping a Mini-14 carbine to his shoulder to blast Ricky, and the youth's scoped Husqvarna was aimed exactly the wrong way.

The Angel shrieked and dropped the blaster to clutch at his bearded cheek, where the steel tang of one of Jak's concealed throwing knives sprouted between his fingers. He fell back out of sight as blood streamed over his hands.

Jak turned and showed white teeth to Ricky in a nasty grin. "Eyes down," he said, pointing to the floor where Ryan was shouting not to open fire yet. "Watch back."

He turned back to the door.

"Ryan said no chilling unless necessary."

Jak shrugged.

"Gonna cut," he said. He didn't even glance back at his friend.

"What now?" Mildred asked.

Krysty shook her head. "I don't have a clue."

They crouched behind the top row of seats, some distance from the entrance nearest the Joe's main door. Fortunately, most of the audience of hundreds upon hundreds of Angels were too raptly intent on the show down on the floor to bother looking for random intruders, though they had seen a group of eight or ten head for another exit, evidently intent on smoking out the sniper.

"Perhaps we should withdraw to the corridor," Doc suggested. "That way we might have an easier time defending the doorway."

Krysty shook her head. She could feel her sentient red hair hugging her scalp in tension.

"If they start roaming the lobby, we're stuck out in the open," she said. "I think our best bet is to hold tight here."

She heard a shout from directly below.

"Hope you're right, Krysty," Mildred said, "because here the bastards come!"

As the Angels' sec men closed in, Ryan and J.B. put themselves back to back with the reflex born of long habit.

"Still sure we want to try not chilling them as much as possible?" J.B. asked.

"Yeah."

It wasn't that Ryan had gone soft and runny to the core. It was that he was more than up to simple arithmetic. And that arithmetic told him that a thousand pissed-off Desolation Angels versus his hearty band of seven warriors equaled them all becoming bloody mush very quick, no matter how skillful, hard or cold they were. When he'd walked into this situation, he'd done so knowing full well that it was one he and his friends would never cut and blast their way out of.

Now I just have to hope I didn't get it too far wrong, he thought as from the corner of his eye he saw Leto elude another furious rush from his gigantic father. And that we can somehow walk away.

An Angel half a head taller than Ryan reached out a beefy hand to grab him. Ryan's hand darted out, caught the thumb and peeled it straight back up against the forearm. The man squealed like a pig as it broke.

Ryan smiled. He'd said not to chill Angels if possible. He hadn't said anything about hurting them.

If they wanted to play rough, let them pay in pain.

But his jaw was immediately rocked by a pile-driver punch from his blind left side. Yellow lightning lanced through his skull as his head snapped clockwise.

He lashed out with an instinctive side kick. It connected, and his unseen assailant grunted. Ryan widened his stance, trying to blink away the dazzle patches floating behind his eyes.

Another Angel, dreadlocks streaming, came flying at him from the right, aiming for a head tackle. Ryan caught the Angel's arms and twisted his hips hard left, throwing the wiry brown-skinned man into the burly shaved-head who was bent over clutching his booted balls.

From the corner of his eye he saw Leto evade another clumsy, roaring rush by his father. Red Wings staggered several steps, visibly fighting his own tremendous momentum before he managed to stop. He turned back.

"Stand and face me, you cowardly little shit!"

Leto stood and faced him. He held his arms out to his sides. "Here I am, Father," he said. "Come get me."

Ryan was busy weaving left and right, evading grabs and

blows, snatching limbs and vests to help steer his attackers into each other. That was the thing about an all-on-one—or two—pile-on attack, it was hard not to get in each others' way.

Of course, all this bobbing and turning made his head feel as if it were about to spin off his neck. But he kept his feet and his focus against the dizziness by force of his vanadium-steel will.

Ryan saw J.B. bring the butt of his 870 hard up under the jaw of a huge Angel with blond locks flowing past door-filling shoulders. The man's eyes closed and his head snapped back. He reeled away as J.B. wheeled smartly to bury the muzzle of the scattergun in the solar plexus of another outsize sec man.

Ryan had said "no blasters." J.B. had correctly taken that to mean don't shoot anybody. They weren't going to win by playing nice. Or fair.

Then hands simultaneously caught both of Ryan's arms from different directions. A booted foot sank into his hard gut. As the air whooshed out of him and he doubled over at the impact, he saw more Angels clambering over the wall to join the assault on the outsiders.

Even as Ryan heard Red Wings bellow again, and his vision started to grow black from the edges in, he knew that this time, it wasn't going to be enough.

Sometimes it didn't work.

Sometimes nothing worked.

Sometimes all the tactical savvy, the cunning, the skill, the courage, the plain determination to survive…weren't enough.

RICKY KEPT PEERING doggedly over the iron sights of his DeLisle, switching aim from Angel to Angel in an attempt to keep covering whichever seemed the most immediate threat to his friends.

He got plenty of shots. By his own reckoning, which his insecurities wouldn't allow to be anything but conservative, he could easily have dropped three of the sec men swarming J.B. and Ryan. He had heard Ryan's order to hold fire, and he understood the reasoning; as long as the Angels weren't shooting, it would be self-chilling, as well as sentencing his friends to death, to open fire.

But if one of the sec men looked as if he was about to put either of Ricky's friends and idols down for good, the youth was determined to drop the hammer and take the consequences.

From behind he heard a strange sound, a furious squalling like a wildcat fighting a wolf. He looked back over his shoulder.

The Angels had tried to grab Jak the conventional way and promptly snatched back hands streaming blood from the gashes inflicted in them by the jagged glass and metal bits he had sewn into the fabric of his jacket. Now one of them had grabbed Jak by the ankles and yanked his legs right out from under him, dropping him on his back half in and half out of the door to the stairs.

Ricky got up, turning. Yelling and slashing with his knives, Jak was dragged rapidly out of Ricky's sight onto the stairwell, where the sound of stomping ensued. More Angels crowded in the door to get at Ricky.

He actually managed to drop two of them, one with a buttplate thrust to the bridge of the nose and another with a baseball-style swing of the flat of the butt against the shaven sides of a ginger top-knotted head, before they reached him and clubbed him down with huge, hard fists.

Chapter Twenty-Seven

Krysty screamed in fury and frustration as hands seized her biceps from behind. She flung her head back rapidly, trying to head bash the nose of the man who held her. Her red hair, uncoiled long again, lashed about her face and shoulders like snakes.

But two men had grabbed her from either side. Her head whipped air, so hard she felt a twinge in her neck.

The three of them had fought furiously as Angels swarmed up over the seats at them. Doc jabbed with his sword stick. Mildred swung her M16 by the muzzle brake two-handed, knocking Angels backward over the seats and sending them reeling back stunned and bleeding along the walkway to either side with the sheer power of her stocky frame—and her rage—despite the longblaster's lightweight synthetic stock. Krysty used her MP5 like a riot baton, jabbing with the muzzle, bashing with the butt, kicking and punching with her not-inconsiderable strength and skill where she thought it'd do the most good.

But even with their backs to the wall, their foes came at them from both sides and the front. Their advantage of height and position was quickly lost as Angels dashed up the stairs on either side of them to close in.

Krysty side kicked the man who had her right arm. He turned to take the brunt on his hip and the meaty part of the thigh and hung on. She saw Doc felled by a sucker punch to the back of his head.

She twisted her body left, ignoring the pain as her right arm was cruelly yanked. She intended to put an aimed kick into the man who had her left arm. But he stepped back as she turned.

Beyond him Mildred was tackled from behind into the backs of the top rows of seats. She gasped as the chair tops hit her in the belly and doubled her over.

A blow to the temple made Krysty's vision blur and her head reel. A woman flew over the top row of seats to grab her legs in a tackle.

It was all over but the pounding.

IT'S ALL OVER, Ryan thought as more smelly, sweaty bodies piled on top of him, pinning his back to the floor.

Some of the Angel newcomers circled like wolves around a campfire, looking for the chance to put the boot in. But the Angel sec men, now that both Ryan and J.B. had been dragged down, were able to keep that from happening as they wrestled to fully subdue the pair.

Ryan glanced out from under a rank, sweat-sopping armpit to see the tall, gaunt prosecutor standing by with his staff, fingering his long gray beard and looking grim. Ryan guessed he wasn't happy not to be able to order the outlanders chilled on the spot. But the man was currently intent on watching the battle between father and son for supremacy of the Desolation Angels.

He heard a bellow of pure hate-filled rage, laced with a bright thin peal of sheer frustration.

Several of the sec men on top of him turned to look. His head was freed up enough for him to raise it and look for himself.

Fifteen feet away, near the wall between the floor and the stands, Red Wings stood with pale columnar legs braced. His son, looking like a child, in fact, had his legs clamped around the sides of the gigantic, heaving chest. His arms were wrapped around Red Wings' neck.

The giant had his bearded chin pressed into his collarbone, preventing Leto from choking him. This could be done even to a man as immense as Red Wings, whose neck was armored in muscle and fat. If you knew the sleight of it. Fists like mallets pounded at the much smaller man.

But Leto clung on grimly.

"You nuke-withered fool!" Red Wings howled. "You're gonna ruin it! We coulda conquered the whole damn rubble!"

His agonized cry, surprisingly high-pitched for a man with a voice like a volcano with indigestion, seemed to shake the floor beneath Ryan, and the whole arena around them.

"No, Father," Leto said. "We couldn't."

And he plunged the Bowie Ryan had given him through the side of his father's tree-trunk-thick neck. All the way in, until the brass cross-guard dug into freckled, greenish, mottled skin.

Then with a grunt of effort Leto pressed the blade down between his father's jaw and his chest, cutting free of his throat into the open air.

A river of blood, an ocean of blood, shot down the front of Red Wings' chest and belly to splash on the floor.

The bloodshot green eyes rolled up. The huge knees buckled, first the left, then the right. The mighty lord and master of the Desolation Angels fell forward onto his face with a vast, sodden thump.

Leto jumped clear at the last instant to stand looking down at his father's still-heaving body.

Ryan saw tears start down his tan cheeks.

"But we can secure our place in the Rubble for years to come," he said. "And that's what I mean to do."

The prosecutor was staring in sheer shocked horror at his fallen master. At Leto's words he shook himself visibly and cracked his staff loudly three times hard on the concrete.

"The Maximum Leader is dead!" the prosecutor trumpeted. "Long live the Maximum Leader—Leto of the Angels!"

Leto shot him a scowl, but the crowd took up the chant.

Turning to the crowd, the blond young man raised both arms high. His father's blood rolled down his right forearm from the knife clutched in his fist like retrograde red vines.

For a moment he stood and accepted the crowd's acclaim. Then he brought his arms down, crossed them in front of his chest—taking care not to stab himself in the process—and flung them out from side to side in a fast, decisive gesture.

The chant cut off.

"I promised my father," he declaimed, "that I will make the Desolation Angel Nation strong—a power to endure for decades. And I will. Will you help me?"

"Yes!" the Angels roared.

Leto nodded. He turned back to gaze broodingly on his father's elephantine white body. The clamor began to diminish as the crowd grew curious about what their new lord would say or do next.

"Might as well get off us, boys," Ryan heard J.B. say. "Seeing as there's been a change of administration and all."

Ryan felt the men who still lay on top of him twist as they looked to their leader for support. Leto nodded.

Ryan sighed as the weight came off. It had taken a power of effort to breathe with all that rank beef piled on his chest.

Leto came up and offered his left hand. Ryan considered

the fact he still held the red-dripping blade in his right. Then he reached up his own left hand.

The two grabbed each other forearm to forearm. Despite Ryan's greater height and weight, the young Angel boss hauled him right up to his feet.

Ryan nodded his thanks, then he jerked his head toward Red Wings.

"You did him a favor, you know."

Leto nodded. "I know."

A door was opened in the wall around the former rink. Angels escorted Ryan and the rest of the companions out onto the floor. Their various bruises and scrapes showed that the treatment they were getting now was considerably gentler than it had been just a few moments earlier. Ryan scowled when he saw how both Krysty's beautiful green eyes had been blackened.

But she smiled like the sun. "I'll be fine," she said through puffed, bleeding lips.

"You should see the other guys," Mildred added with sullen triumph.

"It's true, Lord Leto," a limping black Angel said. "They fought like Dead Elvises on jolt."

"Everybody fit to fight?" Ryan asked his companions.

"I got my pins under me," J.B. said.

"While I have certainly felt better," Doc said, "I am not dead yet."

The others all acknowledged they were holding up. Claimed to be, anyway. Ryan turned to the Angel lord.

"So where do we stand, Leto?" he asked.

Before the man could answer, the prosecutor came sweeping up, as grand as a baron and twice as important.

"Congratulations," he cried in his most throbbing voice. "Command me, O Maximum Leader!"

Ryan couldn't help noticing he didn't kneel or anything.

Clearly, he reckoned the new boss would need to lean hard on somebody as he got his feet under him. Ryan knew the type well. He was the sort who'd never sit a throne and was fine with that, so long as he could be the power behind it.

Leto smiled and nodded at him. "Ace," he said. "Grab yourself a blaster and head for the front line. There's still a war going on."

The face of Leto's prosecutor-turned-sycophant went just one or two shades of gray lighter than his beard. His dark eyes got wide in their deep, dark sockets.

"But, my lord! I can serve you and our Angel Nation so much better here!"

Leto looked him hard up and down.

"No, you can't," he said. "You turn your coat too quick."

Ignoring the man's sputtering objections, he turned to the sec men who stood nearby looking none too sure of themselves.

"Get him a wep and see him to the fight. If he tries to wiggle out, then cut him loose to leave Angel land in any direction he wants—forever."

The graybeard couldn't quite conceal the gaunt man's smile of relief.

"Minus his balls," Leto added. "Since he'll have shown he's got no use for them anymore."

As the crestfallen former prosecutor was hustled away by maliciously grinning sec men, Ryan said to Leto, "Thought you were the boy arguing that the Angels of all people understood something other than a boot in the teeth."

Leto laughed. "Sometimes it takes the boot to get their attention," he said. "Just as happy to get that part out of the way."

He looked at the knife in his hand. "Somebody get me a rag."

He picked the least obviously befouled—or at least the driest looking—of the half dozen handkerchiefs instantly proffered him. He wiped the Bowie's long blade clean of his father's gore. Throwing the bloodstained rag to the floor, he tossed the knife in the air, caught it by the blade and held the hilt out to Ryan.

"Thanks," he said.

"Keep it," Ryan said. "I can always pick up another."

Leto shrugged and stuck the Bowie through his belt.

"Hope you'll still feel that way when you hear what I've decided. I've reconsidered. We still need peace—you're right that we can't fight the whole nuking Rubble and survive, much less win. But I see now that peace will never be possible with Michaud and Bone in charge up in that funky stone fortress of theirs."

Ryan looked at him hard a moment. Leto's gaze met his squarely.

Chapter Twenty-Eight

"Are you sure this will work?" Leto asked.

He and a group of a half dozen Angels were lying up in some trashed-out buildings a few hundred yards mostly east and a little south of Hizzoner's HQ with Ryan and the companions, watching the looming limestone structure through windows and gaps in the roofless walls. Late-afternoon shadows threw the figures of barricades and men toward the broken masonry walls in ever-attenuating form. And one hulking vehicle.

"No," Ryan said. "What I am sure of is this gives us our best shot."

"Even after we didn't persuade a single gang to join us?"

Ryan showed him a smile and a nod. "Oh, yeah."

Though you may not be pleasantly surprised at how things shake out from that, he thought. But though he liked and respected the young man he and his friends had helped become the new Angel Maximum Leader—well, that was personal. And not personal enough to get in the way of survival.

And things would fall into place better for the Desolation Angels, more likely than not. If the plan worked.

If it didn't, none of them would be around to sweat it.

"Not much activity," Mildred commented.

"Got enough guards," J.B. said. "At least twenty out in the yard now, just this section. Guarding the gate and the perimeter emplacements, watching the front door, hanging out in that tent."

"Jak says those're most of the sec men he can see outside," Ricky offered, "which means it's most of them."

"Real action's a few hundred yards south, anyway," Leto said grimly.

"If they're getting ready for a big push against us," asked Mikhail, a slim young Angel with a long brown braid down the back of his vest, "why don't they have their heavy hitter down at their staging area just this side of the Seven-Five, instead of parked on their front porch?"

The V-100 Commando sat parked not far from the corner of the temple end of the grandiose DPD headquarters compound. The block-long bulk of the old Masonic Temple and its annex had been surrounded by a barbed-wire perimeter fence. It enclosed a large space on the southeastern side, the one they were looking at. The wire ran down the far side of the street beyond, which Ryan had learned was 2nd Street. It took a bite out of the square cropland southwest of the headquarters, the whole of which had been scraped clean clear to topsoil to deny concealment to an enemy. It then cut across to Cass Avenue, which ran along the side of headquarters nearest the hidden watchers, enclosing what had already been the DPD mustering yard and the busted-up remnants of some flattened buildings to the southeast.

The fortification was still obviously a work in progress. Only a few coils of razor wire were in place, and only the biggest chunks of smashed-up concrete and stone had been removed from the southeast sector. But it was still an impressive job, Ryan had to admit. They had firing pits dug, a big tent set up for a sec squad ready room and actual watchtowers at the southwest and southeast corners of the compound, standing a dozen or so feet in the air on legs bolted or welded together from various lengths of metal rods, beams and trusses. A pair of cargo wags, already loaded with supplies under tarps, sat parked between the tent and the building.

They'd even erected a gate across the main street that led to the battle zone, which was the southern continuation of 2nd Street where it took a dogleg along Temple, the cross street running along the HQ building's southeast side. The gate had the beginnings of a watch shack and was blocked by the flat bed of an old truck, piled with big hunks of busted building. "They got nervous about somebody making a play for their HQ," Leto answered his man. "That's why they fortified the place. They've been sucking in patrolmen from all over their little empire to try to knock us out on the next hit. Even if it means letting some of the gangs around them to the north, like the Jokers or the Brush Park Rangers, tear off chunks of the territory they've conquered recently."

"Could they do that?" Mildred asked. "Take you out with one blow?"

Leto grunted. "That's why I'm along on this crazy train in the first place. We don't know. But given that the allies who helped us against their first push across the expressway have all got cold feet and are holding back, it's not a chance I'm ready to take."

"And it is a chance Hizzoner's all primed and ready to," J.B. said.

"Why d'you reckon your buddies decided to back off from you?" Ryan asked. He had what he thought was a pretty good notion or two, but he wanted a line on how much insight the new Angel lord had.

He felt urgency crawling in his belly like soldier ants. He stamped on it hard. They had hours to go before the time came to make their move.

"You mean, aside from the jack Michaud's been willing to spread around to buy 'em off?" Leto asked. "Or the fact that he's also been bold about sending Bone's SWAT death squads to lay hurt on the lesser players who won't fall into line?

"They—I mean, everybody else in the Rubble—feared my father. He always was a true stoneheart. That worked ace for him, I have to admit—even if it's not my style. But where once they were mainly afraid to fuck with him because they knew what kind of a hammer he had for a hand—and he was always willing to remind you—for the past few years it got to be more and more about his crazy rages. And just general craziness.

"They don't know yet whether to fear me. To get them to accept what a good friend I can be, I need to show the Rubble how much worse I am as an enemy."

"Pulling this off would certainly show them that," Mildred said.

Leto showed his easy rogue's grin. "That's also why I'm here."

"They're also prolly afraid we got more wag-chiller missiles," said Donut, a roly-poly Angel with a shaved head and a perpetual twinkle in his blue eyes.

He took a bite from one of his namesake pastries. The Angels made them in their bakery, using grain grown in the Rubble, and traded for items not grown in the Cobo or one of their outside garden plots. Ryan had no idea where they got their hands on sugar, but the things were tasty.

"Too bad we don't," Donut added. He was one of the Angels' top weaponsmiths, which was why he was along on a job that called for stealth and agility—or one of his pet creations was, anyway. Though Ryan had to admit that when they'd made their way here he'd done just fine in the sneaking department and kept up without showing signs of effort.

"Be core of a good mobile reserve for them," Ryan said. "The Commando. If they can bust a hole in your lines, Bone can exploit it by sending in the big war wag with some cavalry and a phalanx of the SWAT armored boys. Smash right through and drive deep into the heart of your turf, leaving patrol division to roll up your lines."

Then he offered Leto a half smile. "Sorry."

Leto shook his shaggy head. "Nothing shaken. It's not like you can make it any more obvious than the facts do."

"They have been shifting lots of men to their staging area the past couple days," Donut said. "How many you reckon are left inside?"

J.B. took off his glasses and polished them thoughtfully. "Couple hundred blasters at least. Plus the usual array of clerks and jerks, some of whom may know which end the bullet comes out of."

"So enough to leave us all a greasy red smear on the pavement," Mikhail said.

"'Bout the size of it, yeah."

"Right," Ryan said, eyeing the sun as it neared the trees and low, blocky ruins to the west. "Time to shift out of here. Find a place to grab some shut-eye where DPD patrols are less likely to run across us. We've got hours yet before it's time to make our move."

He rose from his crouch.

"Why are we out here so early, then?" the lithe black woman with the katana strapped over the back of her colors asked.

"We wanted to scope out their defenses."

"But weren't you here often enough when you worked for them?"

"Easy, Raven," Leto said in smiling warning.

"Yeah," Ryan said.

Her show of hostility didn't faze him. Leto relied on her and thought her skills would be useful in what they had to do. Liking Ryan and the rest wasn't optional so much as irrelevant.

"But I reckoned they might make a few changes after we split," he said. "And they have. Like this wire perimeter, the gates and all."

"And you're sure you can get us inside?" asked Bronk, a medium-high cinder block of a woman with the pistol grip of a cut-down Mossberg 500 20-gauge pump shotgun protruding over her left shoulder. She had a blunt, frank, freckled face and blond braids hanging over shoulders that would've done credit to a man her size.

"Yeah," Ryan said.

He turned to go. The others looked at Leto.

The Angel boss stood up and went to follow Ryan.

"Still wish we had another wag chiller," Mikhail said as he rose from where he'd been lying in an empty doorway.

"We don't need wag chillers," J.B. said cheerfully. "We're going to raise an ample amount of mischief."

"What kind of mischief?" Raven asked.

J.B. actually grinned at her.

"Malicious."

HERE I AM again, Ricky thought. Getting ready to chill another sentry.

Once again, without making any noise. We all hope.

He lay on his belly in grass moist and fragrant from a rain shower that had passed and left the sky clear before midnight. It had rapidly soaked through his shirt to dampen his belly. He was just fewer than a hundred yards from the northwest side of the Detroit City headquarters. He was surprised even the rank grass, which didn't grow higher than a foot or so most places, hadn't been cleared away.

He had the Husqvarna pointed at Hizzoner's HQ. He just hoped he didn't have to use it. If he did, it meant the plan had blown up and likely had knocked them all into a world of hurt.

It seemed that, as Jak reported—and as a quick circuit through cover at a safe distance by the others confirmed before they bedded down for a few hours—the defenses, as beefed up as they were, were concentrated almost exclusively on the side facing their rival power players, the Desolation Angels.

He understood why that might be a priority. Even resources as comparatively great as those Hizzoner and Bone commanded had resources, and hours in a day weren't anything the richest baron could bank. Still. He could see too clearly how it could turn around to bite Michaud in his broad ass.

Several lanterns hung from poles set next to the yellowish stone wall. They burned with a low, flickering light so dim its orange was almost brown. Ricky wondered if they were running low on fuel, with most of the night gone and dawn not much more than an hour away.

Two sentries with slung longblasters had appeared around the Cass Avenue end of the annex and walked at an angle toward the corner of the main structure. Ricky tracked them with his longblaster. Almost at once a figure began walking toward them.

Ricky held aim on the nearer of the sentries. He had his finger on the trigger. Just in case.

The newcomer was large and portly, additionally bulky in the black body armor and visored helmet of Hizzoner's SWAT. He swaggered up to the two sentries and said something too low for Ricky to hear. The sentries abruptly braced as if coming to attention.

The SWAT sec man casually raised his right hand. Even in the dim glow of the nearest lanterns it was possible to make out that it was a large handblaster with what looked like a big can on the end of it. The farther guard's head suddenly jerked back.

But the second guard just gaped, not even grasping what had just happened right next to him. With quick efficiency the phony sec man turned the fat sound suppresser to almost touch the other sec man's left eye and blew out the right rear curve of his skull.

The clack of a 1911-model .45 action cycling reached Ricky's ears. A second grotesque mound of darkness joined the first on the bare soil at the "SWAT" man's booted feet.

He turned and walked briskly back around the corner of the main HQ. More figures slipped around the corner ahead of him, ran silently past him and quickly dragged the two chilled guards into the deepest shadows in the angle of the two structures. The meaty man in SWAT gear turned and walked back to where he'd come from.

"That was cold," Ricky murmured.

"Yeah," Ryan said. "Ace in the line."

He rose from the grass a few yards to Ricky's right. He had his own weapon ready. He'd been both guarding Ricky and keeping watch lest anything go wrong.

"You ready?" he asked the youth. He was wearing SWAT blacks and visored helmet, too.

"Yes, sir!" Ricky said. Ryan didn't like to be called "sir," but sometimes the kid just forgot himself.

He got away with it this time. Ryan simply turned and took off hunched over for the gap they'd cut in the wire. The rest had already gone through.

Ricky jumped up and ran to follow.

LETO LOOKED UP from beside the half-sunken door. Ryan saw his teeth flash beneath the open visor of his helmet. He wore the third set of SWAT kit they'd found. It fit him like several sacks, but they weren't in a position to be too picky.

Several of the other figures wore patrol uniforms. DPD weren't the only ones who could salvage items from the persistent battlefield. Ryan reckoned it was a good thing the black sec-men suits hid bloodstains so well. Then again, he reckoned a lot of them got blood on them on a pretty regular basis.

"Doesn't it seem stupe to the point of arrogance that they're not really bothering to guard any direction except south?" Raven asked as Ryan joined the rest with Ricky trotting at his heels.

"They likely are relying on distance to act as a buffer and their roving patrols to catch anybody trying to infiltrate from another direction. And yeah. Stupe arrogance sounds about right."

J.B. gestured at Ricky to follow him. He set off along the wall to the southwest. Mikhail and another Angel, a wiry black man named Keiser, went with the pair.

Ryan stepped up to the door. "You up to jimmying the lock?" Leto asked. "I can get more light here if you need it."

"I think I got it," Ryan said.

He walked down the short flight of steps, took hold of the door handle and pulled the heavy sec door open.

Jak immediately slipped inside to secure the dungeon hallway. Raven followed a beat later.

"See, when we checked out of the place," Ryan told the astonished Angel boss, "we sort of fixed it so the door wouldn't lock."

Chapter Twenty-Nine

J.B. ambled casually around the southwest corner of the tall churchlike tower into the part of the compound Bone's sec men *did* bother to defend.

The yard was better lit by lanterns and even some torches, though not by a wide margin. The V-100 was parked well out of the light, though, but incautiously near the 2nd Street wire. Its angular rear end was pointed right at him. Its 360-cubic-inch Chrysler V8 engine throbbed at a low idle. J.B. suspected Bone was still nervous enough about the possibility of the Angels having at least one more wag chiller to want to avoid having it silhouetted by the considerably brighter light streaming from the actual entryway.

Now, had *he* been in possession of a wire-guided antitank rocket like the one that had fried the Commando's baby brother, the BearCat, he would have been tempted to set up in the ruins several hundred yards west of 2nd and get himself a nice flank shot over the fields and weed patches against a target that was backlit by the illumination broadcast from the HQ doors. Anyway, he thought their plan for dealing with the hulking war wag was *much* cooler.

J.B. was dressed as what he was: a civilian tech of the sort they knew DPD hired to do things like maintain their motor pool—and their weps. So he was wearing his usual clothes, except he'd left his trademark battered fedora in the hands of his apprentice, Ricky, still lurking back behind the corner with Keiser and Mikhail. The hat made his silhouette too distinctive now, given he and his friends had been familiar figures in these parts for about two weeks.

Without it, he was just another anonymous tech grunt. No frontline DPD fighter would give him a second glance.

The Commando blaster ignored him as he strolled up on the street side of the armored wag. The man sat perched on the rim of the top blister's hatch with his legs dangling inside, gazing off across the yard, from which the sounds of shouted conversation and other activity floated. A cigarette ember glowed in front of his partially averted face as J.B. walked up to the car's steel flank and started climbing one-handed up the rungs welded to the hull.

"Evenin'," he said softly as he neared the top.

He could smell the stale sweat soaked through the man's black T-shirt. He'd smelled the smoke far off, which was one reason he disparaged those who smoked on watch, even as a man who was known to enjoy a good cheroot from time to time. Or even just an available one.

The man turned his head suddenly and, as expected, looked down. His expression showed mild annoyance, not alarm. He was inside a secure compound, surrounded by barbed wire and hard men with blasters. What did he possibly have to fear from somebody appearing out of the muggy Motor City night?

J.B. showed him by shooting him precisely between the eyes.

The blaster report was satisfactorily quiet. The *clack-clack* of the heavy slide reciprocating wouldn't attract much attention even if the other noise failed to mask it.

The tubby Angels armorer, Donut, had made more than one noise suppressor. Quite competent jobs he'd done, too, by J.B.'s critical eye. The one he'd lent J.B. was attached to a Glock 30. The man's body jerked. The air filled with a stench as his relaxing bowels voided. Hope none of that gets inside, J.B. thought as he grabbed the man by the T-shirt and yanked him over the wag's side.

Below he heard the other three scurrying forward to catch the falling chill. J.B. ascended the ladder. As he reached the top he heard a stifled exclamation of disgust from one of the men who'd grabbed the sec man. It sounded like Ricky.

Be just the kid's luck to find his hand planted on the seat of the dude's soiled pants.

"Marco? What the nuke kind of game you think you're playin—"

J.B. leaned into the hatch behind the blaster. The second crewman was right beneath, his face upturned to stare out the hatch.

The Glock's muzzle-flash illuminated the greatest look of surprise J.B. had ever seen on a human face.

He slipped inside. Landing on the chill, he stepped off and took a look around. The place reeked. J.B. detected stale smoke, sweat, rancid human grease, burned propellant and lubricating oil. The methanol fuel the engine had been modified to burn made the interior smell like the worst sort of gaudy, though with less vomit. The chill's excrement didn't help any.

He heard a tap against the outer hull. That'd be Ricky, letting him know they'd stashed the first dead crewman in the shadows out of sight of the main yard around the built-up corner. Anybody who happened to come this way would spot him, but then again, they'd already ensured it was unlikely a sentry would until watch change, a little more than an hour away. If somebody did happen along— well, that was just the way of the world. And they'd deal with it accordingly.

They always did.

J.B. let out a low whistle. A moment later Ricky's head appeared as a darker shape against the starry sky.

"Get down here and help me boost this guy up to our Angels pals," J.B. instructed. "And this time, mind not to give him a boost up by the seat of his pants."

"Right," Ricky said.

"Oh—and where's my hat?"

The fedora struck him in the face a touch harder than strictly necessary.

Once they got the chill clear of the compartment, J.B. took stock of the machine. He nodded. It might still smell like a stickie's outhouse in a slaughterhouse, but the inside was spotless, and a quick check showed everything seemed to be operating well.

The two Angels clambered inside. Mikhail wrinkled his nose and adjusted his wire-rimmed specs. The dull glow of the instrument panels was enough to show Keiser's dark face take on an ashen look.

"You two get acquainted with our shiny new ride," J.B. said. He settled into the driver's seat. "Ricky, get back up, poke your head out, keep a watch outside."

"What happens if somebody talks to me?"

"Point to your throat and act like you got sudden-onset laryngitis," J.B. said. "Damn, Mildred's started to get me to talk like her. All medico-like."

"But what happens if somebody gets suspicious?" Ricky asked nervously.

"Son," J.B. said gently, "we're inside a twenty-two-thousand-pound armored car, with an automatic blaster up top that'll shoot through a building. We're the biggest, baddest dog in the yard. What do you think happens?"

"Everybody good?" Ryan asked.

The outer door was shut again. Ryan had fixed the

jammed lock so that it caught again. It still had a nice push bar to let them out, and they didn't want anybody coming in at a bad time. The door wasn't used much, obviously, but Ryan didn't want to leave any more to chance than he had to.

Low-voiced assent came from the others. Leto stood beside him as the two group leaders ran their eyes over their contingents, just to make sure. The lanterns in here weren't any brighter than the ones right outside, but that was the same light anybody they encountered down here would be seeing them in. So it evened out.

Ryan, Leto and Donut were still dolled up in their scavvied SWAT armor. Donut had Raven's katana strapped over his pack as if bringing in a confiscated wep. Its rightful owner would follow him in line. She had on her Angel colors, with handcuffs closed but not locked on her wrists before her. She had an exceedingly sullen expression on her handsome, high-browed face. Ryan didn't know if that was acting or not.

Then he corrected himself. He didn't know how much was acting. She still wasn't thrilled about strolling into the belly of the beast alongside five of its extremely new hired blasters.

But it was the normally sunny blond-braided female fireplug of an Angel known as Bronk who asked, "You sure you know where we're going?"

She was playing prisoner, too, with the handcuffs closed around her massive wrists. Ryan hoped they wouldn't fall open and give the game away.

"Yeah," he said. "We spent a lot of time in this building. We know where Bone's office is and where Michaud's quarters are. Not that we ever got an invite up there. Plus we know a lot of other things about this building."

"It's crazier than you can imagine," Mildred said. "Makes

you wonder what those old Masons were smoking when they designed the place."

She had on a patrol-division uniform and wore a DPD ball cap to conceal her distinctive beaded plaits. Otherwise no attempt had been made to disguise her features. She was far less strikingly distinctive than Krysty, and a stocky black sec woman was not an unusual sight in Hizzoner's headquarters.

Krysty had her unmistakable fire-red hair piled into a foul knit cap to hide it. Her cheeks were smudged with grime, her eyes downcast, and she wore a shabby coat that looked as if it had been used to fend off wildcats and smelled as if a dog had been the last wearer. Doc had shed his long frock coat for a similarly disreputable jacket and wore a ball cap pulled low over his stringy silver-white hair, which was also distinctive in his way. The two would shuffle along with faces downturned, as was pretty standard operating procedure for captives of the DPD.

A growl came from within the black cloth hood that covered Jak's head. He was antsy and bordering on claustrophobic about being surrounded by stone walls underground as it was. But it was necessary, as were the black gloves that concealed his albino hands, which were fake manacled, too.

Ryan, Leto and his friends had debated trying to walk in openly, with the Angels playing sec men who were triumphantly parading their captures, the renegade blasters. They had decided quickly that gave them poor odds. It attracted too much attention, which was the last thing they wanted if this already crazy plan was to have the faintest hope of coming off. So they had to go the other way and ensure that nobody they came across would make anything of Ryan's crew.

The final Angel was also dressed as a simple sec man.

He was an enormously tall, leanly powerful black man with a shaved head called Friendly. Ryan reckoned it was one of those opposite nicknames, like calling some giant dude Tiny. As far as he could tell, though, Friendly didn't really act the *opposite* of his name, so much as he seemed entirely uncommunicative. Still, the way his eyes glared at a body out of sockets sunk deep into a scar-cheeked skull of a face did not encourage intimacy.

He did look natural in the uniform. Enough that, everybody hoped, combined with his forbidding appearance, not even his nominally fellow sec men would care to look close enough to notice how high his sleeves and pants legs rode. The Angels hadn't exactly had a chance to tailor their salvaged clothes for this mission.

Everybody checked out, they set off down the hall. At once, Leto said, "Visor down, Donut."

"But you got yours up, boss!"

"I don't have a giant beard like no sec man from Bone's crew anybody's ever seen. Tuck that damn thing down inside your blouse while you're at it. Anyway, I'm gonna be trotting alongside the prisoners well to the back. Nobody's gonna see my face."

"I got mine down, too," said Ryan, who brought up the rear. The heft of the M4 in his hands did little to reassure him. Not because of its light weight, but because if he actually had to use it, odds were they were all well on their way to staring up at the ceiling while they cooled down to room temperature. "Tip your head back and look out beneath the damn visor."

A low, piteous moan came from behind one of the heavy, closed doors along the corridor.

"Some poor locked-up bastard is not having a good day," Bronk said.

"Well," Ryan replied, "it might just be fixing to get better pretty quick. Depending on how good a day we have."

Just as they reached the end of the corridor, a man strolled around the corner. He was dressed in a threadbare suit complete with necktie, and he was peering at a thick sheaf of papers clipped to a clipboard as if he could actually read in that light.

He noticed the procession quick enough and stopped.

"Prisoner transport," Leto called from down the hall. He sounded a little jaunty for a SWAT man, but he wasn't along for his acting skills. "Stand clear, please!"

That *definitely* didn't sound like any of Bone's elite coldheart corps Ryan had ever heard, but the clerk obediently pressed his skinny shoulders back against a sweating stone wall.

"Visors down is strictly contrary to regulations!" he announced snippily.

They ignored him. As Donut passed him, his eyes got wide behind his specs.

"What's that under your visor? A *beard?*"

He turned and raced off the way he had come, hollering at the top of his lungs, "Help! Help! Intruders!"

Chapter Thirty

Calm as you please, the fat, bearded Donut raised his visor with his black-gauntleted left hand.

With his other he brought up his .45 and shot the running clerk through the back of his head. The man sprawled forward onto his face. He slid all the way into the far wall, leaving a smear of blood on the floor.

"Nice shot," Mildred said.

"Thank you," Donut replied.

She sighed. "Too bad we're blown now."

"We aren't," Ryan rapped. "Necessarily. Leto, secure the next corridor. If somebody answers his yapping, try to bluff them. If that doesn't work, Donut can chill them. Mildred, Friendly, help me haul this chill into one of the empty cells."

Raven shot a hot-eyed glare over her shoulder at him. Little as she liked the whole scheme, she liked her new boss jumping to the one-eyed outlander's command even less. Like at least a couple of the others, Mildred knew, Raven had been hardline Leto loyalists back when that had tangible risks. She gathered it had been a factor in who Leto had picked to come along on this suicide mission. He only asked the men and women he trusted all the way to the bone.

But Leto smiled at the woman as he trotted to obey. He seemed to have that rarest of gifts: an ego outsize enough to boss around a bunch of outlaws like the Desolation Angels and the sense to know when to stuff that mighty ego back down and take orders from someone who knew the terrain and the job better than he did.

Bottom line was, Ryan and his crew were seasoned experts at this. Leto and his Angels weren't. But it took a genuine man to realize that—and act on it. Mildred reckoned the mullet-headed little surfer dude could be dangerous, a real power in the Rubble.

If he lived through this harebrained adventure.

A door halfway down the corridor stood ajar. The three dragged the chill into the pitch-black room and shut the door on him. Friendly followed orders and pitched in the same way he did everything else, without speaking and with a glare on his face. He was ready enough to do what was asked of him, even if he did look fit to scare a vulture off a dead white-tailed doe.

If anything, she thought, he acted the slightest bit put out at not being tasked to shift the dead man by himself.

"Nobody coming," Leto reported. "I don't think anybody heard him."

"Random cries for help and screaming aren't uncommon down here," Krysty said without raising her face. "Trust us on that."

"Yeah," the Angel boss said.

"Everybody back in place," Ryan said. "Donut, lead on."

The armorer faltered. "There's an awful lot of blood."

"Notice all the dark stains on the floor, Donut?" Mildred asked.

The fat man looked down in alarm. He hadn't closed his visor yet.

"Spilled blood isn't rare down here, either," she stated. "And nobody who comes along in a minute or two is even going to notice this patch is still fresh unless they slip in it. Then they'll just cuss and carry on."

"SOMETHING'S HAPPENING," RICKY reported.

"Define 'something,'" J.B. demanded.

Ricky had instinctively ducked. Reluctantly he forced himself back up to peer over the blister-hatch rim.

"They quit loading stuff onto the wags."

"And?"

"Well, there's a bunch of sec men with longblasters coming out of the building and piling inside on top of the cargo."

The two wags' engines coughed to life. They'd been modified to burn ethanol, Ricky knew. He didn't know much about wags yet—his mountainous, tropical home island didn't boast many of them, in working condition, anyway—but under J.B.'s tutelage he was learning when and as he could.

"And now there's a SWAT officer coming this way. He looks like he wants to talk to us."

He looked down inside the dimly lit compartment.

"What are we gonna do? I don't think he's going to fall for the lost-voice thing."

"Wait'll he gets near, then blast him," J.B. said casually, as if he were remarking on a change in the weather.

"But everybody'll notice!" J.B. had handed him the suppressed Glock, but too many sec men and grunt techs in civilian clothes were running around for him to have a prayer of getting away with shooting an elite sec man in the face.

J.B. grinned at him. "Then rock and roll, son. It's what you're up there for. And you know you want to do it."

Well, that's true, Ricky thought.

"Lopez?" an imperious voice demanded from outside. Knuckles rapped on the hull. "Lopez, FitzGibbons, if you taints are sleeping on the job, I swear by blessed Stephen I am going to peel the hides off your lazy backs and roll you in salt and apple vinegar!"

Ricky popped up. A man with a face like a hatchet was glaring up at him beneath the open visor of a SWAT helmet.

He looked puzzled. "You're not Lopez. If you're not authorized to be in there—"

"Oh, shut up," Ricky said. He raised the Glock and pulled the trigger three times.

At least two of the heavy bullets hit flesh and bone from the blood Ricky saw squirt out. The lantern light touched it with crimson and fire as the officer collapsed with the utter bonelessness of the well and truly chilled.

"Shit!" Ricky yelled. "A dude's running for the alarm."

J.B. throttled up the engine. "Well, drown it out," he said.

It actually took Ricky a confused eyeblink before he got it. Then he crossed himself and grabbed the pistol grip of the M240. Long practice as a rifleman made Ricky lean into the blaster and snug its butt against his shoulder. That turned out to be right. The sights were nothing like what he was used to, but he'd figured them out, too. Well enough for short-range work, anyway.

And for this big bad boy, anything less than a thousand yards was pretty close range.

The blaster was mounted on the blister on a kind of sliding ring. It slid around readily enough once Ricky gave it a good tug. He swung the M240 left.

He started firing short bursts. Despite the dazzle of the yellow muzzle-flare, which looked to be the size of a man, he used the dust kicked up by the 7.62 mm bullets striking the yard to walk them right into the sec man just as he reached for the handle of the Klaxon-style alarm. They cut right across the small of his back.

His upper torso actually folded over backward as he went down.

The two cargo wags sat parked with their rears toward the V-100. The supplies loaded onto them had come out of what Ricky thought of as the annex building, which occupied the northeastern end of the block that the mighty Temple took up. Sec men began to bail from the one nearer the structure. Muzzle-flashes winked as they fired at Ricky.

Bullets cracking past his ears really kicked his heartbeat into overdrive. He swung the M240 toward the wag, loosing a burst at a man who stood in the middle of the yard with more balls than sense, firing a semiauto longblaster from his shoulder. He completely missed, but the man instantly dropped his weapon, turned and raced full-speed to dive into a fire pit by the Cass Avenue wire.

Ricky gave another round of fire to the other wag, which was already starting to roll. He thought he scored a couple hits on the crates stacked inside, but not on the sec men lying and kneeling on them and shooting at Ricky. Then he got the barrel aimed at the wag by the annex.

Not even three or four direct torso hits from 147-grain copper-jacketed bullets traveling more than twenty-seven hundred feet per second was enough to knock a man around. But the sec men did tend to go right down as the bullets tripped through them. He pulsed quick bursts, shifting the barrel left and right. Men dived frantically aside or threw up their arms and fell.

In a moment no men were visible around the wag. A half dozen or so bodies lay on the ground. At least one man he'd shot was wailing like a wounded woman.

Mebbe it *is* a woman, Ricky thought. He shoved that aside. He couldn't afford to let it matter.

He fired a couple bursts into the canvas shell stretched

over what he suspected were improvised hoops into what he hoped was the cab.

The other wag had peeled away and was gathering speed on a run toward the gate. The crew there had been brave enough to roll the wag-bed barricade out of the way to allow the supply truck to escape.

Ricky caught it with a burst into the engine compartment just as it rolled through. It promptly exploded into yellow flames and stopped.

"Woo-hoo!" Ricky said, throwing his arms up in triumph. "I got 'em! I got 'em!"

"Great, kid," J.B. called from below. "Don't get cocky."

A bullet spanged off the sloping front deck of the war wag, snapping Ricky back to reality even more definitely than his mentor's voice. He grabbed back onto the machine gun.

Men were shooting at him from various directions. A lot more came tumbling out the grandiose front door and down the steps.

Ricky turned the machine gun on them. The quick-pulsing rips of fire cut them down like wheat. Within a matter of seconds the survivors had turned and fled back inside.

He eased off the trigger. He had been strict with his fire discipline, never once letting off more than four rounds at a time. He was proud of himself. He hoped J.B. was, too. But he also felt an instinctive need to let the barrel cool so that it wouldn't burn out.

The waves of heat making the air shimmer above it, so intense he could feel it on his cheeks and hands, might have had something to do with it, too.

Blood ran in a river down the ancient, weathered stone steps. It lay in a lake at their base, not just on concrete but on earth too saturated with the stuff to drink any more down. Bodies lay sprawled all over the steps. Some writhed, moaned or howled in intolerable pain. Some just lay.

Ricky's ruthless execution of the sec men on the Temple's door step had won him a few moment's respite, though. All the sec men in the yard had taken cover. For the moment, at least, no one was shooting at him.

That ended as a burst of full-auto longblaster fire snarled at him from one of the firing pits by the gate. Bullets bounced off the Commando's sharp prow and cracked or howled past his ears.

He heard and felt a click from below. "Got a new box of ammo bent onto your belt," Mikhail said. "You're good to go."

"Thanks," he said.

Then, riding a wave of exaltation and sheer power—and just a hint of nausea and regret—he began to systematically sweep the yard clean of human life with his relentless fire.

"J.B.," RICKY CALLED.

The Armorer sat at his ease in the driver's seat. The kid seemed to have everything under control. It would've been nice if one of the Angels had opened a firing port to shoot out on the off chance he could see if anybody came out of the HQ to aim a rocket launcher at them. But on the whole he was just as glad they hadn't; he preferred to let Ricky do the brunt of the blasting. It was too easy for a bullet to come in one of those ports, small as they were, and then they just bounced around forever, and help whoever happened to get in their way.

"What is it?" he called back.

Ricky had blazed through the second box of ammo. The skinny Angel with the ponytail and the glasses promptly clipped the loose link of a fresh box onto the tail end of the belt in the receiver of Ricky's weapon and swapped the full box into the empty one's place.

"I—I don't think there are any more targets left."

"Ace," J.B. said. The kid sounded a little sick, which was to be expected. J.B. wasn't big on history—he left that kind of thing to Ryan or Doc—but even he knew that men had been appalled by their first exposure to the terrible power of a machine gun. "How's your barrel?"

"Hot. But I think it's cooling off enough that in a little while—"

"All right." J.B. turned, took hold of the wheel and revved up the engine. "Brace yourself."

"What about us?" Keiser asked. He and his partner sat on fold-down seats aft of the gunner's steps.

"Grab hold and hang on tight."

He goosed it. No one would ever mistake the eleven-ton war wag for a slingshot dragster, but the burly V-504 V-8 engine did give it a surprising jolt. He slewed the vehicle counterclockwise as it accelerated.

"Uh, J.B.," he heard Ricky say over the throaty roar of the V-8. Peering through the forward vision block, he slowed and straightened out the wheel. "You're— That's the Temple door!"

"Ramming speed!" J.B. sang out, and put the hammer down.

RICKY DUCKED ON the shooter's step, clinging to the M240's butt as if he was a drowning man hanging on to a log. He kept his knees bent and hoped for the best.

What he got was a grinding crash so loud it felt as if his bones rang in harmony. The only thing that kept him from being dislodged and flung on top of J.B. was the vertical butt that smashed into his face to the right of his nose. It sent a white sheet of pain shooting to the back of his skull but arrested his momentum enough to let him hang on.

His consciousness drifted for a moment. When it came back, the first thing he was aware of was the powerful engine gunning, the sound of stone squealing and cracking under pressure and the smell of burning rubber.

"We're stuck, kid!" he heard J.B. shout through the ringing in his ears. "Your wep should be clear. Get the nuke back up there and start blasting."

The pinging of bullets striking the armor galvanized Ricky. Had he still had his wits about him he might have thought twice about sticking his head outside the comforting confines of his giant steel cocoon into what sounded like a hailstorm of lead. But he was still fuddled by the impact, and adrenaline sizzled in his veins like bacon frying on a griddle.

He was seized by a sudden terror that someone might manage to torch off the fuel tanks. Then he, J.B. and two Angels would be cremated alive inside an inescapable oven. Whatever vague misgivings he might have had to exposing his fragile skull—feeling more fragile than ever after colliding with the machine gun—to blasterfire vanished. He popped up through the hatch like a prairie dog.

Acrid limestone dust swirled around the trapped V-100. Flames flickered yellow from all sides of the ornate, cavernous lobby. The bullets flying by sounded like fireworks, loud even over the sounds of the blasts that launched them. Grit blasted free of the door arch behind him peppered the back of his head and neck like birdshot. It stung.

He whipped the machine gun around and ripped out a quick random burst. The dust was sucked into a vortex in front of the muzzle. Whether that actually got it out of the air quicker or not, he didn't know. But suddenly he was able to see targets.

He swung the M240 to bear on a knot of four sec men standing roughly thirty feet away. How they'd missed him so far, he had no clue, but the roar of the 7.62 mm blaster seemed to have shocked them into momentary inactivity.

Blood sprayed in all directions from their bodies and heads as he hosed them down.

Because there were targets everywhere, he swung the blaster all the way around to the right. His mind was pretty well alert now, and he reasoned that because it was more comfortable for him to turn from right to left than clockwise, that might help him shoot better.

He swept the lobby side to side, firing bullets in quick spurts. Most of the sec men threw down their blasters and ran away before the death stream could reach them. Not all who ran made it; the bullets didn't stop just because they happened to be heading toward someone's back instead of his front. Or her front—Ricky could see some of the officers were women. But at least the ones who ran had a chance.

The ones who stood and fired their weapons didn't. Ricky methodically cut them down, the jacketed rounds shattering ribs and skulls, pulping lungs and livers and hearts, breaking limbs or even tearing them off.

At least the machine gun was loud enough to drown out the screams.

Abruptly it was done. No targets remained standing, kneeling or aiming at him. The lobby's only occupants were the dead or the dying.

All Ricky could hear was the ringing of his ears, the pounding of his pulse and the oddly musical chiming of spent casings bouncing on the brown-and-tan checkerboard floor.

Then through the grandiose hall that led to the cathedral itself strode a solitary figure. Its tall, lean form was bulked around the torso by SWAT armor. The light of many lanterns glittered on a narrow bald skull.

"I'll be darned," Ricky said, his voice sounding as if it came from a very distant place.

"What the nuke is going on here?" Chief Bone demanded. "Have you lost your mind? I will fry your nuts like eggs, you little shit—"

Then he stopped blustering and began screaming. He danced like a spastic puppet as bullets sleeted through him. The Kevlar armor didn't seem to slow down the pointy slugs.

But then, Ricky shot him a great many times indeed.

And he always remembered to do it in short, measured bursts.

"OKAY," RYAN CALLED from the rear. "It looks as if this is where we split."

Ryan had led them through the bizarre maze of Detroit City headquarters, to a place where the corridor opened onto yet another of the building's myriad high-ceilinged, echoing halls. All of them were different, though there was plenty of polished hardwood, gilt and black-and-white checkerboard floors for some reason. On the whole, despite the Michaud family's obvious efforts to restore the place to its once-upon-a-time grandeur, it all still looked like a chipped, faded and ultimately cheap elegance, like an aging gaudy slut's painted mouth.

With evident relief Donut shoved up his visor. "Ugh," he said. "I hate smelling my own breath and sweat. Are we sure it's a good idea to split our forces? I mean, I always thought—"

"Yeah," Ryan said. "You're not supposed to do it. Except when it's what'll work. This is when."

"Take it easy, Porkins," Leto said. "It's been sheer luck

nobody's got suspicious of all of us roaming the halls in a giant herd like this. We need speed and stealth. Our total number of ten won't mean anything if we get spotted. Plus we got two targets."

"Porkins?" Mildred said in disbelief. "His real name is Porkins?"

"Like we discussed," Ryan said, ignoring her. "Donut, Raven, Bronk, Jak. You're with me. The rest go with Leto."

Krysty walked to him with her face upturned. They kissed passionately but briefly.

"I hate that we have to go separate ways, lover," she said.

"Yeah, but you're my second-in-command with J.B. busy elsewhere."

"I hate that we're not with the group that goes for that handsy bastard Bone," Mildred said.

"But our plan is so ace," Krysty told her.

Mildred gave her a narrow look. "If you say so."

"Sure you trust your woman with Leto?" asked Raven with a sneer.

"I've got no problem with that."

"What's that sound?" Donut asked, looking up.

The hard rapping repeated itself. It sounded like a giant mutie woodpecker attacking a redwood.

"Machine gun," Ryan said. "That's Ricky and J.B."

He started to say more, but then a Klaxon began to sing its rising-falling siren song.

A door opened beside Donut. A little guy in sec-man black stepped out, stuck the muzzle of an MP5 between the front and back halves of the weaponsmith's Kevlar apron, where he was too portly to fasten it fully closed, and held the trigger down.

Chapter Thirty-One

Donut's plump, bearded cheeks jiggled. He made gobbling noises as the bullets spiked through him. The spittle flying from his mouth turned abruptly pink.

He collapsed.

The Klaxon continued to wail mindlessly. Mildred thought of the legend of the banshee.

As Donut fell, Raven uttered a scream of rage. She had already shed the unlocked handcuffs and was stepping up to reclaim her sword. Now she ripped it out of the scabbard, cocked her arm back and cut the sec man's dark crew-cut head off his shoulders in a single backhand slice.

Mildred acted by sheer instinct. She swooped in and grabbed the suppressed handblaster from Donut's slack fingers before he fell on it and buried it under three hundred pounds of swiftly cooling flab.

Even as she marveled at the way she'd pulled off a move she couldn't have reproduced if she practiced for two weeks straight, she stood up. She tipped the front-heavy wep up toward the ceiling and squeezed back the slide half an inch with her left hand. The reassuring gleam of brass met her eye. She let the slide slam home.

Mildred was first and foremost a wheelgun expert, but she knew her way around an autopistol. The first thing a person did after picking one up was to check to see if a round was chambered. Though she had watched with her own eyes as the Angels armorer swapped out the partially depleted mag after he shot down the fleeing bureaucrat, it made no difference. A good shooter did that—and she herself would yell louder than Ryan or even J.B. at anyone in the group who failed to follow the practice.

That took but a second. She shifted her left hand to cover her right. Then, pushing the blaster and its long, thick suppresser out before her in an isosceles stance, she strode through the still-open door.

The room the now-headless sec man had burst through led into a small office. It looked more like the sort of thing she'd have expected to see in her own time, not the random Gothic/renaissance/Arabian Nights fantasyland so many of the HQ's interior spaces were, allowing for the fact that the illumination came from a pair of lanterns instead of the long-dead fluorescent lights overhead.

Two more men were inside. One sat behind a desk, gaping in surprised alarm. The other was coming out of a chair, drawing a handblaster from a hip holster.

She shot that one through the head. The bullet hit his temple at an angle that should have taken it to the far rear corner of his skull.

Without waiting to see its effect she switched aim to the man behind the desk. He was getting up now. He had a double-action revolver in his hand, rising fast.

It didn't rise quite fast enough. She shot him once through the open mouth. As his head snapped back, Mildred dropped aim and fired again for the center of mass.

As he collapsed over the desk, she turned back to the first sec man. She put another bullet in his head before he hit the floor.

Time had slowed as if some god had grabbed it by the future and the past and stretched. Now it snapped back into place. Mildred continued into the room, swinging her blaster left and right.

"Clear," she called.

"Nice work, Mildred," Krysty said as the woman came back into the hall. The others had gone into defensive crouches, with blasters ready, facing up and down the passage.

She nodded curtly to her friend. Inside she was a strange seethe of emotion. It wasn't the fact of sudden death of someone she barely knew. She was used to that. It was how sudden Donut's death had been. In her current state, keyed up by the seemingly hopeless odds of completing their mission and living, the shock had knocked her momentarily loose from her moorings.

Outside, a full-on firefight was raging.

She offered the .45 to Leto, who had come up to stand near Ryan and over Donut's corpse. He shook his head.

"Keep it," he said. "You're handy with it. And he'd want it going to someone who can use it right. Poor Donut."

To Ryan he said, "Well, we're blown now."

Mildred knelt over the fallen Angel. He lay on his belly with his face turned from the wall. His staring blue eyes told a pretty persuasive story, but she pressed two fingers against his neck by his ear to find the basilar artery, most accessible given his position.

"Poor Harry," Bronk said. "He didn't deserve that."

"Nobody does," Krysty said. "Except for the likes of Bone."

"You take your people back out the way you came," Ryan said. "Clear out and head back to your lines."

"What about you?" Leto asked.

"We still got people here. We don't leave without them. Anyway, we came to do a job. We got this far. I mean to do it."

"Let's go, Leto," Raven said. "No point in throwing

your life away. This was a crazy-stupe idea from the start."
She shot Ryan a death glare.

"No," Jak said. "Not found."

"Somebody set off the alarm," Mildred stated.

"Nobody else has come close to us since the alarm start going," Krysty added.

"Even if nobody knows exactly where we are," Raven said, "the whole nuking building knows we're here."

They heard voices from outside their field of vision in the larger room. Making a snap decision, Ryan gestured the group into the room Mildred had so recently rendered vacant. He and Leto grabbed Donut's ankles and dragged him in with them.

There wasn't much they could do about the giant pool and smear of blood.

Mildred crouched and poked her head around the door, just enough to see out. A knot of men and women came dashing into the chamber from the right, some still hauling on black sec-man blouses.

Somebody else appeared in the mouth of the far corridor. Mildred reflexively started to shrink back, but he didn't look her way.

"Attack, attack!" he yelled, waving a frantic hand. "Move it! Angels comin' over the wire!"

He turned and raced off with the others right on his heels.

"We are, are we?" Raven said. She cocked an eyebrow at Leto.

"News to me," the Angel boss said.

"Could they be victims of mistaken identity?" Doc asked.

"Mebbe," Ryan said.

"They probably think Ricky and J.B. in the war wag are part of a general attack," Krysty told them.

"Yeah," Ryan agreed. "Key is, they think their troubles are all on the outside. So let's push on."

"Weren't we going to split up here?" Leto said.

"We were. Conditions have changed. We need to see what's happening. We can always split later."

Leto nodded briskly. "Ace."

"What about disguises?" Bronk asked.

"Where we're going right now," Ryan said, "nobody's going to see us."

"WHAT IS THIS PLACE?" Raven asked, looking all around by the light of the lantern she held. It was one of the two they had scavenged from the office whose occupants Mildred had so efficiently disposed of.

The area was narrow but high ceilinged, with walls of stone that were cool to the touch. It twisted left and right suddenly and without explanation. Then again, the open corridors in this insane building tended to do that, too.

"What it looks like," Ryan said. He was bringing up the rear again with the other torch. "Secret passage."

Jak led the way because he knew it best.

Raven looked back, and for once he saw something other than anger—whether repressed or not—in her dark eyes. This time they seemed to hold a mixture of wonder and disgust.

Or maybe I'm letting my imagination run away with me again, he thought.

"Seriously?"

"Jak and Ricky found them during our downtime when we were bunking here," Krysty said. "They're veined all through the building—all fourteen floors of the tower. It's quite clever, really."

"So Michaud and Bone gave you the run of the place, huh?" Raven asked. She was back to her nasty, skeptical self. Ryan wondered if that was her natural state, or if they had made her that way.

"They went snooping around where they weren't supposed to," Mildred said. "They're like that."

She touched a wooden door as she passed. "The passages open into all kinds of rooms. Secret entrances."

"Who'd build something like this?" Bronk asked.

"Masons," Mildred said.

"Who're they?" the powerfully built woman asked. "Some kind of gang?"

"More or less."

"Don't the mayor's people know about these passages?" Leto asked.

"Bet Hizzoner does," Ryan said. "And Bone. I suspect they keep the info to themselves and discourage their own people from prying into things. Jak and Ricky said most of the ones they found didn't seem like they'd been used in years."

"This one's sure dusty," Mildred said, stifling a cough.

Like a ghost materializing from the darkness, Jak appeared in the gleam of Raven's lantern ahead of the party. He held up a thumb.

"Shut it, people," Ryan said. "We're there."

He squeezed past the others to join Jak at the front of the line. His own lantern light quickly showed a doorway capping off the secret passage.

"Here," he said, handing off the lantern to Leto. "Take this back a bit and dial both the lanterns down so we don't get backlit."

He caught another furious look from Raven, but Leto nodded. He tapped the woman on the arm, and they both moved back a few steps.

"Somebody's still shooting out there," Mildred said. "A lot."

"Smell smoke," Jak added.

"Let's see what's going on then."

The secret doors were meant to be opened by feel. Ryan opened this one in the dark and cracked the door.

The light that instantly streamed in was yellow and too bright and flickered too much to only come from the lanterns that lit the great lobby twenty-four hours a day.

The little antechamber beyond had been stripped of most of its bizarre and gaudy decorations. What remained was age-cracked wooden wainscoting somebody had tried to oil and polish back into a semblance of respectability, walls painted what once had been white and a single heavy carven wood sofa with some lumpy modern-made pillows. Beyond, the lobby looked as if it gave entry not to a cathedral, but hell. The yellow glare danced like fire demons on the high walls and elaborately figured ceiling. A bareheaded SWAT officer ran by carrying a longblaster in one hand and hollering something over his shoulder. The blasterfire seemed to be coming mostly from the left.

The stink of burning alcohol and propellant was overpowering.

"I don't like this, Ryan," Krysty said.

"Me, neither."

He moved cautiously forward. The others followed.

When he looked out he first checked right because that seemed to be where the traffic was coming from. People were running through the hall from the cathedral toward the front. None of them glanced his way.

He realized the SWAT riot helmet he wore had a lot to do with that. He wasn't the only DPD officer who sported an eye patch. But they seemed completely focused on whatever was happening at the front of the building.

Then he looked that way. It felt as if a mailed fist punched him in the gut.

The V-100 Commando was stuck in the arched main door with its pointy snout sticking into the lobby, and it was puking yellow flame and greasy black smoke from every opening.

Chapter Thirty-Two

"J.B.!" Mildred cried.

"Ricky in trouble, too," Jak said.

"Somebody's coming down the passage," Raven said from the secret door, her voice low and urgent. She drew her katana.

Jak turned back and slipped past her into the passage. He and the volatile sword-wielding Angel seemed to have an understanding.

Then he said, "No shoot!"

A moment later J.B. strolled into the antechamber.

"Oh, my God!" Mildred exclaimed. She threw herself at the Armorer and grabbed him in a fierce hug. He returned her embrace and gave her a quick kiss.

"I'm here, too," Ricky said, also emerging into the light and taking a sidestep to avoid the pair.

Krysty went and gave him a hug. He blushed. She knew it was cruel to risk exacerbating his crush on her, but she was glad to see they were both alive, and he seemed to need the appreciation.

"Ace on the line," Ryan said. "How?"

"Once we cleared the lobby out," J.B. said, detaching himself from Mildred, "we popped smoke and left the wag to our Angel buddies. Then we ducked off into one of these hidden passages, and here we are. Reckoned we'd find you here."

Although they'd lost their gear in the treacherous arrest by Bone and Michaud, they still had their considerable cache of "excess" C-4, black powder, safety fuse and blasting caps they'd squirreled away while working for the self-proclaimed mayor. J.B. and Ricky had spent some time whipping up a few surprises for their enemies out of that trove.

"What about Mikhail and Keiser?" Leto asked.

J.B. shook his head. "Don't rightly know. I think the barrel finally burned out by the time we found the secret entrance. If they got out then, they should be ace."

"What took out the war wag?" Ryan asked.

"Turns out Hizzoner did have at least one wag chiller, even if the Angels don't. Somebody hit the car with an M72 LAW. Went right up."

"You came at just the right moment," Krysty said. "Despite how worried we all were about you, it's time to split up and go after Michaud and Bone."

Ricky and J.B. looked at each other and grinned.

"Not much need to go after Bone," J.B. said.

"Why not?" Leto asked.

"Because he's already as full of holes as an old flannel shirt in a drawer full of moths."

"I chilled him!" Ricky said. His eyes gleamed and his cheeks flushed red.

"He tried intimidating somebody who was sitting in an armored fighting vehicle behind a 7.62 mm machine gun by yelling at him," J.B. said.

"He's just out there to the right," Ricky said.

Ryan peered cautiously out of the little room. "There he is, all right."

He ducked back inside. "Even I forget how much blood there is in a body."

"So who exactly are the Detroit sec men shooting at?"

Doc said. "And more to the point, who is shooting back at them?"

"No idea," J.B. replied.

"Right," Ryan said as another squad of sec men trotted toward the front door. "Then we all go after Hizzoner. Now."

"You sure you're up for this?" Leto asked Raven, which puzzled Krysty because the woman seemed constantly eager for a fight.

"Never more sure," she said and slammed her sword home hard in its scabbard.

"ACCESS TO THIS floor is strictly restricted," a voice barked from above as the little party headed toward the midfloor landing above the sixth floor.

Two sec men in full SWAT armor with open visors stood glaring down from the next landing, beating their side-handle batons suggestively against the palms of their gloved hands. The ancient Masonic Temple's seventh floor was the exclusive preserve of Hizzoner, Mayor Michaud.

Ryan didn't find it easy to see with his own visor down. Fortunately, the landing was well lit by two kerosene lanterns, so he was able to make out the way the guards' eyes bugged out of their faces when they actually saw who was walking between Ryan and Leto in their full-on SWAT drag.

Krysty was anything but vain, but she had also never been particularly shy about her voluptuous body. From voracious reading as a kid, Ryan had gathered that people back before the Big Nuke had been a lot more uptight about nudity than people were these days, and temporal refugees Mildred and Doc had confirmed it.

However casual they might be about nudity here in the citadel of the self-proclaimed city government of Detroit, it was unlikely the two SWAT guards had ever seen anything that could compare to what they were seeing now.

Krysty had thrown off all attempts at disguise. Her hair was free and whipping defiantly about her shoulders as she marched with head up between her apparent captors. Her face was still smudged, but that went with the image she was trying to project: of a woman captured by bitter enemies who hadn't submitted easily and gotten roughed up double well in the process.

Her stained man's shirt, it seemed, had suffered particularly in the struggle. It was torn open so far her entire left breast was in plain view, and her right kept slipping in and out of view as she climbed the stairs.

"Is that—the renegade coldheart slut?" asked the guard to Ryan's right.

"Yeah," Ryan growled. "Got brought in just before all the excitement started down below."

"What was all that all about, anyway?" asked the second guard, who had an impressive auburn mustache.

"Not sure," Leto said from Krysty's right side. "We were already in charge of the prisoner when the alarm started. Our priority was to get her to Hizzoner as soon as she got processed."

"Heard somebody say some of the Rubble-rat gangs were attacking the perimeter," Ryan said.

From the corner of his eye he saw Leto's faceless helmet twitch ever so slightly as the Angel boss resisted the impulse to look at him in surprise. The keen-witted young man had caught the ring of truth to Ryan's statement and was starting to wonder.

Let him, Ryan thought.

"Not our job, anyway."

The Klaxon had cut off right before they came out of the warren of secret passages to the main stairs. By this time there was a rousing firefight going on in the main lobby—and outside as well, to judge from the sounds that filtered through the thick limestone walls.

As they started up the stairs, a couple groups of hastily dressed and armed men passed them going the other way. Because the two remaining SWAT-armored members of their party walked in the lead, nobody questioned why they were walking *away* from the fight.

On the third and fifth floor they'd encountered individual men racing down the stairs, probably bearing messages from above. J.B. and Mildred had chilled them with the suppressed .45s. Then the group had paused on the fifth-floor landing to set up this final charade.

They continued to march up the steps. It was a little crowded, with the three of them trying to walk abreast, so to speak. Behind them tramped Bronk and Friendly—who still hadn't uttered a syllable in Ryan's hearing—in their patrol uniforms.

The sec man with the auburn mustache held up a hopeful hand. "Cop a feel before you go?"

"Those are some *prime* goods," the other guard said.

"Sure," Ryan said. "If you want to explain to the mayor why you got your fingerprints all over his shiny new playmate."

"Uh—" The guard dropped his hand. Then he and his partner reluctantly stepped to either side to clear the way.

To Ryan's surprise, the corridor beyond was clear of guards. Apparently Michaud—and his now-late sec boss—had relied largely on intimidation to keep intruders out of Hizzoner's private sanctum. Naturally, though, there would be more sec when they reached Michaud's rooms.

Ryan felt the opposite of relief. This is too easy, he thought.

THE TWO GUARDS stood crowded together in the doorway, staring single-mindedly after the four escorts and their flame-haired captive.

It placed them in an absurdly easy position for Mildred and J.B. to step out on the landing below, sight on the gap between the backs of their polycarbonate helmets and the beginning of their body armor and fire a kill shot each.

They fell where they stood without uttering a peep.

J.B. and Mildred stood aside to let Ricky and Raven slip past as the noise of their heavy slides reciprocating echoed down the stairwell. They sounded as loud as gunshots to Mildred, though she knew they were far from that. They didn't *sound* like gunshots, though, and that made all the difference. If there was even anybody in position to hear them, which she doubted, especially with the battle raging outside.

I know they were brutal coldheart bastards, Mildred thought as she, J.B., Doc and Ricky followed the two scouts, who had quickly made sure the guards were truly chills and moved on. And no doubt extrasadistic, to make Bone's first team and Michaud's personal detail. It still makes me feel a bit better about shooting a man in the back to know that he died watching Krysty's perfect rear end work its moon-white magic as she walked away, Mildred thought.

"Krysty really is a pro," she murmured as she and J.B. hauled the dead guards to the sides of the door, out of sight from the hallway beyond. "The way she cut open the rear of her jeans like that, just for that added level of distraction."

"The woman's good," J.B. agreed, straight-faced. He showed no signs of interest himself.

He knows what's good for him, she thought.

MICHAUD'S RESIDENCE LAY down a blessedly short corridor from the last turn in their path. Though Krysty and the others had gotten a basic idea of where it lay on the seventh floor while they still worked for Hizzoner, Jak and Raven had had to scout a couple times to find the right route. She was constantly amazed at how labyrinthine the giant old building was.

When they turned the final corner, she gave her head a toss, partly to make sure she had the proper look of defiance on, partly to hide the restless stirring of her sentient hair.

Four guards stood flanking the door, arrogant in their black SWAT armor. Like the ones by the stairs, these held batons ready, though each man had a longblaster slung.

These guards reacted the same way: initial barking followed immediately by big, staring eyes. Just before turning the corner Krysty had pulled open the right side of her much-abused shirt a little farther to enhance the effect.

"We were ordered to bring this one straight to the mayor!" Ryan barked. "Let us in."

The guard nearest Ryan nodded instant acquiescence. Krysty had to force down a laugh at the way his head bobbed while his eyes stayed locked as if gyro-stabilized on her naked breasts. He reached a gloved hand and knocked a fast but complicated pattern on the door, which was covered in what appeared to be a brass sheet, engraved in curious geometric patterns, dominated by a curiously intricate cross and a symbol with a drawing-type compass and angle ruler with a giant *G* in the middle. From the sound of it there was thick hardwood behind the metal.

Krysty heard heavy locks being disengaged. The door opened.

Inside stood the last thing Krysty had expected to see: an Asian-looking woman almost as tall as Krysty in stiletto heels, with jade-green eyes and black hair flowing down over a black leather bustier almost to the tops of a pair of black thigh-high boots. Dawn light pouring through huge windows outlined her graceful form.

She tipped her head to one side and slowly smiled. Then she turned her head.

"It's the red-headed mutineer woman, Claude," she said. "They've caught her and brought her right to you."

"Splendid!" Hizzoner called from behind her.

The woman stepped back, pulling the door open.

Ryan raised a heavy boot and kicked the door open. It knocked the woman sprawling backward against the side of a huge bed.

Krysty heard two clacks from behind, coming one on top of the other, as J.B.'s and Mildred's handblasters cycled after firing a single suppressed shot each. Both guards immediately to either side of the door grunted and collapsed.

Then came the sound of soft feet rushing forward. She heard ripping sounds, gurgling. Then liquid splashing on the black-and-white checkerboard floor.

Jak and Raven had just chilled the other two sentries with their blades.

Ryan stepped into the room, drew his M4 one-handed and fired a quick burst into the ornate ceiling to make sure he had everybody's attention. Leto unslung his big riot shotgun and leveled it.

Krysty took a large step forward and to her left. She drew a compact autopistol from where she'd kept it concealed tucked into her pants, its cold muzzle pressing uncomfortably between the cheeks of her half-exposed backside, with the untucked tail of her shirt to hide it. She aimed the blaster at the man on the bed.

The sight that met her astonished eyes instantly wiped away any trace of regret, either for helping beguile sec men to their deaths or helping Ryan with his brutal treatment of the slinky doorkeeper.

The room was a bizarre and gaudy fantasyland even by the standards of the old temple. She had the impression of the usual hand-rubbed hardwood paneling and the metal ceiling of gilt and silver and deep indigo blue, both on the floor and parts of the wall. But there was also a fireplace with a gilt mantel, and flanking the bed stood two obelisks, fluted like Greek columns and topped by malachite globes, as well as nightstands and sturdy chairs.

But the bed was the centerpiece. And not because its size—Krysty thought it had to be ten feet by ten—dominated the spacious, high-ceiling room. Behind and on either side of the bed stood, or sat, or reclined on silk cushions at least a dozen women dressed in a variety of what she could only think of as fetish outfits: a bare-legged nun, at least a pair each of white-clad nurses and plaid-skirted schoolgirls, saucy maids, garter-belted dominatrices like the still-stunned Asian woman, a pair in tentlike baby-doll nighties who were clearly nude beneath.

Six women lay sprawled on the red satin spread of the bed, some asleep, some clearly drugged to stupor. These were all quite young, though Krysty noted with some relief they were all clearly in their twenties.

That didn't make her feel any more charitably inclined to the man in the gold-trimmed deep-blue silk robe sitting with his back propped on pillows against the high, wide headboard.

But the somnolent young women scattered with casual contempt at his feet and around his legs were all entirely nude. Whatever the status of the women in fantastic outfits was, clearly the naked women were something they were not: captives.

"Get your hands up, you fat bastard!" Krysty yelled.

Hizzoner Claude Michaud smiled insouciantly.

"Why should I, dear girl?" he asked in a voice of calm reason. "If you meant to chill me, you would have blasted me the instant your male escort kicked open the door. Might I hazard a guess that he's another former employee of mine named Ryan Cawdor?"

Ryan took off his helmet and tossed it aside with what Krysty recognized as a look of relief.

"Yeah."

Leto likewise discarded his helmet. "And I'm Leto, new Maximum Leader of the Desolation Angels."

Michaud nodded courteously to him. "I have heard descriptions of you. They don't quite do credit to your... presence."

The others were coming in behind and spreading out along the walls. Friendly and Bronk had already winged out left and right to stand alongside the two men in SWAT armor.

Some of the bizarrely clad women sashayed forward as if to surround the bed protectively.

"Stay where you are!" Ryan snapped.

"What are you going to do, you big handsome one-eyed devil, you?" asked the doorkeeper. She rose gracefully from where his door kick had thrown her against the bed. The trickle of blood from where the door had hit her nose looked disturbingly natural, trickling across her equally red lips. "Shoot us?"

"If we have to, honey," said Mildred from Krysty's left, "we will."

"It was an admirably constructed ruse," Michaud said in his voice of honeyed oil. "But to what do I owe the honor of this little pageant if it's not meant to murder me?"

"It's still an option," Ryan growled. "That 'murder' thing."

"We want to negotiate with you," Leto said. He lowered his shotgun and looked questioningly at Ryan.

Seeing no resistance, Ryan shrugged. "Right. Put them down. Keep eyes peeled and shoot at the first sign of trouble."

He lowered his own carbine.

"Negotiate what?" Michaud asked.

"An end to this war," Leto said. "It can only drain us both to the point the other gangs in the city will see us as potential prey and jump on us. If that happens, neither of us wins."

"Perhaps," Michaud said. He smiled. "But what if I win?"

"Doesn't seem likely from where I stand," said J.B. from Krysty's right.

"And what do you offer by way of inducement for me to negotiate with you?"

Leto pushed his head slightly forward on his neck and stared as if suspecting the mayor was stupe. "Your life, to start with."

Michaud laughed heartily.

"Time to start taking this seriously, Michaud," Leto said. "The time we're willing to waste on you is limited and running out fast. So what's it going to be? Yes or no?"

"I do not negotiate with terrorists. What do you have to say to this?"

Then he whipped out a tiny black handblaster and shot Ryan three times in the chest.

Chapter Thirty-Three

Ryan whipped up his right gauntlet. "Hold fire!" he rapped to his people. Then he felt gingerly where the bullets had struck him.

"You do know I'm wearing your own SWAT armor, right?" he said. "And that's a what? A blaster that fires a .25-caliber bullet?" He grinned.

"Except for, nice grouping, Your Honor. Okay, haul his butt out of bed. It's time this got real."

He gestured. Bronk and Friendly started forward. Fetish maidens moved to bar their path.

"Indeed it is," Michaud said.

"Do what he tells you, you fat murdering rapist bastard!" Raven shrieked.

In a single bound she was up on the bed, knocking the hapless doorkeeper sprawling again, this time to the deep blue floor. Raven waded right across the still-unconscious naked women to kick the blaster from Michaud's hand. Then she pressed the tip of her bloody sword against the wedge of hairy chest visible at the top of his robe.

He had paid more than a cursory glance only to Krysty, Ryan and Leto. The others he had flicked a mere glance over and dismissed. But now his cheeks became ashen, and his eyes bugged wide.

"Aaliyah?" he said.

A plump black woman in a platinum bob wig and white

nurse's costume picked up a candlestick and struck Raven over the head with it.

And it all went to glowing nuke shit at once.

Friendly had grabbed a willowy Latina in a formfitting red dress with a slit clear up to her rib cage by the wrist. "C'mon, honey, out of the way," he said.

She tugged furiously. He was as immovable as granite.

But the tug had been a blind. It gave her cover to turn half away from him.

When she turned back she whipped around with a commando-style dagger protruding from the bottom of her fist and buried it in his sternum.

He bellowed like a scalded buffalo bull and back-handed her with all his enormous strength. Her neck broke with a loud snap. She was flung atop the bed like a rag doll.

The nude young women she fell across were scarcely more limp and passive than she was.

Bronk was advancing along the other side of the bed when Friendly was stabbed. As she turned to look, the black nurse whipped out a MAC-11 and emptied its magazine into her from four feet away. The little machine pistol lacked its customary counterbalancing suppressor. The noise was loud as hell.

The Angel threw her head back, cried out in agony and fell.

The MAC's slide locked back from an empty chamber. Then the nurse's head rocked back with a blue hole over her left eye as Mildred shot her.

Staggering, Friendly grabbed the dagger's hilt with both hands. A pale, blue-eyed waif of a woman in an absurd pigtailed blond wig and blue-and-white *Alice in Wonderland* pinafore dress held out a snub-nosed .38 in both hands and blasted all five shots from the cylinder into the huge man's torso.

Ryan was trying to swing around his M4 to bring her down. The room was full of screams, curses and hurtling bodies. He had to take a step back as two women, one dressed as a cowgirl with a hat hanging behind her neck by a chinstrap and the other another nurse, jumped up on the bed, sprinted over the limp bodies and launched themselves at Krysty in a flying tackle as she tried to line up a shot on Hizzoner.

A splintering crack came from Ryan's blind side. He snapped his head around in time to see a shiny wood panel explode before a massive black boot. He snapped the carbine that way and a figure lunged out of the concealed niche at him.

A whistling blow of a side-handle baton slammed against the right side of his chin and sent him smashing straight down to the floor with blackness and purple lightning vying for space in his cranium.

But he kept his presence of mind enough to fire a long, shuddering burst into the center of the immense, blocky, black figure that loomed suddenly over him. From around the room he heard echoes of the first clash as other bodyguards kicked their way out of similar concealment.

The figure didn't so much as rock. Suddenly Ryan's blurry eye focused enough to realize that it was a sec man wearing Type IV body armor, a kind of apron with pockets down the front holding ceramic-steel plates. Ryan's regular SWAT armor was Kevlar, with only a single trauma plate over the center of his chest.

Of course he'd shrugged off the burst of point-blank 5.56 mm rounds. That armor would stop pretty much everything short of a .50 cal.

"Take the rest alive!" yelled Michaud, who remained

in bed. Probably he felt that was still the best way to stay out of danger for the moment. "Don't mark the women up too bad, and you can play with them!"

Before Ryan could switch his aim to the sec man's lower legs, the boot came down right at his head. He had to roll violently aside to avoid the stomp.

He caught quick glimpses of some of his friends. Krysty was rolling around in a furious kicking, punching tangle with the two women who had jumped her. Doc was reeling around trying to dislodge a tiny woman in a French maid outfit who clung to his back with her legs locked around his chest, holding a fistful of his hair with one hand and punching his head with the other. Ricky flung himself at a sec man in assault armor like the one who'd clubbed Ryan, and he got stiff-armed onto his butt on the floor for his troubles.

Leto raised a handblaster to the other sec man who had appeared on the far side of the bed near the outer wall. He fired two shots into the man's chest. The sec man, not even bothered, stunned him with an overhand club blow to the head.

And then Friendly rose from the floor, roaring like an angry grizzly bear with blood streaming from his mouth and nostrils. He lunged at the sec man who'd struck down his Maximum Leader, put his shaved head down and stuck his right shoulder into his midsection. He locked his arms around the heavily armored figure and drove him bicycling backward.

The sec man windmilled into a tall, wide window past the head of Hizzoner's bed. The metal framework holding the glass was strong, but it couldn't resist the berserk power and fury of the dying Angel, nor the combined masses of two big men. The framework tore free of the stone, and the two men flew out the seventh-story window in a flurry of sharp glass fragments.

Ryan saw Ricky tackled by a fetish guard in a pink baby-doll nightie. Doc went to his knees, stunned. Then Ryan rolled back to his right side.

His mind was still fuzzed by the baton blow, his reactions not as crisp as he needed them to be. The heavy-armored sec man's boot caught the M4 before it came to bear and ripped it out of Ryan's hands. It clattered on the floor out of sight.

Suddenly a figure interposed itself before the enormous sec man and the supine Ryan. It was J.B., hat defiantly in place. He held something in his hand that sputtered. Before the guard could react to J.B.'s sudden appearance from his blindside, the Armorer had grabbed the neck of the shirt he wore beneath his armored apron, yanked it open and stuffed the little object down inside.

"Get clear," the Armorer called to Ryan, a heartbeat before following his own advice and diving back in the direction of the doorway. Ryan rolled frantically away, fortuitously landing on the backs of the legs of the cowgirl, who was sitting pinning one of Krysty's arms while her nurse partner sat astride the redhead's hips, pinning her as they beat her.

The guard stood staring down at himself in horrified disbelief. He dabbed at his armor-plated chest with his unwieldy black gauntlets, going, "Buh! Buuuuh!" in mindless panic.

The fuse burned down to the cap stuck in the C-4 chunk J.B. had jammed inside his armor.

The deafening detonation blew out the other window glass in the mayor's luxury suite. It also blew the sec man's arms and head right out of the armholes and neck of his armor, if not entirely to shredded pieces. Blood

fountained upward and to both sides, along with clouds
of pulped organ and splinters of bone.

EVERYONE FROZE AT the terrific noise. Ricky felt as if he'd
been clapped over both ears with frying pans. The blonde
who straddled his body reeled.

He was physically stunned by the sharp and echoing
crack of the plas ex going off—muffled only a little by the
armor, which had largely had the effect of concentrating
the blast's energy into puréeing the whole upper half of
the man's body and squirting it out the available apertures.
But the kid was less mentally disoriented by it because it
didn't take him completely by surprise.

He had seen what his mentor was about to do, and he
was similarly equipped.

Ricky took advantage of the oh-so-brief pause in the
head punching and boot stomps to fish out his own C-4
chunk and the little spring-and-gear striker he had fash-
ioned himself in emulation of his teacher, J.B. He lit the
tiny sprout of fuse and sent the chunk skittering between
the legs of the sec man, who had taken two steps back as
if physically driven by the force of his companion's detonation. Then he grabbed the woman in the peculiar pink
lingerie, who had recovered enough to be cocking her
fist again.

"Stop hitting me!" he yelled, then rolled them both to
his left, away from the sec man and the improvised bomb
beneath his boots. Fortunately, the good old inverse-square
law guaranteed that the blast energy of the plas ex would
taper off rapidly with distance, especially in the open air.
Not so fortunately, at least where Hizzoner's special bodyguard was concerned, it didn't dissipate fast enough to
help *him*.

Unmuted by cloth, metal or flesh, this explosion was much louder than the first.

Dissipated though it was, the blast wave stung like a vicious full-body slap when it hit Ricky and rolled on. Luck had him roll just far enough—just past being on his back again—that his nearer eardrum wasn't aimed directly at it, or his eardrum would have been burst for sure.

He still felt as if he'd been picked up about ten feet and dropped on pavement.

Fortunately, nobody else in the room was in better shape.

When his sense and senses, all of which had been bodily booted out of his body by the shock, came swarming home again—in a momentarily confused form—he glanced back over to where the sec man had been. The man's armor hadn't helped him. His legs had stuck unprotected out the bottom because death from below was not something it was designed to deal with.

The blast had wrenched the left leg off at the hip and traumatically amputated the right one just below the knee. He was still spraying blood in rapidly diminishing clouds as he rolled around thrashing his arms on the mayor's formerly pristine indigo floor.

Ricky became conscious—very—of the blonde, still atop him, leaning down to press her small, pointy breasts in their thin chiffon against his chest.

"You saved me," she murmured. He could just hear her through the ringing in his ears. His head hurt. "How sweet."

She kissed him once on the lips.

Then she head-butted him. Yellow light stabbed through his skull as his nose broke.

A boot came whipping up from Ricky's left, clocked

the bodyguard on the right pigtailed side of her head and knocked her clean off him.

"SORRY, HONEY," KRYSTY said to the woman she'd just kicked in the face. Her voice came to her as if from the other end of a well through the ringing in her own ears. "Be glad I didn't feel the need to chill you."

The two women who'd taken her down had probably been as surprised by Krysty's almost-manlike strength as Krysty and her crew had been by their sudden, vicious attack. Now the cowgirl lay moaning next to Ryan, clutching her broken jaw, and the nurse was facedown and stunned with her left arm visibly dislocated.

Everybody in the room seemed to be moving at half speed. The two blasts, especially the second, had had a terrifically disorienting effect on everyone. Not just the two men they blew into bloody ruins.

And the blood was everywhere, floors, walls, even the ceiling. It was spattered on the women bodyguards in their bizarrely lascivious outfits, all of whom were down now. The naked bodies, brown and white, strewn casually on the bed, some of whom were beginning to stir and slobber and make incoherent sounds as they returned to something like consciousness, were dappled in red. The mayor's fantasy boudoir looked as if big bags of blood had exploded in it.

Which literally is what happened, I guess, she thought.

Violent motion drew her eye left. There was one massively armored guard still on his feet, and Ryan was face-to-face with him, holding his wrists in his own steely grasp, wrestling for control of the folded-stock longblaster he had unslung.

Ryan hooked a boot behind one of the sec man's ankles and threw his weight into him. Still stunned by the explosions, the guard hadn't recovered all his balance yet.

He went right over backward and cracked his head on the walnut baseboard behind him.

Krysty winced. That sounded fatal enough. But then Jak was on him from somewhere in a catamount leap, slicing his throat with a single savage swipe of a knife.

When Krysty had been a little girl, growing up in the mountains of Colorado, her uncle Tyas McCann had an expression he sometimes used: "He's a man likes to wear a belt as well as suspenders."

Jak was that way, too. Only, when it came to chilling.

RYAN GOT TO his feet a little slowly. He felt as if a giant had picked him up by the ankles and used him to beat another giant to death.

He looked at Hizzoner. Mayor Michaud still sat at the head of his bed, enthroned in silken pillows. He was dabbing blood from his features with a purple silk handkerchief. Otherwise, he looked entirely unmoved by the impossibly grisly scene before him.

"That's it, Mayor," Ryan rasped. "It's over."

Michaud smiled beneath his mustache.

"Oh, Mr. Cawdor," he said. "What an optimist you are. But I think not."

From the right side of the bed Ryan saw a sudden stir of purposeful motion. It wasn't more than a few feet from him.

A woman with long, dark hair, dressed as a nun, who apparently had been lying stunned along with her fellow bedmate/bodyguards, suddenly reared up. She hauled with her the limply unconscious body of Raven, the ferocious Angel woman, who still managed to keep her katana in her limp fist, as if it was naturally attached to her.

And then Michaud had the woman's body held in front of his as a shield on the bed and the abbreviated barrel of the dead nurse's MAC-11 stuck up under the angle of her slackened jaw.

"Throw your weps down, everybody," he said in a voice of confident command. "Or I blow her empty head right off!"

Chapter Thirty-Four

Ryan looked Hizzoner dead in the eye, then he grinned and shrugged.

"Go ahead," he said. "She never liked me, anyway."

"Wait!" Leto said, climbing to his feet. He made an uncertain job of it, and Ricky had to go help steady him. His long face, always more compelling than handsome, was a hideous mask of blood. Some of it was likely his, Ryan judged.

"Don't chill her. I do care."

"Do you, boy?" Michaud said nastily. "You honestly don't have any clue what you're dealing with in this treacherous little bitch, do you?"

He extended the machine pistol one-handed to aim at Leto.

Raven's eyes snapped open. She dug her left elbow sharply into the mayor's short ribs, where his flab didn't protect him so much. Then she yanked her head free of his momentarily slackened grasp.

Grabbing the hilt of her long, curved sword with both hands, she rolled to her left and swung hard. Ryan heard an ax-striking-cordwood kind of sound.

The mayor's hand, still clutching his blaster, flew off his wrist and fell on the bed. Blood gushed from the stump to soak the face and strawberry-blond hair of one of his drugged playmates, just as she stirred and raised her head.

"You know I don't like it when you do that!" the nude

woman cried. Then she curled into a fetal ball and lay whimpering.

Hizzoner stared in flat incomprehension at his spurting wrist. Raven sprang to her feet. She cocked the katana back and drove it deep into his capacious belly.

His eyes bulged huge. His mouth opened to spew saliva and gargling, choking sounds of inexpressible agony as she twisted the blade inside his guts.

"Fuck you, Daddy!" she roared.

She ripped the blade free and held it up over her head in a two-hand grip. Cast-off blood spattered across the elaborately worked gilt ceiling.

"This is for what you did to Mommy and me!" she screamed, then split his face in two with a single brutal stroke.

"This is all getting pretty complex," Mildred said.

"WHAT IN THE NUKE," Leto demanded, peering into the bright morning sun, "is going *on* out there?"

Leto and Raven and Ryan and his companions stood in a little concrete-walled pump house—long since looted of its massive and massively valuable piping and pumps—that stood in a weed-choked field a hundred yards southeast of the DPD HQ wire. The ancient builders of the Temple had included a secret underground escape route. Ryan reckoned it was only natural that they should.

Jak and Ricky had found it, too—or what they took for the entrance to one—during their nocturnal rambles. It had only been bad luck that when they escaped, they didn't have ready access to it.

Though the way it turned out, he thought, maybe it was the very best kind of luck.

"Sounds like a pitched battle, Leto," Raven said.

Because it was. Blasterfire snapped from all around the

Temple complex perimeter and crackled and popped in vicious reply from firing pits and windows within.

The Commando was still smoldering, Ryan noticed.

"It looks like half the gangs in the Rubble are attacking police headquarters," Leto stated.

"Reckon that's because that's just what's happening," J.B. said.

Leto and Raven stared at him.

"There's something you're not telling us."

J.B. looked puzzled. "Of course there is!"

The familiar pull of the straps of his overladen backpack at Ryan's shoulders reassured him. Before departing the none-too-friendly confines of the late Hizzoner's fantasy castle, they'd located their missing gear and weapons. It was all in an impound room on the ground floor. Nobody had had a chance to pick through it yet, which seemed hardly surprising under the circumstances. Bone and his merry men and women had had plenty else to think about.

And that was before half the gangs in the Detroit Rubble had attacked them.

"Remember how," he said to Leto, "after the spectacular failure of our final attempt to drum up some allies, your man Raúl reported we went out again on an errand of our own?"

"You mean the one when you ran away in a hail of bullets," Raven said.

"That one, yeah."

Leto shook his head ruefully. His face was clean, other than a few stubborn traces of congealed blood in the crevices and crannies of his face. But his long, shaggy blond hair was still an ugly shade of pink, even after cleaning it. Somehow the City of Detroit managed to supply fresh running water to the lower two floors of their massive fortress. Mildred had nagged the whole group into sluicing off in a communal bath before going after their possessions, which Ryan for one was fine with. Blood felt bad when it dried on the skin. And the salt got itchy.

It hadn't been a security risk, at least. Everyone in the whole rad-blasted building was either pointing blasters at their enemies or hunkered down somewhere deep inside the Temple's convoluted bowels, hoping they went away.

"All right," Leto said, "I remember Raúl telling me that. What has that got to do with—" he gestured out the door "—this?"

"We went back and dropped the word on the street in a few key places," Ryan said, "that the Angels were gonna hit Hizzoner all on their lonesome. This morning, in fact."

"You traitors!" Raven screamed. "Leto, I told you you couldn't trust these bastards!"

Leto looked at her.

"Oh," she said.

Then she shook off her momentary chagrin to fix Ryan with an even angrier than usual stare.

"Well, I still don't have to *like* you!"

"No," Ryan said, "you don't. You did fight like a devil alongside us, though. And that's all we asked of you."

After a moment she said, "Yeah. You, too." She still looked at him meanly, though.

Leto was frowning, but obviously in confusion, not anger.

"But I don't get it," he said. "Weren't you risking all our asses if some snitch told Bone we were coming?"

"I'm sure someone did," Ryan said. "Likely multiple someones. Think it through. If they even took the warning seriously, they were expecting this—" he gestured at the battle outside "—not somebody attacking from within. Anyway, they were preoccupied with their big push against you that they planned to launch today."

"Why didn't they at least put the whole nuking perimeter on high alert last night?" Raven asked.

"What were the most two salient characteristics of your da—that is, the mayor and his chief of police?" Mildred asked.

"Rape and murder?"

"Well, apart from those."

"Arrogant stupidity," Leto said promptly.

"There you go."

"One wonders how such arrogantly stupid men could have amassed so much power," Doc said mildly.

"They inherited a lot of both," Leto pointed out.

"Amazing how far brute force and animal cunning can take you if you put your mind to it," Ryan said.

"As my father's last few years proved," Leto added.

"Leto," Raven said, "I don't understand. They all turned us down cold. But here they are, doing just what they told us they *wouldn't* do."

"Not so surprising," Leto said. "As our friend Ryan said, think it through. If they joined us openly for an attack, and we lost…"

"Right," Ryan said. "We're out of here."

"Back to the Joe?" Raven asked.

"No. Now that the mayor and his troops are off our backs, it's time we shook the dust of this ville off our boots. What about you?"

Leto glanced at Raven. Then he grinned and gestured at the trap door that led down to the tunnel from the embattled HQ.

"I'm going back."

"You're what?" Krysty and Mildred said in unison.

"It's self-chilling and nothing else," J.B. warned.

"Naw," Leto said. "I've got a plan."

He looked to Ryan. "You know the story of how Claudius

got to be Roman Emperor after Caligula got chilled by his own Praetorian sec men?"

"Yeah. I've got to admit, I'm surprised you do."

"Well, you know, my father wasn't always like that. Always had more temper than was good for him, but he was a smart man."

"I know."

"He brought me up to be a full baron's son. He always wanted the Nation to become a proper barony. So I got a broader education than you might've expected."

"And what about you?" Mildred asked. "Is that what you intend? To make sure the Desolation Angels have a ville of their own?"

"I reckon I got a shot at it. So long as we don't piss our strength away on fights we don't need to be in. And if we're someday gonna unite the Rubble, I reckon we got a much better chance of doing it by setting such a good example everybody wants to join up. Rather than trying to hammer and grind everybody into submission the way that fat freak Michaud and his predecessors did."

"So what about Claudius and Caligula, then?" Ryan asked.

"I'm gonna go back and drag some likely bureaucrat out from behind an arras and proclaim him mayor," Leto said. "Then he and I are gonna negotiate a peace treaty. A nice, lasting peace treaty."

"What about these boys and girls?" Mildred asked, gesturing at the attacking gangs.

"Looks as if they have already commenced fighting with one another," Doc observed.

Leto tipped his head briefly sideways. "Best get back before they start to win, then. Raven, you can clear out if you want. Head back home and let the people know what we accomplished here."

"No way," she said. She stepped up beside the Angel boss and slipped an arm through his. "You're not getting rid of me that easily, lover."

"Well, I've gotta try to protect my dainty little flower of a future wife best I can, don't I? You men know what it's like."

"Yeah," both J.B. and Ryan answered simultaneously, after only a moment's hesitation.

Chapter Thirty-Five

Ryan ducked as a burst of full-auto fire thudded into the thick masonry wall. A few bullets cracked in through the window over his head.

It was a long burst. When it stopped abruptly, he came up with his Steyr already pointed toward where he'd seen the woman with the M16, a block away.

Through the scope he saw that she had her head down and was fumbling to swap the magazine she'd just exhausted for one that was loaded. He drew a bead and fired.

Just as the trigger broke, he saw her look up, which meant that instead of hitting her on the crown of the head, the 7.62 mm bullet hit her smack in the middle of the forehead.

She had already fallen to the cracked and weed-grown sidewalk when he brought the longblaster back online. He promptly crouched back into cover of the stub wall as more bullets came his way.

They had been besieged since late the previous night. Fortunately, they'd found cover in the ruins of a sturdy two-story building standing by itself on a corner, with only rubble plots and patches of low weeds immediately surrounding it. The structure was small enough for the seven of them to keep an eye on the situation and lay down fire at need in all directions. Some of the second story was actually still standing, though the way the ceiling sagged in places didn't make Ryan confident that it would stay that way for long.

"Who's out there right now?" Krysty asked. She was

hiding behind a wall at ninety degrees to Ryan. She had a lever-action .44 carbine she'd kept from their haul from the late Hizzoner's arsenal.

Mildred called an answer from the other room. "We got the girl gang, the ones with the generic vests with the homemade logo that's either a screaming head or a really badly drawn chicken and the Dead Elvises. What we did to piss those boys off I don't know."

"Perhaps the Elvises blame us for provoking the general internecine warfare that has overtaken the entire Rubble," Doc suggested mildly. Then he straightened enough to fire a fast-aimed shot .44 round from his LeMat before ducking again. "Ha! Be banished, brigand!"

"Well," J.B. said thoughtfully. He had his back turned to Ryan, shooting the other way as targets presented themselves. "They're not exactly wrong."

"Ryan, I'm getting low on ammo," Krysty reported.

The one-eyed man grunted. He was running low himself.

"I thought your notion was to avert a war," Mildred said.

"Hey. I reckoned, better a lot of little wars than one big one," he said. "Just didn't reckon on that particular wildfire spreading so far, so fast. Anyway, my main thought was getting our asses out of the ville alive."

He glanced up, only to see yellow muzzle-flashes flickering everywhere in the early-morning sun.

"Got to admit I may've screwed up that last part, though."

Jak came into the room with Ryan. "Girls fight Elvises now," he reported.

"That's good," Mildred said, "because here come the Chickenheads!"

Ryan came up again enough to flash sight on a fat guy waving an ax over his head with both hands and drop him.

Then he had to get down fast because the charging gang laid down such a withering return fire.

He was just wondering whether to swap to the SIG, which had a much higher rate of fire than the Scout, plus he had more ammo for it, when he heard the engine roar, accelerating hard and fast and getting quickly louder.

He risked a glance up. A skirmish line of a dozen gangers was approaching down the street, firing as they came.

Around the corner behind them came tearing a big old honking rhinoceros of a power wag, with gigantic knobby tires and firing ports in the armored box behind the cab. The Chickenheads turned in surprise and consternation.

The wag bore down on them. A woman leaned out the passenger-side window. She blasted away at them with an MP5-K held by fore and rear pistol grips.

"Get outta my way, you street rats!" Patch screamed.

The Chickenheads did their best. They scattered like actual chickens from a charging bull. Not all of them made it.

The wag barely bobbed as its tires drove over them.

"That's a Unimog," Ryan muttered. "You'd have to reckon he'd have himself a Unimog."

Four other, less imposing, wags rolled around the corner behind the first wag. Fire flashes danced from their cabs and compartments as others sprayed bullets at the now-fleeing gang members. The monstrous lead wag braked to a squealing, bucking stop before Ryan and the companions' hideout. Its tire cleats ripped up chunks of frost-heaved asphalt.

Patch still hung out the window, menacing the entire street with her machine pistol and her scowl. A black-haired head appeared above the far side of the driver's compartment. White teeth showed beneath a dark mustache.

"Going my way?" Nikk, the scavvy boss, called cheerfully.

"So I take it our deal's still on?" Ryan asked.

"Yeah. I keep my deals. 'Less I can't. You know the drill."

"Yeah."

"What took you so long?" Mildred called, rising from her firing position in the ruined building.

"Hey, you know, it's the Deathlands. Nothing ever happens on schedule. Also, you're welcome for us saving your sorry asses."

"We could've handled them," Ryan said.

"Sure, sure," Nikk said with an indulgent chuckle.

"What's going on in the wider world?" Mildred asked, shouldering her pack and stepping into the street. She still held her ZKR 551 ready in case more attackers popped up.

Nikk threw a hand in the air. "This. Everywhere. Gangs are fighting each other all through the Rubble. Like packs of rabid dogs. Never seen anything like it. We got a power of blasting to do. And that's before we even get to Windsor."

"This is your fault, isn't it?" Patch said.

Ryan shrugged. "Yeah."

"You got to admit," Nikk said as the rest of the party emerged from the building, bowed beneath the weight of their packs, "there's a certain irony in our having to rescue you right after you signed on as extra sec on my caravan."

"Go figure," Ryan said.

Actually, he had. He had foreseen this might be happening when he made another side trip the night they had finally thrown in the towel on trying to find allies for the assault on Hizzoner. One he never did mention to Leto—need to know and all that. Which was why, when they returned to the giant blocky building near Angel Land, which they had since learned was a predark TV studio, to strike a deal with the very scavvies who had evicted them from it, he had specified a rendezvous at this previously scouted, easily defensible position.

"Don't know why you bother with them, Nikk," Patch said sullenly, slipping back inside. "We ran 'em off quick when they came to call."

"Well, we had the drop on them, too, you might remember," her boss said, slipping back down behind the wheel of the enormous wag. "And I reckon anybody who can face down the wrath of the whole Desolation Angel Nation and get away with all their parts has exactly the skills we need for the road ahead."

Patch grunted and locked her eyes ahead.

"Does everyone hate you wherever you go?" asked Zander, a burly scavvy with a shaved head and a steel hoop dangling from the lobe of his left ear, who hopped down from the second wag to help the new members of the team load their traps aboard. Other scavvies had climbed out to pull sec.

"It's a gift," J.B. said.

"Scoot on over here," Nikk told his second-in-command. "Climb in with us, Ryan. Her ass is skinny. You'll fit fine."

With poor grace Patch opened the door and slid over. "My ammo's coming outta your pay!" she told Ryan as he clambered in.

For a fact the seat was wide enough they could mebbe have fit another person in without crowding, Ryan thought.

"What about our pal Leto?" J.B. asked through the window.

Nikk chuckled again.

"Seems like the shiny new boss of Angel Land found himself a shiny new mayor to do business with. By the time the sec men the last mayor had mustered just north of the Seven-Five came back and ran off all the dozen or so gangs that were laying siege to the place, the Desolation Angels and the City of Detroit, so called, were allies, joined at the hip for all eternity. And the new Hizzoner never even welched with his whole army right outside."

"No surprise there," Ryan said.

"Boy's got a sound head on his shoulders," J.B. observed. He resettled his hat on his head and turned to find a spot in one of the scavvy wags.

"So it looks like your boy Leto is liable to find himself and his Angels sitting pretty and posed to take over the whole dark-dusted Rubble after all," Nikk said, grabbing the stick and thunking the wag into first. "If he pulls through the current shitstorm of crazy, that is."

Ryan cast his eye out the window of the Unimog as the beast snorted and rolled onward. The bodies of fallen attackers crunched and squelched beneath its tires.

Blasterfire rattled, faint with distance. Then Ryan heard another quick burst from just a block or so away. Somewhere, a quarter mile or so to the west, a brown ball of smoke rolled suddenly into a sky that was clouding over. A moment later the boom of the explosion rolled over them.

"If," Ryan agreed.

* * * * *

AleX Archer
THE DEVIL'S CHORD

The canals of Venice hide a centuries-old secret some would kill to salvage...

In the midst of a quarrel on a Venetian bridge, the Cross of Lorraine is lost to the canal's waters. Suspecting a connection between the cross, Joan of Arc and Da Vinci, Annja Creed's former mentor, Roux, sends the archaeologist to search for the missing artifact.

After facing many difficult situations when retrieving the cross, Annja discovers that the artifact is fundamental to unlocking one of Da Vinci's most fantastical inventions. But the price Annja must pay to stop this key from falling into the wrong hands may be her life.

Available July wherever books and ebooks are sold.

GOLD EAGLE®

GRA49

AleX Archer
CELTIC FIRE

The theft of a whetstone and the murder of a curate seem like random crimes, but the troubling deeds are linked by a precarious thread...

Annja Creed, archaeologist and host of television's *Chasing History's Monsters,* is in the U.K. when her mentor, Roux, interrupts her sojourn with news of the thefts. He's certain that the thirteen Treasures of Britain are wanted for their rumored power. Roux tasks Annja with locating and protecting the treasures before the wrong person finds them. Meaning she must stand against a woman fueled by madness and the fires of her ancient Celt blood—and a sword as powerful and otherworldly as Annja's own.

Available September wherever books and ebooks are sold.

GOLD EAGLE®

GRA50

The Executioner

Don Pendleton's®

ARCTIC KILL

White supremacists threaten to unleash a deadly virus...

Formed in the wake of World War I, the Thule Society has never lost sight of its goal to eradicate the "lesser races" and restore a mythical paradise. This nightmare scenario becomes a terrifying possibility when the society discovers an ancient virus hidden in a Cold War–era military installation. Called in to avert the looming apocalypse, Mack Bolan must stop the white supremacists by any means necessary. Bolan tracks the group to Alaska, but the clock is ticking. All that stands between millions of people and sure death is one man: The Executioner.

GOLD EAGLE®

Available August wherever books and ebooks are sold.

GEX429

TAKE 'EM FREE
2 action-packed novels
plus a mystery bonus

NO RISK

NO OBLIGATION
TO BUY